Stratton tried to recover his composure.

He'd had no idea Jennifer Rodas would come back so damn fast. She'd almost caught him. There was no need for secrecy—he was conducting a legitimate investigation of a murder—but he'd learned a long time ago he could accomplish more by flying under the radar screen rather than across it.

His goal had simply been to slip into Leonadov's office and check it out. An in-and-out recon job to be double sure he'd missed nothing, and he'd screwed it up royally.

Never let them see your face, Meredith had taught him. *And if they do, never let them see your eyes.*

He'd not only stared at Jennifer Rodas, he'd caught her gaze and held it. Or to be more accurate, *she* had held his.

He was out of shape and out of practice. If he didn't watch what he was doing, he was going to end up dead as well.

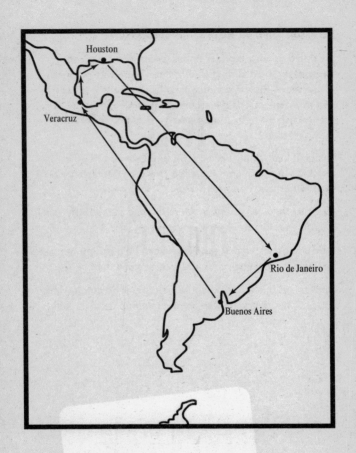

Signature Select™
SAGA

KAY DAVID

NOT WITHOUT PROOF

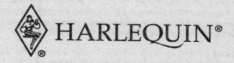

HARLEQUIN®

TORONTO • NEW YORK • LONDON
AMSTERDAM • PARIS • SYDNEY • HAMBURG
STOCKHOLM • ATHENS • TOKYO • MILAN • MADRID
PRAGUE • WARSAW • BUDAPEST • AUCKLAND

ISBN 0-373-83671-6

NOT WITHOUT PROOF

Dear Reader,

When I first starting thinking about THE OPERATIVES as a series I tried to put the idea out of my mind and forget all about it. How can assassins—people who kill for money—be the object of anyone's affection? What kind of love story could come out of characters like that? Like a lot of things I'd rather not think about, however, the stories refused to be ignored and the harder I tried, the louder the thoughts became inside my head. Finally, I abandoned my resistance and the first of the series became the book you now hold in your hand.

Not Without Proof starts THE OPERATIVES saga. Each book is set in a different South American country and each features a hero or heroine who works as an assassin. Led by Meredith Santana, the group was formed to fight battles that cannot be resolved in any easy way. Following *Not Without Proof* will be *Not Without Her Son*, *Not Without the Truth* and, finally, *Not Without Cause*. The characters in each story are linked by their organization and by their skills, but mostly by their need to carve out goodness in a world that sometimes seems without it.

Stratton O'Neil, the hero in *Not Without Proof*, is a killer, as are the other members of the Operatives. A former soldier, he entered the murky underworld of assassins because he wanted to see justice prevail, even when it looked impossible. In his opinion, the simplest form of justice was often the best and most effective. While on assignment, however, he makes a tragic mistake and everything he had always believed in—including himself—disappears in an instant. He gives up and decides to spend the rest of his life paying—in agony—over an error he can never correct. His guilt becomes a hair shirt he never takes off.

Jennifer Rodas is a good woman. Her life is a little dull at times, but she's always believed in doing the right thing, even if it costs her. When her boss, Ami Leonadov, asks for her help, she gives it gladly because the diamond dealer has always done the same for her and her family. When she finds out Ami isn't the man she thought he was, Jennifer is left with a lot of questions...and a building number of corpses. The appearance of Stratton O'Neil only adds to her confusion.

Diamonds and intrigue. Murder and travel. Killers and lovers. THE OPERATIVES has it all, and I hope *Not Without Proof* will have you hooked from the beginning. Step into the world of the Operatives but be warned: you might not want to leave anytime soon....

PROLOGUE

February
Houston, Texas

THE DIAMOND WEIGHED almost ten carats.

Sitting atop the desk, the gem was round and cut precisely, the fifty-eight perfect facets reflecting the low light overhead with an amazing brilliance. The color was just short of summer butter, delicate enough to give the stone a treasured elegance yet bold enough to triple its value.

The three men sitting around the desk were wholesale diamond dealers, people who made their living selling and buying intrinsically useless pieces of carbon that were worth thousands, sometimes hundreds of thousands, of dollars. None of the three seemed particularly interested in the diamond at the moment, though. They were discussing something much more compelling.

They were discussing murder.

Outside the high-rise office building, the weather suited their conversation. A northern had blown in that afternoon dropping the temperature from fifty-five to thirty-two in the space of an hour. Texans were accustomed to drastic weather changes, but this one had been unexpected and when the wet roads had become icy, the streets and freeways had turned into battlegrounds, the SUVs and pickups morphing into deadly weapons. Houstonians liked their ice in tall glasses splashed with Scotch. They didn't know how to handle it beneath their tires.

"I told him to be careful, to keep his eyes sharp. There is evil in this world," the dealer in the center said solemnly, "but did he listen to me, an old man? No, of course not." He patted his yarmulke anxiously, aligning the small black circle with nervous fingers. His name was Ami Leonadov and he was seventy-eight years old. He was the one who'd brought the diamond. Tilting his head toward the empty chair at his left, he spoke with sadness. "C.J. was a good friend for many years. For him, I would have wished a better death."

"How much do you think he told them?"

The second man, Luis Barragan spoke in English just as Ami had, but it was not the native tongue of either. Barragan had flown in from Mexico City, his home, that morning and he was weary, his accent heavy.

Before Ami could say anything, the last man, silent until now, answered for him.

"Anything would have been too much! Anything!" His voice was harsh and the other two stared at him. They were embarrassed by Joseph Wilhem's bluntness and considered him obnoxious but they had needed his money. Of the four of them, Joseph had the most to lose—or win. He lived in Argentina now, his family all refugees from the wrong side of Germany, another fact Ami and Luis tried to overlook.

"We should have our wills in order," Wilhem said in disgust. "We're walking dead men."

Luis Barragan sent Ami a frightened look. The older man made a calming motion with his hands and shook his head imperceptibly. "You are overreacting, Joseph, just as you always do. C.J. was murdered by thieves. They robbed him and then they killed him. He told them nothing because there was no need."

"How do you know this?" Wilhem's expression was suspicious. "If it's gossip, I don't believe it."

"I talked to the police and the IDDA," Ami replied.

"The IDDA?" The pitch of the German's voice went up another notch. "They're involved?"

"Another dealer called them." Ami shrugged. "He was scared—I think it must have been that new fellow on six—and they may send someone to help the police as an added precaution. The IDDA want their dealers safe as well as their stones."

The majority of diamond brokers in the building, and around the world, obtained their goods from a privately held New York firm, the International Diamond Dealers Association, mainly because they had no other choice. The IDDA more or less controlled the supply of diamonds, from the ground to the diva's finger.

"The police told me his death was the work of a heartless *farbrecher*, a criminal, nothing more. C.J. would have had no reason to bring up our plans while he was being robbed. The act, as horrible as it was, had nothing to do with us."

"And what if it wasn't just a thief?"

"No ears but ours have heard what's been said in this

room. The project is safe," Ami replied. "You see too many ghosts."

"That's because they're there!" His face flushing a deep red, the German rose abruptly, his hip hitting the edge of the desk. The furniture was sturdy—Ami's late wife had brought it with them from Russia eons before—but the desk moved under the force of Wilhem's anger, its legs scraping across the cheap linoleum with a nerve-etching screech. The diamond rocked with the movement then rolled to one side, acting as a prism to cast a perfect rainbow against the opposite wall.

Ami stood slowly. He wasn't as tall or imposing as Wilhem. He enjoyed eating too much and in his slippers he reached five-six, maybe five-seven on a good day. He had the advantage over the other man, though, because he was the one who'd brought the deal to the table.

"If you want out, Joseph," he said in a dignified voice, "please say so now. We cannot proceed if we do not all agree."

The German frowned fiercely, as if he were actually considering the question, then he shook his head just as Ami had known he would. "I don't want out," he said gruffly. "But I *am* worried."

"Don't you trust me? Is that it?" Ami shook his head with a mournful expression. "Have I not reassured you enough? Have you not seen with your own eyes? What is there to fret over?" He held his hand out toward the yellow diamond. "The stone is everything I promised it would be, no?"

His words hung in the air between the three of them and, one by one, they turned to the diamond. They stared at it until Luis, soothed by Ami's calm manner, chuckled nervously and spoke. "It *is* everything you said, Ami, *and* it isn't."

The tension broken, Ami smiled indulgently at his friend's simple joke then he patted Wilhem on the back. "Very soon, we're going to be rich old men, Joseph. Relax and accept your future."

"When I know for sure that I will have a future, then I will accept your advice." Wilhem's expression was dark, his voice even more so. "Until that point, I wait and see. If you two are as smart as you think you are, you will do the same, otherwise we might be joining our old friend C.J. long before we're ready."

CHAPTER ONE

April
Somewhere in California

THE RINGING PHONE CUT through the silence of Stratton O'Neil's rundown beach rental like a Stryker saw on high.

Stratton didn't move. Sitting in a deep armchair, staring at the waves as they rolled in, he listened to the sound with a detachment one notch short of depression.

The machine came on, his message played, and a woman's voice filled the room. He'd listened to too many people for too many years. The need had left him, but the habit was still ingrained, her grating accent a detail he noted without thinking. New Jersey coast, he thought indifferently, but trying for Upper East Side.

"This is Lucy Wisner with IDDA in New York. Mr. O'Neil, please call as soon as possible. You've been recommended to us by a former client and we're in need of your services. This is a matter of some urgency so please contact us quickly." She read off four telephone numbers, then hung up.

Lucy Wisner had called twice before and left messages, begging him to phone her. Stratton had no idea who she really was or what she wanted, but he knew one thing for certain—she was a liar. None of his former clients would have given his name to anyone, unless it was to warn them to stay as far away from him as they could. He hadn't worked in almost two years.

And he had no intention of ever doing so again.

He drained his coffee mug then set it on the floor. His hand hit the bottle of Jack he'd left there the night before, and he picked up the whiskey and held it in front of him, the breaking sun highlighting its deep amber color.

For the past two years, he'd kept the bottle close. It was an ever-present reminder. The seal was intact but he harbored no illusions. At some point, he'd break down and open it. He knew himself too well to think otherwise.

The phone rang a second time.

The New Jersey accent came from across the room. "This is Lucy Wisner again. I forgot to give you the cell number of my assistant. His name is—"

Stratton dropped the bottle and grabbed the portable receiver in its stead, his irritation finally overcoming his lethargy. "I don't want the number of your assistant or any of the other half-dozen numbers you've left here, lady. Leave me the hell alone," he said without inflection, "and don't call here anymore." He started to punch the off button, but stopped as her pleading voice sounded again.

"Mr. O'Neil? Stratton O'Neil? You actually answered! I need to talk to you—"

"Why?"

"We want to hire you." She spoke quickly, as if she was afraid he was about to hang up. Which he was. "A valuable member of our organization—"

"What organization?"

"IDDA," she replied. "The International Diamond Dealers Association. We broker diamonds to wholesalers all over the world. One of our dealers in Houston has been murdered and we were told you could help—"

"Told by whom?"

"That's confidential information. I can't tell you."

"That's just fine," he said, "because I can't help you. I'm no longer in the 'helping' business."

"I'm sending you a first-class ticket, Mr. O'Neil. Our offices are in New York. We'll pay you just to come talk to us."

"You aren't going to pay me squat," he replied, "because I'm not going to New York or Houston or wherever you said you're from. I'm not going anywhere but to hell and I don't want my progress slowed."

"WHAT DID HE SAY?"

Lucy Wisner looked up from her desk and shook her head at the man leaning against the doorjamb. In his custom-tailored suit and two-hundred-dollar haircut, Ian Forney looked exactly like what he was—the successful CEO of a multinational business with sales in the billions.

He was her boss and her lover, and she despised him.

"He won't come," she said in a dismissive way. "He's not interested."

"Did you offer him money?"

She narrowed her dark eyes, intentionally making them as hard and shiny as the pear-cut diamond she wore on a chain around her neck. "You heard me, didn't you? I told him a ticket was on its way, but he didn't give me the chance to explain."

Ian smiled. "He'll come."

"What makes you so certain? He sounded as if his mind was made up."

"Maybe it is, but when he sees the check you'll include with the ticket, he'll unmake it."

"Money doesn't motivate everyone, Ian."

"Of course, it does," he answered easily. "The trick is to figure out the *right* amount. Once you do that, you can buy anyone."

She arched one eyebrow but stayed silent. If she spoke, she was afraid she'd say something she'd regret. Ian was so full of himself he made her sick. When they'd first hooked up, she'd thought he was different but he wasn't. He was a carbon copy of every self-centered, egotistical bastard she'd ever known.

He dropped his gaze to the neckline of her blouse then slowly brought it back up. "Trust me on this one, Lucy. We can buy Stratton O'Neil. He's a washed-up has-been. He's a loser and the organization he worked for fell apart because of it."

"What kind of business was it?"

He laughed coldly. "I wouldn't call the Operatives a business, sweetheart, unless you consider death a product."

Lucy felt herself blanch but she didn't blink. "What are you saying, Ian? Are you trying to tell me these people were mercenaries or something?"

"'Or something' might cover it," he answered. "Until he went wacko, he and his buddies made a living from killing third-rate dictators and inconvenient drug lords on the q.t., mostly in South America where those kinds of things can be more easily accomplished. Our own precious government used them on occasion, as well, but only when they had plausible deniability. You do know what that means, don't you?"

"I'm well aware of the definition of plausible deniability," she said coldly, "but what I don't believe in are assassins."

"Fine," he said petulantly. "But that's exactly what the Operatives were."

"If that's the case, why didn't we hire them to begin with?"

"Haven't you been listening? They're no longer in business because of Stratton O'Neil's incompetence." He hesitated. "But they wouldn't have worked for us regardless. They don't kill just anyone. According to my source, their targets have to deserve what they're getting."

The office fell silent as they both considered the meaning of his words. Lucy broke the silence. "So what did this guy do that was so bad?"

For the first time since their conversation had begun, Ian looked uncomfortable. "My sources wouldn't tell me but I got the impression that whatever it was, it must have been pretty unbelievable."

"You're crazy. This is fantasyland stuff, not to mention illegal."

Ian's attitude was back in place. "Illegal, oh my God! You're right! We wouldn't want to be doing anything illegal now, would we?"

Her anger rose at his mockery. "Who are these sources? And how do you know them, anyway?"

"I just do," he said smugly. "And that's all *you* need to know. Stratton O'Neil has a price. I know what it is and you'll double it. He'll take the job and he'll do just what we want. A month from now, our little situation will be solved."

"I'm not sure I agree."

"That's your problem then, isn't it?" Forney straightened then adjusted his cuffs. "Because I know I'm right. I have it on excellent authority that he's the perfect man for us. No one can screw up a job better than Stratton O'Neil and that's exactly what we need."

June
Houston, Texas

JENNIFER RODAS sat at her desk and stared out the window of her sixth-floor suite. The office building where Leonadov Diamonds was located sat just off Westheimer, one of the busiest streets in Houston, but Jennifer faced the north and below her stretched a high-priced residential area. The older homes, large and well maintained, occupied shady lots with backyard pools and extensive landscaping. In the morning, after the traffic slowed but before the heat set in, a parade of uniformed nannies pushed shiny strollers up and down the wide sidewalks that were lined with flowers. They met in groups of two or three and talked briefly. Some of them would head to the park at the end of one of the streets but others disappeared beneath the limbs of the magnolias and live oaks to return home with their precious cargo.

Jennifer propped her chin on her hand and wondered, as she had hundreds of times before, what it would feel like to live in one of those million-dollar homes. Did live-in help and money to spare make life perfect? Were children and a husband all you needed to be happy?

Before her mom had left two years ago, Jennifer would have never even dreamed of asking herself those questions. She'd known the answers then, but things had changed and now she wasn't sure of anything. Death had a way of doing that to you, she supposed.

She closed her eyes for a moment and let the sadness push its way past her defenses. Had it been two years or an eternity? It felt like both. When her mother had remarried and moved to Arizona, Jennifer had been more than willing to take over the care of her twin sister, but as time and Julie's condition had progressed, she'd become increasingly overwhelmed. Left paralyzed by a car accident the night of their high school graduation, Julie was cared for by a trio of nurses. The settlement from the lawsuit had been generous—the driver of the other car had been high on PCP—but nothing could make up for the life she would never have.

Then six months ago, Julie had suffered a heart attack and died.

Set adrift without warning, Jennifer now found herself at loose ends, paralyzed by inertia as surely as her sister had been by her injuries.

Should she move out of the house and find her own place? Should she quit her job and get another? Should she go somewhere different and start all over? There were so many options that she could only do nothing.

A lot of her friends had told her she didn't know how lucky she was to have a glamorous job and a life of her own. They thought her days were filled with champagne and sparkling jewelry and men dripping with money.

The reality was a lot different. She was an assistant, a glorified secretary, nothing more, nothing less. Sure she knew a good diamond from a bad one and sure, she occasionally met a rich client but he was there because he was in love and he wanted to buy another woman something special. At the end of every day, Jennifer went home alone.

A soft knock pulled her attention from the window to the doorway. The man she worked for stood on the threshold and she immediately forgot the children and homes below. Ami Leonadov looked exhausted, almost sick, and a familiar alarm rose inside her. She didn't know when it had happened, but after she'd emerged from her fog of grief she'd been shocked to see that Ami had aged as if years had passed instead of months.

"You're daydreaming," Ami Leonadov said with a smile. "How do you get all your work done and have time left over to daydream?"

She'd asked him repeatedly if he felt all right and his answer had been the same each time. *I'm fine, sweetheart, fine. You worry too much....*

She didn't bother to ask again. "I have a very understanding boss," she said, returning his smile. "He lets me get away with a lot."

"That's because he needs you so much." He sank into the chair in front of her desk with a sigh. "This office would fall apart if you weren't here. I don't know what I would have done if you hadn't come in after your dear mother left, God bless her soul." He shook his head in mock sorrow.

Jennifer laughed with a rusty sound. "Ami, for

heaven's sakes, she got married and moved to Arizona! You make it seem like she was carried out feet first."

"Arizona or the hereafter," he shrugged, "between you and me, the difference, I don't see it. They're both too quiet, too far away and way too hot. She should have stayed here!"

Jennifer shook her head. "It's your fault, Ami. If you hadn't been such an angel and helped us all these years——"

"Angel, smangel." He discounted her words but the pleased look that crossed his face told her how much her teasing meant to him. "What are you? Trying to make me blush?"

He might have brushed off the compliment but no one could have been more understanding or more patient than Ami Leonadov had been. She'd always suspected that he'd been halfway in love with her mother, but when she'd announced her pending marriage, he'd actually paid for the ceremony and her move, as well. Other than Thomas, Ami's son, Jennifer was his sole employee, but she had needed time off, whether it was to take Julie to the doctor or to pick up medicine or a thousand other details Jennifer had had to deal with, Ami had simply shooed her out of the office, no questions asked. He'd also given her quarterly raises and a bonus, too. When she'd questioned his generosity, he'd told her they'd had a very good year. She kept the books, though, and she knew the truth. Business hadn't been *that* good.

"I don't care what you think," she answered lightly. "In my eyes, you'll always be an angel. I'll never be able to pay you back for all your help."

"Well, I have a way you can begin, sweetheart," he said. "I need a favor—" he put his hands on his knees "—and it isn't such a small one, I'm afraid."

"You name it," she said, "and I'll do it."

"I'm thinking you should ask what it is first."

"Okay," she said. "What is it?"

"I have a problem and I must go to Rio de Janeiro next month. I have business there. Important business. I'll be gone a week, maybe two."

Terrible words had shot into her mind the minute he'd said *problem*. Words like cancer or bankruptcy or divorce. Those were problems. A trip out of town was not a problem. Relief flooded her.

"Don't worry about a thing," she said promptly. "I can take care of the office just like before—"

"But that is the problem, you see. I don't want you to stay here," he said. "I need you to go with me, Jennifer."

She leaned back in her ancient office chair, the springs squeaking their protest, as she looked at him in surprise. He traveled a lot but he'd never asked her to go with him before.

"You want me to go with you? To Rio de Janeiro? Rio as in Brazil, Rio?"

He nodded. "I know you don't like to fly, but I don't have anyone else I can ask. I will handle the expenses, of course, and even give you extra pay. I don't want to go alone this time."

As he spoke, his accent had begun to thicken. *Want* came out *vant* and again she was struck by his weariness.

She spoke carefully. "Why do you need me to go with you, Ami? Is something wrong?"

"No, no, no." He waved away her question as if it was

an errant gnat. "Nothing is wrong. Everything is perfect."

Noting iz vong. Everyting iz purfeck.

She stared at him. "Are you sure?"

"What's not to be sure of?" he asked. "I'm an old man, that's all. I have to go a long way away and I want someone young and helpful with me."

"What about Thomas?"

"I said *young* and *helpful*. He's neither."

"But he knows the business better than I do—"

"I want you, not my son." He spoke with insistence, his vehemence growing under her steady stare. "I want you," he repeated. "You speak Portuguese and I need someone I can trust to interpret for me."

"What about the man you used last time? I thought you liked him."

"I did like him." He folded his arms and looked at her above his glasses, the picture of stubbornness. "But now, I want you."

Jennifer nodded slowly, her guilt piling up. After all he'd done and now here he was, offering her an expense-paid trip to a beautiful foreign country and she was acting as if he were making her work overtime without pay. She did hate planes but so did a lot of people and they managed to travel. She could only imagine what her friend Cissy would have to say about this.

Ami stood awkwardly, resting his weight on the arms of the chair before pushing himself up. "I know it's asking a lot," he said. "You're still mourning your dear sweet sister and trying to get your life in order but I wouldn't ask unless I needed you, Jennifer. Think about it and let me know as soon as you can. If you can't go, then I must find someone else."

Jennifer nodded then waited for his parting shot. Ami never left her office without teasing her about something, but he surprised her this time. He shuffled out and closed the door behind him without another word.

JENNIFER HAD MADE PLANS to meet her best friend for lunch that day but after Ami left her office, she thought about canceling. With a single look at Jennifer's face, Cissy McGinnis would know something was bothering her and if Jennifer didn't tell her everything, Cissy would drive her crazy until she did. The woman had the persistence of a bloodhound and nothing could dissuade her once she was on the scent of something she thought might prove interesting. Which was, by definition, anything about which she didn't know the last and smallest detail. When she found out about Rio, she'd give Jennifer so much grief she might end up going just to get away from Cissy and her nagging. She'd already told Jennifer in no uncertain terms that she was going to shrivel up and disappear if she didn't get a life for herself. Cissy's definition of *life* included exotic travel, expensive clothes and men, any kind, as long as they had money.

Jennifer procrastinated until it was too late to call Cissy and stop her from leaving the boutique she managed at the Galleria. Navigating the lunchtime traffic down Westheimer, Jennifer wondered if she could possibly keep the proposed trip a secret, but by the time she reached Chimney Rock and turned into the parking lot of their favorite Chinese restaurant, she knew she was fooling herself to even hope. She and Cissy had been friends since they'd both been stuck in the Sparrow reading group in Mrs. Barnes's third grade class at Westside Elementary. The Redbirds were the best readers, the Bluebirds were okay but the Sparrows, bless their brown and ordinary little hearts, couldn't read a word. The two little girls had bonded instantly.

Cissy was waiting for her at the table in the corner. "You're late. I already ordered." Looking up from her menu, she started to scold Jennifer some more, then she stopped abruptly. "What's wrong?"

"God, can't I even sit down first?" Jennifer dropped her purse into one of the empty chairs and pulled out the one next to Cissy. "How do you do that?" she asked. "How do you read me so well?"

"Believe me, it doesn't take a genius," Cissy snorted. "You wear your emotions like Post-it notes." She tapped her forehead. "Your forehead says 'I'm worried,' and your mouth says 'I'm afraid.' Your eyes are the dead giveaway, though. Right now, they're screaming 'I'm upset but don't ask me why.'"

The waiter appeared at Jennifer's side and poured her a cup of hot tea. She gave him her order, grateful for the interruption, then he was gone, way too quickly.

The minute he left, Cissy spoke. "So what's wrong?"

"I'm hungry and tired," Jennifer said in a lame attempt to turn Cissy's attention to something other than herself. "And I'm worried about Ami. I'd just like to go home and get in bed and pull the covers over my head."

As Jennifer spoke, Cissy's gaze softened. She'd been right beside Jennifer through all her troubles, helping any way that she could. She reached over and squeezed Jennifer's fingers. "I know that's what you'd like to do, sweetie, but you can't. You have to get out and mix things up. You need to mingle. You need to live!"

Arching an eyebrow, Jennifer tried to make light of her friend's advice. "I thought that's what I had been doing for the past thirty years."

"Nope. You've been taking care of everyone but yourself," Cissy replied. "After your dad left, it was your mother, then after she moved, it was Julie. I bet your boss is next, too. I can already tell—"

"You can't tell anything," Jennifer interrupted, suddenly grumpy. "And as far as Julie went, what was I supposed to do? Throw her out to the curb and wait for someone else to pick her up? It doesn't work that way, Cissy."

"That's not what I mean and you know it. Don't be a turd." Cissy focused her green eyes on her friend with a steely determination that made Jennifer groan. Cissy had the bit in her teeth and nothing would stop her now.

"Julie's gone, Jennifer. You did your best with her but you need to move on because time is passing. You've placed your own goals on hold for far too long and in the process you've gotten older. If you don't start making plans, you're never going to have the life you want."

Cissy's words stung but as usual, she was right. Right enough, in fact, for her rebuke to make Jennifer recall her gloomy thoughts just before Ami had come into her office. Jennifer looked down at the cup she clutched in her hands.

She *did* need to move on, but where exactly was she supposed to move on *to?*

Cissy read her mind. "You're never going to have a life if you don't find a man first."

"That's ridic—"

Interrupting her, the waiter placed bowls of hot-and-sour soup before them, steam rising from their surfaces like curls of white lace.

Cissy started talking, preventing Jennifer from protesting more. "Is it? You wouldn't even have to look that far," she said pointedly. "Most women would be thrilled to be in your situation."

Jennifer groaned. They'd been over this before, too. "I don't date people I work with and you know that." She picked up her spoon. "It's not professional."

Cissy rolled her eyes. "Ami would be thrilled if you went out with his son. You're using that as an excuse."

"No, I'm not," Jennifer said stubbornly. "Every women's magazine I've ever read tells you not to date coworkers."

"You must not be buying the same ones I am. The ones I read would tell you to jump on Thomas Leonadov quick before someone else does. He's nice looking, he has money, and he drives an expensive car. What else do you need?"

"I don't know." Her spoon halfway to her mouth Jennifer paused, cocked her head thoughtfully then widened her eyes as if in surprise. "Wait, I got it! How about…liking the guy?"

"What's not to like?"

Jennifer sighed. "You're relentless."

"I only want to see you happy."

"Then don't bug me about Thomas."

Cissy insisted on returning to this topic because

Thomas *was* everything she said he was and probably more. In fact, women were always calling the office asking for him. Even her mother had loved him but Jennifer didn't feel the same way.

She'd been twelve the year her mom had gone to work at Leonadov Diamonds and Lorraine Rodas had insisted her daughters come down and meet her boss and his family. Jennifer, the quieter of the two, had been content to let Julie do all the talking. Her sister had been gorgeous and very outgoing. Like every male they'd ever met, Thomas hadn't been able to take his eyes off Julie. Jennifer had never forgotten the incident, although she still didn't know why. She'd never resented that kind of thing. Rather, she'd been grateful. She hated having any attention turned on her but his eyes had held an acquisitiveness she hadn't liked.

Her negative feelings about Thomas had never wavered after that but Cissy had refused to accept that as a good enough reason for Jennifer not to want to date him.

"There's nothing wrong with Thomas," she said stubbornly.

Jennifer looked at her friend. "You're absolutely right."

"But you'll never go out with him, will you?"

Jennifer shook her head.

"You ignore all my advice, don't you?"

"I don't ignore it," Jennifer said with a grin, "I just don't follow it."

"Well, if you don't watch out, you're going to end up being one of those old women who collects strays and gets all her romance from books." Cissy fluffed her napkin with a fussy movement, her irritation clear. "You have to get out more. Life isn't going to come to you, you know."

The waiter whisked the bowls away and replaced them with overflowing plates. Jennifer waited until he moved out of earshot. "I need more time to figure it all out. I'm not like you, Cissy. I have to think about where I want to go from here."

Cissy pursed her lips, then picked up her fork. "That's fine but while you're thinking, everyone else is doing. Be careful or you'll get left behind."

After that, Cissy changed the subject and they finished their meal without incident. Standing outside on the sidewalk, they hugged and said their goodbyes, Cissy slipping on her sunglasses.

"Do you want to hit the sale at Foley's this weekend? They're going to have all their shoes fifty percent off. I keep thinking about those cute white sandals we saw at the beginning of the season. You know, the ones with the little bow?"

Cissy continued describing the shoes, but Jennifer stopped listening. It was happening again.

The skin on the back of her neck had begun to tingle and she tensed, every muscle in her body going tight as she froze in place. She waited for the feeling to pass but it didn't, so she turned slowly and let her gaze slide over the parking lot and then the sidewalk. For the past few weeks, sometimes at the office, sometimes in her own neighborhood, out of the blue she'd get the distinct feeling that someone was watching her. Holding her breath, she'd look, just as she was doing now, but she never spotted anyone who even seemed vaguely familiar or more importantly, anyone who seemed the least bit suspicious.

She'd told herself she wasn't being paranoid; security issues came with the job. Their business could be dangerous. Ami had taught her to be careful and aware of her surroundings, and her mother had reiterated his advice.

"The bad guys know all the diamond dealers are in this building and they recognize the faces, too," she'd told Jennifer when she'd taken her mother's place. "Never let your guard down and always watch the people around you. It doesn't matter if you're carrying stones or not, they assume you are and that makes you a target."

For the past two years, Jennifer had religiously followed their advice and consequently she'd developed a pretty good sense of what went on around her but this unrealized dread was beginning to bug her.

"Okay, that's it!" Cissy's voice pulled Jennifer's attention back to the two of them. "Something is wrong, isn't it? I let you off too easy and I knew it! Spill it, Jennifer. Spill it right now."

Jennifer hesitated then did as Cissy demanded. It was easier to explain the trip than her imagined stalker. "Ami's going to Brazil next month and he wants me to go with him."

Cissy's mouth dropped and she grabbed Jennifer's arm as if to steady herself. "Oh my God," she squealed. "Brazil! How cool is that?"

"Way cool, I'm sure," Jennifer answered dryly. "But you know how I feel about airplanes."

Cissy whipped off her glasses, her eyes narrowing.

"Yes, I do and I think it's pathetic," she said bluntly. "Do you want to be a hermit?"

"No, that's not what I want, but—"

"You haven't gotten a thing I've said! You're at a turning point in your life, Jennifer! Are you going to let everything pass you by or are you going to go out there and start living?"

Jennifer stared in amazement at her friend; she hadn't seen her friend this wound up in quite a while. Stabbing her sunglasses in Jennifer's face, Cissy continued. "You know what you're doing? You're just continuing down the road to martyrdom that you started on when Julie got hurt. I thought you might overcome it by taking care of her these last few years, but you did just the opposite. Your guilt has only grown over time!"

Cissy paused to catch her breath, and Jennifer felt herself blanch, the painful accusation stinging sharply. Cissy must have noticed, because she winced, apparently realizing she'd gone too far. But the words had already done their damage, and no matter how much she might regret them, she couldn't take them back. Jennifer stared at her in stunned silence.

"Oh, my God," Cissy said quietly. "I am so sorry, Jennifer. I don't know what came over me. I shouldn't have—"

"Is that what you really think about me, Cissy? You believe I feel guilty about the accident—"

Backpedaling quickly, Cissy interrupted. "I've made you mad enough already. I'm not going to make things worse by answering that."

"That's not fair! You can't say something like that then refuse to explain."

Cissy batted away Jennifer's words and replaced her glasses. "You're pissed and you have every right to be. I was way out of line and once again, my big fat mouth has gotten me in trouble. I really am sorry, sweetie." She leaned over and brushed her cheek against Jennifer's. "And you're right—it *isn't* fair but I'm not saying another word."

Making a fast escape, she murmured goodbye and a moment later, all that lingered was her perfume.

Cissy's remark stayed with Jennifer the rest of the day, pushing everything, including the weird sensation she'd had outside the restaurant, out of her mind. Cissy knew Jennifer almost better than she knew herself and whenever she said something like she had at lunch, Jennifer did listen, even if Cissy thought otherwise. In this case, however, Cissy was dead wrong.

Jennifer had moved Julie into her home after their mother had left because it was the right thing to do. Jennifer had *never* felt guilty over what had happened because there was no reason for her to feel that way. Sure, she'd been behind the wheel the night of the accident and yes, they'd both been too excited to pay attention to what they were doing, but the other driver was the one who'd broadsided them. He'd run a red light and hit Julie's side of the car going sixty miles an hour, paralyzing Julie and breaking Jennifer's right leg.

There had been no way Jennifer could have avoided him. Her mother, the police, even Julie had told her so time and time again. She'd *didn't* feel guilty over what had happened.

Cissy was wrong.

CHAPTER TWO

JENNIFER WAS SETTING the burglar alarm before leaving the office a week later when the front door rattled. She stepped out of the closet where the system's controls were hidden and glanced at the video display behind her desk.

A small vestibule fronted the offices. To enter or leave, visitors had to step first into a locked area that was monitored with a discreet camera. Jennifer could release the inner door if she wanted, but if she didn't know the person she could turn them away by using the intercom or by simply ignoring them.

On the screen, she saw Thomas Leonadov.

"I left my keys at home," he said, looking up at the camera. "Can you let me in?"

Jennifer thought about saying "no" or better still, pretending she had already departed, but Thomas would have known what she was doing. The outer door would have been locked as well had she not been there. Jennifer leaned over her desk and pressed the button at the base of the center drawer. A loud buzz filled the office, then the lock clicked open. Interior security cameras stationed at various spots along the hallway allowed her to watch him enter the reception area then stroll toward the back. She straightened as he stopped at her open door.

"You're working late," he said as a greeting. "Things been busy this week?"

Jennifer wished she'd waited until tomorrow to make that one final phone call that had kept her, then for some reason she found herself wondering if he knew about the trip to Brazil.

"It's summertime," she answered. "Things have been pretty steady with last-minute brides. I've been sending out a lot of parcels."

He picked up an invoice that had been lying on her desk and idly opened it. Jennifer started to protest then held her tongue. On paper, Thomas wasn't listed as an owner of Leonadov Diamonds, but everyone knew he was the heir apparent.

He dropped the bill back on her desk. "How's the bottom line looking these days?"

"It's looking very good. Your dad's a smart businessman. He always makes money."

"That's true. I think he could be making more, though."

She shrugged. "Maybe so, but he's content, and that's all that matters to me."

He tapped his fingers on the edge of her desk, his expression unreadable. "You're a loyal employee, Jennifer. You always have been."

"I like your dad." Uncomfortable in the face of Thomas's compliment, she tried to change the subject. "He's a nice guy. There is something that concerns me, though."

"What?"

"I think he looks tired," she answered. "Is he feeling okay?"

Thomas laughed lightly. "He's going to outlive all of us, Jennifer, believe me. He's a tough old bird but to answer your question, he's doing fine. I actually went with him to his last appointment with the cardiologist and the doc pronounced him extremely fit for his age."

Jennifer hid her surprise. To her knowledge, Thomas had never gone to any of Ami's doctor's appointments in the past. Maybe he was beginning to appreciate his father more. She felt her long-held opinion of him shift slightly. "That's good to know," she said with relief. "I was beginning to worry about him."

Thomas shook his head. "Don't, because there's absolutely nothing wrong with him and here's the proof. He gave me these last night." He pulled two tickets from his pocket and held them out to her. "He actually had a date lined up but she canceled so he offered them to me instead. I don't guess you'd be interested in coming along, would you?"

Jennifer looked at the tickets he held. They were for the Rockets' game that Friday. The basketball team had made the playoffs and the whole town had been fighting to get inside the Toyota Center to see them.

"Oh, my gosh," she said in surprise. "How did he manage to snag those?"

"I have no idea." Shaking his head, Thomas read off the seat numbers. "I think they're right off center court. Do you want to come?"

Jennifer's refusal was on the tip of her tongue then she thought about Cissy's warning. *If you don't watch*

*out, you're going to end up being one of those old
women who collects strays and gets all her romance
from books.*

A Rockets game with Thomas might shut that little
voice right up, Jennifer decided, and it might even be
fun. If he'd taken his dad to the doctor, then Thomas had
clearly changed somewhere along the way and she
hadn't noticed. Maybe she should give him a second
chance.

She hesitated and Thomas spoke again.

"I promise we won't even call it a date," he teased.
"We'll say it's an employee appreciation reward. Dad
will be thrilled. He's always trying to find ways to make
you happy."

His remark hit Jennifer squarely. Ami did value her,
as a person and as an employee. If going to the game
would make him happy, too, then she should do it, especially since she'd grown more sure, after calling the
airlines, that she wouldn't be able to sit on a plane long
enough for it to get to Brazil. Twelve hours, the woman
had informed her, from Houston to Rio. Twelve long
hours! She'd be a total nutcase.

"I'll even throw in a hot dog and a beer."

Jennifer looked up, her decision made. "That's not
necessary," she said with a smile. "I'll buy dinner. You
provide the tickets."

BY THURSDAY, Jennifer had begun to regret her decision
to go out with Thomas, no matter what they called the
evening. And on Friday afternoon, she was desperately
dreaming up excuses.

The pipes leaked in the kitchen and I didn't notice

until the house flooded. Too irresponsible sounding, she decided. How about *I had company come in from Oklahoma and I can't leave them behind?* She chewed her bottom lip then shook her head. Knowing Thomas's persistence, he'd probably just whip out more tickets. For half a moment, she considered the old standard *my grandmother died* but Thomas knew that both of her grandmothers had passed away years before.

She nibbled at the edge of one fingernail. If they hadn't argued Jennifer might have called Cissy and begged her for some help, but considering everything that had been said, Cissy didn't seem like the one to turn to right now. They hadn't spoken since their lunch and that was highly unusual.

The phone rang, saving her from sure and abject failure in the excuse department.

"Leonadov's," she answered automatically.

"I'd like to speak with Mr. Leonadov." The man's voice was deep and flat, and for some bizarre reason, Jennifer remembered her sense of being watched.

"Ami or Thomas?" she asked.

"Ami, please."

The way he said Ami's name pricked her attention even further.

"May I say who's calling?"

"He doesn't know me," he said. "But I have some questions for him about a mutual friend."

"I'm afraid he isn't in at the moment. I'd be happy to tell him you called if you'd like to leave your name and number."

The man said, "I'll call back later," and then he was gone. Jennifer replaced the receiver then glanced down at the caller ID display, something she should probably have done before answering the phone.

Unavailable.

The outside buzzer sounded, and she glanced at the monitor with distraction. Thomas waited in the vestibule.

He was holding a bouquet of roses.

Her concern about the phone call evaporated instantly. "Oh, God." She dropped her head into her hands and moaned. "What have I done?"

No one answered so she forced herself to hit the release button. Thomas stepped inside and came directly to her office.

"I brought you these," he announced, holding up the flowers in case she'd missed them. "I know we said this isn't a date, but I saw them and couldn't resist. They're a perfect match to that pink sweater you wear a lot."

She stared at him in surprise. Thomas noticed what she wore? She came around her desk and reached for the flowers. "Thank you, Thomas," she said. "You didn't have to do that."

Her voice died out as he continued to clutch the flowers without handing them over. A sly smile lifted his lips. "How about a kiss in return?"

The childish remark was so typically Thomas that Jennifer stiffened and cursed to herself. How could she have been so naive? Nothing had ever been simple with Ami's son and she was a fool to have thought it could be.

Cissy would have laughed, pecked him on the cheek and grabbed the flowers, but Jennifer couldn't make herself do something like that. "I don't think that's part of the deal, Thomas."

He hesitated and for one wild second, she thought he might grab her anyway, but he laughed instead and dropped the flowers on her desk. "Oh, Jennifer, I was kidding! You need to lighten up. I said this wasn't a date, and I meant it. Don't be so uptight."

Instead of relieving her anxiety, his reply only made her feel even more uncomfortable. She backed up. "Maybe this isn't such a good idea," she started. "I do have a headache and it's going to be a late night."

"That's not going to work." He shook his head. "You promised." He held his hands out. "I'll be on my best behavior," he said solemnly, "and that's *my* promise."

Jennifer desperately wanted to say no but Cissy's voice came once again. After another moment's hesitation, she conceded, then silently chastised herself all the way to the restaurant. Dinner was awkward until Thomas switched their topic of conversation to business. By the time they got to the game and settled into their seats, Jennifer had relaxed enough to see that his attitude had been nothing but gentlemanly. She ended up enjoying the evening even though it was past midnight by the time Thomas brought her back to the building. As she took his hand and stepped out of his Cadillac SUV, she had to admit, he'd lived up to his word.

"I appreciate you asking me to the game." She looked up at him as they walked toward her car. "And I appreciate the flowers, too."

He shook his head and waved off her comment. "I shouldn't have brought them. I didn't mean to make you feel uncomfortable."

They reached her Camry. "It's not you, Thomas," Jennifer said. "It's me. I haven't dated much and I'm out of practice."

He moved to wipe a dust speck off her car, which also took him closer to Jennifer—a fact she told herself meant nothing.

"I'd be happy to provide you with some."

Without cause, her earlier uneasiness returned full force. "I don't know if that's a good idea or not," she hedged.

"I think it's a great one."

He raised his hand to touch her cheek but she pretended not to notice. Her heart pounding with sudden anxiety, she turned and stabbed her keys into the lock on the driver's side door. "Well, I'll consider it," she said in a rush. "And thanks again—"

She opened the car door and stepped behind it, using it as a barrier. "I had fun," she said, climbing behind the wheel. "I'll talk to you later."

She started to close the door, but he put his hand on the window. "Wait! Aren't you going to get your flowers? They won't last the weekend. You should bring them home."

"I'll get them tomorrow," she answered. "It's late and I have to get home and feed my dog."

His eyes seemed to darken or did she imagine it? "Okay," he said reluctantly. "Then I guess I'll talk to you on Monday."

She pulled the door shut and locked it, gaily waving

to him as she reversed out of the parking space and drove away.

She didn't exhale until she was home and standing in her entry with the door bolted behind her. If he ever came over, she'd have to rent a Doberman.

STRATTON DIDN'T OPEN his mail most days but the pile was growing too large to ignore. He was also pretty sure that hidden somewhere in the stack of envelopes there was more than one notice that his phone, his electricity and probably his gas were going to be cut off if he didn't take some kind of drastic action that involved money he didn't have. Telling himself he couldn't get up until he finished, he'd sat down at the desk that morning to tackle the problem. But so far sitting down was all he'd done.

The task seemed too daunting. There might actually be something in one of the envelopes that required a decision and he was a little light in the decision-making department these days.

As if someone wanted to test the truth of that, the doorbell rang and then the phone joined it. Which to ignore first? He chose the phone, but then he surprised himself by ambling toward the door. A uniformed courier stood on the porch.

"Stratton O'Neil?" the man asked, thrusting a clipboard at him.

The phone continued to ring as Stratton scribbled "John Lennon" on the line beneath the man's finger then he handed the board back and exchanged it for an envelope. Stepping inside again, he slammed the door.

This was the third delivery he'd gotten, but the first

he'd accepted. As he walked back to his desk, he ripped open the envelope and tipped it upside down, a first-class ticket to New York falling into his hand along with a letter. The phone stopped ringing as his machine picked up and Lucy Wisner's voice rang out. She'd called once a week since April. He was getting to where he almost looked forward to hearing her nasally voice.

"Mr. O'Neil, I've sent you another packet of information and a ticket to New York. As usual, it should be arriving by courier anytime now and I'd like—"

Stratton dropped the ticket on his desk and picked up the phone, the recorder stopping automatically. "You're a very persistent woman, Ms. Wisner." He paused. "But the answer is still 'no.'"

"Oh, my God, is that really you, Mr. O'Neil? I can't believe you answered. Did you receive my packet? Did you open it this time?"

"It just got here but you've wasted your money."

"Did you open it?" she repeated.

She was getting to know him, he thought. "Yes, I did."

"Including the enclosed note?"

"No."

"Please open it, too. I'll hold."

Hooked despite himself, Stratton put the phone down and tore the edge off the smaller envelope. Inside there was a single piece of paper. A check, he realized, pulling it free. For fifty thousand dollars. He felt a flicker of interest but not because the money mattered in the usual sense. In his Operative days, he'd required exactly half that much to even look at a case. Whoever was behind IDDA knew his rate and had doubled it.

He lifted the receiver and cradled it between his ear and shoulder, his hands still holding the check. "Your organization is well-informed, Ms. Wisner, but I'm still retired."

"An innocent man has been murdered, Mr. O'Neil. We understand that you no longer do what you did before but we need help and we were told you might be interested. We need someone who can help us make things right."

Stratton would have chalked her words up to coincidence if he believed in random connections, but he didn't. Nothing like that ever happened outside of movies. Turning very still, he took the phone and thought of Meredith Santera. She'd run the Operatives and when he'd left, her warning had been simple. "You'll never get a chance to *make things right* if you leave now," she'd said. "Don't walk away like this. You'll end up regretting it."

When she'd first called in April, Lucy Wisner had told him a former client had recommended him. Had Meredith given these people his name in some well-meaning but misdirected attempt to help him? If she had, she should have known better. He was past help, hers or anyone else's. Meredith had a soft spot, though, buried deep beneath the frozen piece of ice she called a heart. He'd seen it once or twice in the ten years they'd known each other.

"Mr. O'Neil? Are you there?"

He wanted to say no, but he didn't. "I'm here."

"We have a very tight-knit community of dealers and the murder of one affects all of them. They're going nuts down in Houston and rightly so. If this isn't solved, our business is going to suffer but more importantly, we want the people who did this arrested. Mr. Singh was a family man and his death has left five children without a father."

"What makes you think I can help?"

"We've been told that you know how things like this work," she sidestepped.

His pulse took a jagged leap. He should hang up, he told himself, right now. Why hadn't he realized the potential for disaster much, much earlier? He was losing what little edge he'd had left after abandoning the Operatives. His eyes jumped to the envelope on his desk. They even knew where he lived, for God's sake.

So what? What do you care? You've been killing yourself by inches for the past two years.

"Mr. Singh was knifed just outside his home." She obviously didn't understand why, but Lucy Wisner seemed to sense she'd gained Stratton's interest and she wanted to take advantage of the opportunity. "We aren't sure, but we believe he had a large parcel of stones with him since some of his inventory is missing."

"And the police?" he asked in spite of himself.

"They've done nothing," she replied. "Some random crimes have occurred in that neighborhood recently and they're attributing the killing to a local gang."

"You don't believe them?"

"Actually, we think they're right," she said, surprising him.

"Then why hire me?"

"As I said, we've had calls from several other dealers in Houston. They don't trust the police and *they* don't believe them. To maintain their goodwill we'd like to hire you to make sure everything possible's being done. You'll be our eyes."

"So this move on your part is purely PR?"

"Oh, no. No, no, no, Mr. O'Neil." She sounded genuinely indignant. "The IDDA does feel confident that the Houston Police Department knows what it's doing but we want to give them as much help as they need."

"Then this is PR"

She hesitated then spoke flatly. "The money spends the same either way, doesn't it, Mr. O'Neil?"

His eyes fell to the bills on his desk. "Yes," he answered slowly. "I suppose that it does."

"Does this mean you'll come to New York?" She tried to hide the eagerness in her voice but failed.

"No," he said. "I won't come to New York. But I will cash your check and I will go to Houston. If I find anything, you'll be called. Otherwise, don't bother me again."

CHAPTER THREE

CISSY PHONED Jennifer the following Wednesday. "Am I interrupting anything?" she asked when Jennifer answered.

"Yes," Jennifer replied. "You're breaking up a deadly boring morning. Thank you for calling."

Cissy giggled then let out an audible sigh of relief. "Whew! Does this mean I'm forgiven?"

Jennifer leaned back in her chair and stared out the window. "There's nothing to forgive you for, Cissy. You were only trying to help and I know that."

She'd given a lot of thought to Cissy's accusation since they'd had lunch and while Jennifer didn't really want to believe her friend had seen something in her she'd been blind to, she'd been equally unable to let go of the idea. And that could mean only one thing. The thought had some merit. She said so to Cissy.

"Well, I really didn't call to talk about that." Her voice was airy as she dismissed Jennifer's words. Too airy. Jennifer knew Cissy was lying and it made her love her friend all the more for it.

"I called to ask about the basketball game," Cissy said in a low voice. "How'd it go? Not to mix my sports, but did you let him get to first base?"

Surprised but not really, Jennifer laughed at the high school phrase. Cissy had hundreds of friends—any one of them could have seen Jennifer at the game. "And just how the heck did you know about that?" she asked anyway.

"I haf my vays," Cissy answered in a bad German accent. "We've got spies, everyvhere, you know...."

"Well, they aren't very good spies," Jennifer answered, "or they would have let you know that it wasn't even a date. Ami gave Thomas the tickets because something came up and he couldn't use them. So I went with Thomas, that's all."

They chitchatted a bit more then arranged to meet that evening to catch a movie they'd both intended to see. Just before she hung up Cissy asked about the trip to Rio.

"I haven't decided," Jennifer hedged. "Maybe we can discuss that tonight."

"If you'd like to do that, I'll be happy to listen."

Cissy's effort to be less domineering was so obvious, Jennifer had to hold back a laugh. "I believe that I would," she said, matching Cissy's tone. "And, Cissy?"

"Yeah?"

"I really do want to talk to you about what you said the other day. I mean about Julie." She paused. "I need to hear more of your theory."

They said their goodbyes and Jennifer went back to work, her heart a little lighter. She hadn't liked being on the outs with Cissy. They were too close to let anything come between them.

JENNIFER WAS POSTING the past month's expenses on a spreadsheet when Ami walked in the following day with an open FedEx box in one hand and several parcels of diamonds in the other.

"Look at these for me, will you, sweetheart, then send them out this afternoon to those ganefs in Dallas. Why do I do business with them? Why? They're nothing but a bunch of thieves and crooks. They scream about the prices then scream about the stones. Why don't I tell them to go fly the kite?"

She smiled. "That's a very good question," she answered, "but I have no answer for you."

He shook his head then told her he'd be out the rest of the day, dropping everything on her desk. Ami let nothing out of the office without being double-checked. The stones were weighed twice, matched against the paperwork twice, then examined twice under a ten-power loupe.

Jennifer saved the spreadsheet file then glanced at her watch. It was past lunchtime. She'd grab something to eat then come back and see to the shipment. She loved working with the stones and the task was always one she looked forward to completing.

Locking the diamonds in the safe and setting the alarm, she made her way downstairs to the deli in the lobby where she picked up a salad then got in line to pay. The elevator was deserted when she headed back to the office because she'd waited so late to leave. Without making a single stop, it returned to her floor in record time.

She stepped into the corridor. Then she stopped.

A man stood at the end of the hallway, his hand on the doorknob of the suite next to the Leonadov's. He turned and met her curious gaze, his eyes sending a ripple of unease through her.

Everyone who entered the building not only had to pass by the guarded security desk, they had to present ID, which was then photographed. Sancho Rodriguez was the man who sat behind that desk and he wasn't a rent-a-cop. He was a real life honest-to-God City of Houston policeman. In uniform and fully armed. In addition, each floor was equipped with cameras at both ends and Sancho monitored the comings and goings on a continual basis.

The building was safe.

She had nothing to worry about. Reminding herself of those facts, Jennifer forced her feet to move and she started down the hall. Deep inside, though, she wanted to ditch her salad and run. For the stairs, for the elevator, for another office, she didn't care which.

And she didn't know why.

The man appeared perfectly harmless. He was dressed well in a herringbone jacket over a collarless shirt and he wore black slacks, his loafers polished as nicely as the expensive briefcase in his hand. He looked as if he'd just come from the barbershop, too, his dark brown hair a little too long for her taste but stylishly cut.

Repressing a shudder as they walked toward one another, Jennifer told herself she was acting crazy. Then their gazes met again.

His eyes were light and cold and very, very empty.

She nodded and looked past him, reaching the office door a moment later. Tapping her key loudly against the lock, she got the blade home just as he took the step that would have put him even with her. Her pulse jumping like a madman, Jennifer finally managed to get the damn door open.

Charging inside the vestibule, she abandoned what little pretense of unconcern she had left. Unlocking the inner door, she slipped into the office then leaned against the wall, fear fueling her rapid breathing.

Before she could recover, the buzzer went. Her legs turned to water and she might have slid down the wall, but the sound startled her so much she sprang into action instead. Running to her office, she dropped her salad on the desk then bumped into her chair with such force that she sent it spinning into the corner. She ignored the pain that shot through her hip and stared at the security monitor, her hand at her throat.

In black and white, Cissy stared back, her tongue sticking out, her eyes crossed.

Jennifer cursed then laughed. The laughter held equal amounts of hysteria, relief and amusement.

Cissy walked inside a second later and came to Jennifer's office. "Hey, I was in the neighborhood and—" She stopped abruptly as she took in Jennifer's appearance. "Good God, what's wrong? You look like you just saw a ghost. The face I made at the camera wasn't that scary, was it?"

Jennifer shook her head, her pulse still beating way too fast. "Did you see anyone in the hallway? A man? He had on a jacket and—"

"The hall was empty."

"Are you sure?"

"Of course, I'm sure. What do you think, I'm blind or something? There was no one out there."

"I saw a man."

"And?"

"And he scared me," she answered. "Something about him didn't look right."

"Did you call Sancho? He'd know who the guy was."

"I haven't had time. I just walked inside right now. Are you positive you didn't see anyone? He couldn't have left quickly enough for you to miss him."

Cissy shook her head slowly, clearly seeing Jennifer's distress. "I swear, Jen, there was no one in the hall, no one waiting for the elevator. No one."

"I guess I must have imagined him." Shrugging, Jennifer tried to make light of her reaction then changed the subject. "What are you doing here?"

Cissy didn't press the point. "I only have a few minutes—I'm already late getting back," she said, "but I couldn't wait to hear if you made up your mind about Rio. Are you going or not?"

After the movie they'd talked for some time about the trip and the conversation had made Jennifer realize just how isolated she'd become. Before taking on the responsibility of her sister, she'd had loads of friends. They'd gotten together every weekend, checking out the newest restaurant or the trendiest bar, but, except for Cissy, one by one, they'd drifted away. No, that wasn't right. They hadn't drifted—she'd abandoned them, too busy caring for Julie to have time for anything else.

The result was a lonely life that seemed to be slipping toward paranoia. How else could she explain seeing invisible men and feeling ghostly stares?

"I don't want to go," Jennifer said now, "but I've been thinking…."

"And?" Cissy prompted.

"And I'm going," Jennifer replied, her mind suddenly made up. "I'll dope myself up, get on the plane and wake up in Rio. It's time," she declared. "Time to move on."

INSIDE THE STAIRWELL, Stratton sat down on the top step and tried to recover his composure. He'd had no idea the woman would get her lunch and come back so damn fast and she'd almost caught him. He'd barely had time to ease over to the other doorway. There was no need for secrecy—he was conducting a legitimate investigation of a murder—but he'd learned a long time ago he could accomplish a lot more flying under the radar screen rather than across it.

And if he needed to do something illegal, being invisible worked out better, too.

In this case, his goal had simply been to slip into Leonadov's office one more time and check it out, just as he had done last week. An in-and-out recon job to be double sure he'd missed nothing, and he'd screwed it up royally.

Never let them see your face, Meredith had taught him. *And if they do, never, ever, let them see your eyes.*

He'd not only stared at Jennifer Rodas, he'd caught her gaze and held it. Or to be more accurate, *she* had held his. He cursed and wiped his brow. He'd used fake ID for the cop downstairs but this wasn't the way things were supposed to go.

He was out of shape and out of practice. If he didn't watch what he was doing, he was going to end up dead, as well.

The thought jarred him. Almost as much as some of the things he'd learned since he'd arrived in Houston.

He started down the stairs, his palms sweaty as he slid them down the metal railing.

Emerging a few minutes later, he caught the elevator to the tenth floor wearing a cap he'd pulled from the pocket of his jacket and a pair of heavy-framed glasses, the sports section of the newspaper two inches from his face. He then left the building and made his way to the Ford Taurus he'd rented under a different ID at the airport when he'd arrived. He didn't breathe again until he was on the Southwest Freeway and halfway to the hotel where he'd been staying.

Leaving Jennifer Rodas behind didn't take her off his mind, though. He knew who she was because he had a list of every business in the building, along with their employees, but he'd recalled her specifically because she was Ami Leonadov's assistant. He'd seen her come and go all week long. He also knew Leonadov had been a close associate of Singh. The information had cost Stratton more than he'd wanted to pay but clearly the price of bribery had risen since he'd left the Operatives. Not that it mattered—IDDA would be footing the bill regardless.

Which was, as it turned out, a very good thing, because he was going to be buying a lot of info. The Houston Police Department had not been impressed with him. The cop on the case hadn't wanted to share a cup of coffee with Stratton, much less his file on the murder.

So, he'd been on his own, but that was okay because Stratton preferred it that way. The first thing he'd done after that was to investigate Singh's relationships. Meredith had taught him to plot Venn diagrams of association. Family and business associates were circles that overlapped the main circle of the target's existence.

Seeing where those curves intersected was very important.

In the old days, the target had been just that, a target, but the technique had seemed appropriate here and Stratton had applied it. He now knew everyone C.J. Singh had known. He also knew that the last person who'd seen Singh alive had been Leonadov. And he'd recently booked two tickets to Rio. Was he leaving permanently and taking his young assistant with him? Making his escape while he still could with Singh's missing inventory? Stratton had picked up a few more details before booking a seat on Varig. The move might have seemed drastic to some, but not to Stratton. In the Operatives, they'd investigated any anomaly when it appeared, and Leonadov leaving was definitely an anomaly.

Back at his hotel, Stratton was tempted to call Meredith and talk the case over with her. After giving it more thought, he drank a cup of coffee instead and tried to work out the details and what they meant on his own. He didn't deserve Meredith's help anymore. When he'd walked away from the Ops he'd let everyone down. Meredith, Armando, Cruz… They'd depended on him and in return he'd not only put their lives in danger, he'd caused more tragedy than any of them could have ever anticipated. He was paying for his mistakes and he *would* for the rest of his life, but knowing that fact didn't change anything. He was too late for that.

He finished his coffee. It was too late for a lot of things, he thought. Way too late.

THEIR FLIGHT was scheduled to leave at nine on Wednesday evening. They would make one stop in São Paulo,

Brazil, then continue to Rio, arriving at 10:55 the next morning.

Jennifer looked at the ticket in her hand and shook her head. "How can they say a flight's gonna land at 10:55? Why don't they just say eleven and be done with it?"

"Because that's not how the airlines work," Cissy replied. She rummaged through the suitcase lying open on the bed as if it were her own, which it was. Jennifer had had to borrow it from her. If you didn't like to travel, you didn't spend money on luggage.

"Have you packed your sunscreen? Bathing suit? Raincoat?" Cissy looked up with a sly expression. "Condoms?"

"Condoms?" Jennifer squeaked. "Are you crazy? This is a business trip, not a Club Med jaunt. Not that I'd do that anyway."

"Oh, relax, for God's sake. I'm teasing you. But on the other hand—" she raised an eyebrow "—you never know. You could meet someone interesting and—"

"I'll only be gone a week. And as I've pointed out before, I work slower than you. That's not enough time for me to meet someone, fall in love and start making babies."

"Who said anything about love or babies? I'm talking sex, honey. Wild, all-night, never-ever-forget sex." Cissy snatched an oversize T-shirt from out of the bag and held it to her chest, wiggling it suggestively. Before Jennifer could answer, Cissy looked a little closer at the faded cotton then rolled her eyes. "Then again, maybe you're right. You're never going to get a man sleeping in something like that."

Jennifer grabbed the garment and threw it back into the suitcase. "That's my favorite," she said. "Don't make fun of it. Besides, it doesn't matter. Wild sex or love and babies, I've got to know more than his name before he sees me sleeping in this or anything else."

"You're no fun."

"I know," Jennifer answered. "But I *am* trusty, loyal and recognize it's my duty to be useful and help others. Don't you remember our Girl Scout promise?"

"No."

Jennifer tucked the edge of a blouse back inside the suitcase and slammed it shut, locking it on both sides. "Somehow that doesn't surprise me. But that's okay. I still love you anyway."

Rising from the bed where she'd been sitting, Cissy smiled then hugged Jennifer tightly. "I love you, too, and you're going to have a terrific time," she said. "Just relax and enjoy yourself. This is a once-in-a-lifetime kind of trip."

"I hope so." Jennifer spoke nervously. Ever since she'd seen the man in the hallway, she'd been uneasy, more so than when she'd simply had the trip to worry about and her invisible stalker.

Sancho Rodriguez took photographs of every visitor's ID, he had explained, but not of the visitor themselves. He'd been less than helpful. Something told her the visitor had probably slipped inside without Sancho's knowledge and if that *had* happened, Sancho wouldn't have been too pleased to have that revealed.

She'd talked to the people next door, too. They sold settings and other types of jewelry supplies and a constant stream of customers went in and out. They couldn't remember anyone who matched Jennifer's description.

The doorbell interrupted her thoughts. "That must be the cab." She looked at Cissy as a tiny rush of panic froze her in place.

Cissy laughed and gave her a push. "Then go get it, silly. I'll bring the case."

Five minutes later Jennifer was in the taxi, her suitcase was in the trunk, and Cissy was waving from the sidewalk. Two hours after that, Jennifer was walking down the jetway with Ami at her side. They entered the Boeing 767 and the attendant directed them to their right.

"I'm sorry we're not flying first class, sweetheart." Ami spoke over her shoulder as they squeezed toward the seats. "I've made up for it at the hotel, though. I think you'll be pleased."

Jennifer stopped in front of the row that held their seats and lifted her carry-on to the overhead compartment. "First class? Are you crazy? Why on earth would anyone pay that much money for an airline ticket? Either we're all going to get there or none of us is going to get there. It doesn't matter where you're sitting."

Ami smiled, put his briefcase beside her bag, then slid into the space next to her. "You're absolutely right," he said, "but a pretty girl like you deserves first class. They serve champagne up there and you get dinner on a real plate." He leaned closer and patted her arm, the scent of peppermint coming with him. "Next time, sweetie, we'll sit up there."

"Next time?"

He nodded. "I may have to come back and if I do, I promise you, we'll go first class all the way."

She looked at him, her curiosity piqued. Like all the dealers, Ami was cautious about his business affairs, but in the past few months, he'd seemed even more so. On several different occasions, she'd walked into his office unexpectedly and he'd hastily turned over paperwork so she couldn't read it or hung up the telephone without saying goodbye. He'd even handled a few of the invoices himself, asking her for blank checks that he could make out on his own, telling her the amount later so she could fill in the register without knowing whom he'd paid. She'd thought his actions a little strange, but the diamond world *was* strange. Where else did people consign inventory worth hundreds of thousands of dollars to each other on a handshake and a few good words?

Her mother had warned her, though. "Don't ever ask a dealer too much about his business," she'd said. "If you need to know something, then sure, ask, but if you're just wondering for your own sake, forget it. They can get real nervous real fast."

Her mom's words echoing inside her head, Jennifer carefully framed her question. "Are you working on something special?"

He smiled like a little boy. "I am," he whispered, "but you mustn't tell anyone. It's a secret."

Jennifer nodded then pressed her luck. "Does Thomas know?"

Ami's expression closed, and Jennifer knew she'd stepped in it. "No," he said shortly. "And I don't want him to. It's very important that he doesn't know about this." He seemed to realize how sternly he was speaking and he softened his voice. "Not yet, anyway," he amended. "I want to get the details settled first."

I vant to git ze deetails sittled furst.

Jennifer started to reply but the engines on the jet revved up at that moment, and she jerked her eyes to the window. While they'd been talking, the plane had backed out of the gate and was now on the runway. She hadn't even noticed. That little oval pill Cissy had given her had magically vanquished her anxiety over flying. Over just about everything. Jennifer had four more in her purse if she needed them and four of a different kind to help her wake up. She hoped she didn't get them mixed up.

She turned back to Ami. "I won't say a word," she promised.

"I know you won't. You're a good girl, Jennifer. When this is all over and I'm rich, I'll find the perfect diamond, just for you. We'll have it set in a necklace. And later, God willing, you'll remember the old man who gave it to you after I'm dead and long gone, no?"

"I'll remember you regardless," she said, "but let's hope that doesn't happen for a very long time."

"From your lips," he said, "to God's ear."

CHAPTER FOUR

THEY WERE AIRBORNE shortly after that, but Jennifer felt as if she were floating on a cloud instead of flying in a 767. Nothing bothered her, not even the starched and suited businessman in the seat beside her who had dropped down his tray table and now had his computer—and all its paraphernalia—spread not only across his space but most of the way into her own.

The attendant brought dinner and then the movie came on. When the lights finally dimmed, Jennifer went out completely and next thing she knew, Ami was shaking her arm, gently at first and then with more force.

Her eyes fluttered open.

"Wake up, sleeping beauty." He tilted his head toward the window where a sliver of light outlined the shade he'd obviously pulled down sometime in the middle of the night. "It's almost morning. We'll be in São Paulo in just a little bit."

How could she have slept like she had, sitting straight up between two men in a crowded airplane, thousands of feet above the earth? It didn't make sense. Then she remembered Cissy's pills and Jennifer shook her head in amazement. The miracles of modern science. She suddenly wondered what else she might have been missing out on.

Squeezing past the businessman who looked a little less perfect than he had ten hours before, Jennifer lurched toward the bathroom, carrying her makeup kit. Once inside, she scrubbed her face, brushed her teeth and drew a comb through her hair, looking at herself critically in the mirror. Cissy always insisted that Jennifer looked like another 'Jennifer,' one who was a little more curvy and a lot more famous. Jennifer didn't see the resemblance, though, especially right now. Dark hair and dark eyes, sure, but to her the similarities ended there. J.Lo, she wasn't.

Returning to her seat, Jennifer accepted her breakfast tray from the harried attendant and in no time at all, they landed in São Paulo. As the plane taxied to the terminals, Jennifer looked out the window.

A combination of high-rises and red-tiled roofs covered the landscape, but low mountains could be seen in the distance. On their slopes, she thought she could see the favelas she'd read about, but she wasn't sure. The slums looked more like trash heaps than anything else. She couldn't imagine people actually living in such conditions.

Customs went smoothly. Jennifer had been worried about her vocabulary but the language she'd learned as a child from her Portuguese grandmother, then studied later in college, came back to her easily. As easily, it seemed, as the warm smile came to the agent behind the counter who appeared to appreciate her effort with his difficult language. If the rest of the trip went this way, she told herself walking toward the domestic terminal, she might actually have some fun.

Ami somehow sensed her relief. "You did well back there," he said. "I'm impressed."

Jennifer smiled. "Give me a little time. I'm sure I'll order a mouse for dinner instead of an omelet or ask where the pig is when I really want to go to the port."

They were back on the plane and heading out again in less time than she expected. An hour later, Rio de Janeiro appeared beneath them. Jennifer stared open-mouthed with amazement. The city hugged the coastline, the azure waters of the Atlantic Ocean spread out on one side, the emerald mountains of the *Sierra da Carioca* holding it close as a lover on the other. Along the shoreline, the sandy beaches were ribbons of white silk with luxurious high-rise hotels perched nearby, their aquamarine swimming pools jewels that glittered in the sunlight.

"Oh, my God," she whispered. "Look at that, Ami. It's incredible."

"That's why they called it *Cidade Maravilhosa.*"

He butchered the pronunciation, but Jennifer understood. The Marvelous City was just that and more.

She squeezed his arm in excitement, a wave of anticipation the likes of which she hadn't felt in a long time coming over her.

"Thank you for bringing me here," she said. "I'm sorry I didn't appreciate the offer better. Now I understand."

"We will work hard," he said, "but you will have plenty of time to explore, too. I promise."

Jennifer turned back to the window, her heart suddenly lighter. They hadn't even landed but she felt different already. As if she'd dropped some extra luggage somewhere over the ocean, Jennifer felt a weightlessness replace the worry she'd come to assume. She didn't understand the change and didn't know what to call it, but she made a vow right then and there to make the most of it, whatever *it* was.

STRATTON'S FLIGHT to Rio was uneventful—just as he liked things to be yet he sensed a change in the city from the last time he'd been there. Three years had passed, but even in that short time, the dangerous air that had seemed integral to the country had grown and shifted. Pickpockets and thieves had been the worst he'd had to deal with before. Now there was a restlessness tinged with anger. The poor had gotten poorer and the rich had become more determined to keep what they had. The air felt ripe with a potential for violence.

On the other hand, he could have been imagining things. His reason for visiting was much different now. Before he'd been such a part of that dark world he'd been blind to it.

Either way, it hardly mattered. He needed to be alert and cautious, even more so than he had in Houston. If Ami Leonadov had fled to Rio, he wouldn't be happy to know someone had followed him. From what Stratton had seen so far, the old man was no fool. Stratton wouldn't put it past him to have someone covering his back. He would have, had their positions been reversed.

One thing that hadn't changed in Rio was Ribeiro Gomez. The fixer Stratton had always used had been happy to hear from him last week and even more happy to watch the airport for Leonadov and his pretty young secretary. When the two had arrived that morning,

Gomez had followed them to the Copacabana Palace Hotel, a luxury high-rise right on the beach. The old man had good taste, in women *and* in hotels.

From the airport, Stratton went directly to the Copa. He wasn't worried about Jennifer Rodas recognizing him because he looked completely different from when she'd seen him in the hallway outside her office. It was amazing what a different hair color did to your appearance.

Gomez met him in the marble-lined lobby. Stratton shook hands with the tall, pockmarked Brazilian and they went directly to the bar. The room was loud and noisy, the lunchtime crowd ready for their usual three hour meal. A few fell silent, though, when they saw Gomez. A retired *superintendência* for the Federal police, he had that effect on people and not just because of his scars. There was something inherently scary about the man.

They'd met years before, Stratton telling Ribeiro Gomez the first time they'd worked together that he was an American businessman who sometimes needed help but never needed questions. Despite Gomez's threatening demeanor, he'd respected Stratton's request and over the years, they'd developed a close relationship,

But not too close.

"You look well, *señor,*" Gomez said. "Much time has passed since we have had the pleasure of your company. I was very pleased to take your call."

"I was very pleased you were still here," Stratton replied.

They spoke Portuguese. It wasn't a simple language

to master, but Stratton had a propensity for such things, which had made his life much easier, especially since he'd spent so much time overseas.

They ordered, bottled water for Stratton and a *caipirinha* for Gomez. When the drinks came, he lifted his glass and tapped it against Stratton's. "You endanger your status as an adopted Brazilian, my friend." He nodded toward the water. "That isn't the national drink of Brazil."

"I know, but it'll have to do for now." Stratton shrugged but his answer was enough.

Gomez's spine straightened and what little casualness he'd had in his demeanor disappeared. It was time to do business. He pushed a piece of paper across the bar. "This is the room number," he said. "They have a suite. With two bedrooms."

Stratton pocketed the scrap without comment.

"There was no car rented," Gomez continued. "They took a cab here, checked in and are still upstairs now. Three phone calls have been made, but I couldn't get the numbers."

Stratton raised an eyebrow questioningly.

It was Gomez's turn to shrug. "Things have gotten tighter," he said. "Since 9/11 it takes more money and more effort to get information."

Stratton recognized a setup when he heard one. He'd come prepared, though. He pulled a sealed envelope from the inside pocket of his coat and slid it toward the man beside him. "Maybe that will help."

The packet disappeared into Gomez's jacket so quickly, Stratton's eyes barely registered the movement. Gomez murmured, "I'll see what I can do," then said, "What else do you require?"

"I'm not sure," Stratton replied, "but I'll be in touch. Stay handy."

"Certainly." Gomez stood, straightened his jacket, then held out his hand. "It is good to see you again, *señor.* I hope all has been well during your hiatus."

His gracious words reflected his Latin heritage more than it did anything else. Gomez knew, as did the whole shadowy world they both came from, exactly what Stratton's past few years had been like. It was no secret.

Stratton shook Gomez's hand then dropped it. "I'm still here," he said. "I guess that counts for something but I'm not sure exactly what."

EXHAUSTION HIT Jennifer the minute they walked into their suite whereas just the opposite seemed to happen to Ami. He had her pick her room first then he took the other one, quickly unpacking his suitcase and setting out his briefcase on a desk in the living room where he immediately went to work. A bit dazed, Jennifer wandered around and stared in awe at the twenty-foot ceilings and elaborate woodwork. The hotel was like nothing she'd ever seen before. There was hand-etched shower glass in her private marble-covered bath and fresh orchids gracing every table. The linens on the bed were fine cotton and the nearby couches soft leather. As luxurious as everything was inside, though, nothing could match the view. Staring through the broad window almost hypnotically, Jennifer felt the scene steal her breath.

She stepped through a set of double French doors to the balcony so she could see even better. A pristine beach stretched for miles, the water beyond the white sands so blue that it hurt her eyes. In the distance sharp green mountains rose along the coast. She wasn't sure but she thought she could even see Sugar Loaf. Cissy had shoved a tourist guide into her hands last week, and Jennifer had glanced at it briefly before tossing the book into her suitcase. As soon as she had time, she'd sit down, read it and make a list of places she wanted to see. Ami had said she'd have some free time. Regardless of what else she might visit, the famous mountain and its companion, Corcovado, with the Christ the Redeemer statue on top, were absolute musts.

She turned away from the beautiful vista with reluctance and walked back into the living room. Ami already had the phone pressed against his ear. He was speaking Yiddish and she sat down to wait.

When he hung up, he turned to her. "It's nice, this hotel, yes?"

"Oh, Ami, it's more than nice. Have you seen the view?"

"Not yet, but I will. First things first." He waved a hand over the desk. "I must take care of this."

"Oh, my gosh, I'm sorry. I should have been helping but I was distracted by the sights." She stood. "What can I do?"

"Take a nap, relax, go to the beach, sweetie. I won't need you until tomorrow, maybe the day after. I have to get my appointments lined up first and only I can do that."

"Are you sure?"

"Absolutely," he answered.

His suggestion about the beach sounded good, but her stomach was still jumping as if she'd never left the plane. She headed back to her room to read her travel guide and then unpack. Maybe all she needed was a little time to regain her equilibrium. Opening the suitcase to dig out the book, Jennifer found a gaily wrapped box beside it.

"Oh, good grief," she murmured. A note hanging from the bow was written in Cissy's bold squiggles. "Pretend you're me and have some fun!"

Jennifer sat down on the edge of the bed and lifted the lid off the box. Nestled inside the carefully folded, floral-scented tissue was a pale blue nightgown. It was made of silk and lace, so very little of each that Jennifer knew instantly it must have cost a fortune. She picked the garment up gently and a small square package, released from its folds, dropped to the floor.

Jennifer bent over, then giggled. Ever the optimist, Cissy had tucked a condom beneath the gown. Jennifer fingered the package then tossed it back into her suitcase.

She'd had a serious boyfriend in college, and they'd moved in together after graduation, but every time her mother had called and asked her to help with Julie, he'd gotten angry, telling her that her family was a tangle of needy codependents and she would never understand the concept of personal boundaries unless she first escaped from their tyranny. He'd been a psychology major. She'd told him goodbye without much hesitation.

Since then, all her dates had been casual.

She refolded the nightgown and put it back in the suitcase, pulling out the guide book she'd come to get. Lying down on the bed, she settled in to read, but before she got past the first chapter, she was asleep. When she woke up, the window was dark. Ami had covered her with a blanket and left an envelope with her name on it beside the bed.

> I'm having dinner with my friend, Ioao. A boring old man or I would have asked you to come. Order room service or go out on the town, whatever you like. I'll be late so don't wait up. I exchanged some dollars for you so have fun! P.S. Goods in safe downstairs.

Jennifer set the note aside and opened the envelope wider. A thick stack of foreign currency, the local real, she assumed, was inside. She shook her head at his thoughtfulness then rolled to the edge of the bed, dropping her feet to the floor. She'd order room service, she decided. Going out might be kind of tricky and where would she go anyway? A sound pulled her to the window and she padded barefoot across the room, her toes sinking into the thick carpet.

Beneath her window a band had set up on the beach. The musicians were standing in the sand with their pants rolled up, tuning their instruments. A crowd had already gathered on the wide sidewalk that separated the busy avenue from the shoreline. Dressed in everything from tailored tuxedos to tiny bikinis, some of them had even started to dance without the music.

Even though she was four floors above the crowd, Jennifer caught their infectious enthusiasm. Fifteen minutes later she was in the elevator. At the registration desk, the twenty-something clerk told her about an outdoor café only a few blocks down.

"When do you plan on being back?" he asked after she thanked him.

The question seemed curious to her. "I'm not sure," she said. "An hour, maybe two. Why?"

"Not that late, then." He smiled with relief. "This is a very safe part of Rio," he explained, "but there can be trouble anywhere. We warn our guests to be extra cautious after three or four in the morning."

"After two, I'm nowhere but in bed," she responded.

His dark eyes swept over the sleeveless black dress she'd borrowed from Cissy and lingered on the low neckline. His voice dropped, as well. "A beautiful woman like you? In bed by two?" he asked seductively. "That shouldn't be the case, unless, of course, you are not alone. In Brazil, we're just getting started at two."

The suggestiveness of his remark would have earned him a cool look from Jennifer if she'd been back home, but the way this man spoke made her actually consider what he'd said instead. Was it his accent? His body? His stare that met hers so boldly?

She didn't know but she didn't care, either. Surprising even herself, she spoke, her own voice pitched a little lower than usual. "I'll take that into consideration," she said, "I do understand your nightlife starts later here."

He leaned over the counter. "It does," he said, "but it goes longer, too. You might want to remember that, as well."

She smiled and nodded, then turned away, his stare heating her back until she slipped out the revolving door and into the Brazilian night. She made it to the sidewalk, then giggled out loud. Flirting with a guy ten years younger than herself—man, Cissy would be proud of her!

SITTING IN THE BAR, Stratton watched the interaction between Jennifer Rodas and the hot-eyed clerk behind the desk. He didn't need to hear the conversation to know what was taking place. The guy had practically willed her to come to him from the moment she'd stepped out of the elevator, his gaze never leaving her body. He'd stared at her and no one else.

Stratton would have been suspicious except he had done the very same thing.

Between Houston and Rio, something had moved Jennifer Rodas from "pretty" to "whoa." Stratton told himself it was probably the dress. The simple black sheath was definitely tighter and more clingy than her usual businesslike attire, yet she wore it with a different kind of attitude, as well. With her spine straight and her shoulders back, she looked more confident than she did in Houston. More vibrant. More alive. More sensual.

He polished off his ginger ale, then stood abruptly, dropping a handful of reals to the bar. What was he thinking? There was one reason Jennifer Rodas looked like she did and it was a simple one. She thought she and her elderly boyfriend had gotten away with murder and a fistful of diamonds. Stratton had learned a little more about the "missing inventory" as Lucy Wisner had so casually called it. Singh had had a shitload of high-end diamonds with him the night he'd been murdered. He'd come straight from Leonadov's office before the murder so it was likely the old man would have known. A stash like that could keep him going in Rio for quite a while, especially if Leonadov had managed to bring out his own share of IDDA's inventory in addition to Singh's.

Stratton sent a glowering look in the clerk's direction as he passed the counter on his way to the revolving doors. Busy with a couple who were checking in, the young man didn't notice. Which, Stratton decided, was just as well—he didn't know why he'd done it anyway.

On the sidewalk, he took the calculated risk of turning right. Earlier in the evening, he'd asked the day attendant to recommend a café and he'd steered Stratton to a small place down a few blocks. Knowing how things worked in South America, Stratton made the assumption the night clerk had pointed out the same place to Jennifer. The hotel clerks liked to keep things simple—the proprietors of the nearby businesses paid them a certain amount of money every month and in return, they funneled a certain number of customers to those establishments.

Stratton wasn't disappointed.

Jennifer sat at a table for two near the sidewalk, a tall drink in front of her. She was resting her chin on top of her folded hands, staring at the people as they passed by. Despite her newly seductive air, her expression struck him as sad. He shook his head at the ridiculous thought and crossed the street. She was waiting for her boyfriend, he told himself. Leonadov had left the hotel a few hours earlier but the maid who'd knocked on Stratton's door to tell him so hadn't gotten to him fast enough. The Russian had been long gone by the time Stratton had come downstairs. He had no idea where the man was, but Stratton knew where he'd end up. His mother had once said there was no fool like an old fool, and she'd been right.

Stratton waited on a bench and acted like an American tourist, gawking at the women in thong bikinis who paraded past. It wasn't a difficult task but the whole time, he kept Jennifer in sight. She'd been at the café for almost twenty minutes when the waiter brought her a platter of steamed seafood. She wasted no time before tucking into the food. She either hadn't been waiting for Leonadov or she was a pretty rude date. Stratton quickly settled on the first option.

With no other choice, he watched her eat her dinner but he soon began to regret his voyeurism. What was it about women who ate with their fingers? She cracked open a huge crab claw to reveal the inside then she brought one half to her mouth. Unable to look anywhere else, Stratton swallowed as she sucked off the delicate white meat, using her teeth to strip it completely.

He came to his senses when a young couple sat down at the other end of the bench. Laughing and kissing, they broke his concentration. He rose and moved down the sidewalk, grateful to them for giving him an excuse to leave. With his eyes still on Jennifer, he stopped at a *frescaria* a few yards down the beach and bought one of the icy fruit drinks. It gave him something to do but he was hoping it might cool him off, too.

He was on his second coconut drink when she finally called for the bill. Tossing the paper cup into a nearby wastebasket, he dodged the traffic and crossed the street, jumping onto the sidewalk half a dozen yards behind her as she exited the outdoor patio. She paused for a moment, obviously trying to decide what to do, then she seemed to freeze, her body going taut.

Stratton ducked his head and stared into the window of the shoe store on his left. In the glass, he watched her turn slowly as if she were looking for someone, her gaze carefully taking in the crowd around her.

He wondered suddenly if she wore a hidden earpiece. Was Leonadov talking to her at this very moment? Was she looking for him? Stratton narrowed his eyes at her reflection, then all at once he realized what had happened. He'd seen her do the same thing in Houston but he hadn't understood until right now.

She'd made him.

No, not him. But she realized she was being watched, he thought in amazement. He'd only had one other target who'd been able to sense his scrutiny and he still didn't know what had tipped the man off. Some people just had better radar than others. Stratton moved toward the doorway of the store, then went inside.

A clerk immediately approached him. Stratton pointed vaguely toward a pair of ladies' heels and muttered a size, his eyes locking on Jennifer. The clerk disappeared and Jennifer completed her turn. Unbelievably, she paused as she stared at the shoe store and Stratton went cold.

He stepped back, putting more space between himself and the window. Her eyes lingered a second longer, then her gaze shifted and he breathed again.

Faster than Stratton expected, the clerk came back

with a pair of red satin pumps, their stiletto heels at least
four inches long. Stratton didn't want to lose Jennifer,
but he didn't want to be someone the man remembered,
either. Stratton mumbled *"Por mi esposa,"* in badly ac-
cented Spanish and thrust a wad of reals toward the guy
with an apologetic shrug for his poor language skills.

The salesman's face cleared and he nodded with a
big smile. Leading Stratton to the back of the store, he
counted out the bills that he needed, then gave himself
a five-real tip before handing the roll back. He then
pantomimed his thanks, dropping the shoe box into a
gaily colored bag and passing it to Stratton.

"Thank you," Stratton said in broad English, slightly
louder than he usually spoke. "Thank you, uh, gray-
cieses muc-cho."

The clerk nodded, his smile stretching. Stratton was
out the door a moment later, but Jennifer was nowhere
in sight.

THE CREEPY STARED-AT FEELING had hit her without
warning.

Totally unprepared for the reaction, Jennifer found
herself trembling and frightened. What was happening to
her? Was someone following her or was she losing her
mind? She stepped off the sidewalk and flagged a cab. The
car screeched to a halt causing the driver behind to slam
on his brakes, but no one took notice as the horns began
to blare. Jennifer suspected the nearby pedestrians would
have stopped and looked if everything had gone silent, but
transportation here was a noisy affair. She jumped inside
and gave the cab driver the name of the hotel.

He nodded with a blinding smile, then whipped the

car around in a tire-squealing U-turn. They were in front of the hotel a few minutes later. She paid the fare and doubled it for his tip, fleeing the cab before it could halt completely.

Back in Houston, she'd begun to wonder if someone was setting her up for a robbery, but she had never expected to have the same sensation of being watched here. It made no sense whatsoever.

Even more shaky than she'd been at first, Jennifer hurried up the steps leading into the hotel and entered the revolving door. Her eyes went to the desk but the clerk who'd flirted with her was gone. A young woman had replaced him, and she nodded at Jennifer in a pleasant and totally nonchalant way. Everything—and everyone—looked completely normal, she realized slowly. In addition to the desk clerk, she saw a bell captain near his podium, talking with two bellhops, two maids dusting and a young boy pushing a service cart with the remnants of someone's dinner. Nothing looked even remotely out of the ordinary.

She wanted to escape to the suite, but instead she forced herself to walk at a regular pace toward the small bar off the side of the lobby. Once there, she ordered a glass of Amaretto. She'd never had the almond-flavored liqueur, but Cissy swore by it, telling Jennifer nothing calmed her more than a splash of it over ice.

The bartender brought the drink and Jennifer downed it quickly. A little too quickly, she thought a minute later. The room seemed to spin for a second then it steadied, a slow, easy warmth building inside her. Feeling better, she ordered a second drink. She sipped this one and thought about what had happened.

Until she'd gotten scared, she'd been having a nice time. The food had been delicious and the people watching even more so. Everyone had looked so carefree and happy. And beautiful. Without exception, it seemed, the woman were self-assured and sexy, their dark, shining hair hanging straight, their eyes sparkling as they moved gracefully along the street. The men beside them were equally gorgeous with burnished skin and bold stares. Cissy would have been in seventh heaven.

Jennifer took another sip of her drink, her chagrin at her imagined stalker growing. She'd let her fear ruin what had been a perfectly lovely evening. What the heck was wrong with her? Her mom had had a friend who'd suffered an early menopause, and she'd thought for a while that she'd been losing her mind. Maybe Jennifer was going through something hormonal. She stared into the drink and frowned, unsure which would be worse—a mental breakdown or a chemical imbalance. Draining the second drink, she decided neither one sounded good.

She signed her tab then walked out of the bar, still feeling tense. The tiny elevator took her straight to her floor and when the doors opened, she exited into a hallway that was empty and quiet. Too quiet. Her uneasiness returned full force, but she ignored the warning voice in the back of her mind and went directly to the suite, unlocking the huge mahogany door and stepping inside.

"*Stop,*" the voice in her head whispered. "*Don't go any farther. Turn around and leave right now.*"

"Oh, shut up." She spoke out loud. "You're driving me crazy." Feeling for the light, she found nothing but an empty wall. She cursed, then her fingers brushed the switch.

Light flooded the room, and she breathed a sigh of relief. Until she saw what was on the floor.

She was still screaming when the maid ran into the room.

CHAPTER FIVE

THE BARTENDER brought Stratton a ginger ale, setting it in front of him and nodding before he moved to another customer. Stratton picked up the glass but instead of drinking from it, he stared into the mirror behind the bottles. He could see most of the lobby from where he sat but no one could see him. If the old man came in the back way or through the revolving door, Stratton would be able to spot him.

When he'd left the shoe store, he'd seen a cab make a U-turn and he'd understood instantly. Jennifer Rodas might have a heightened sense of awareness but she knew diddly about disappearing. He'd beat her back to the hotel and waited outside until she'd exited the cab. For one short minute, he'd considered following her into the bar and striking up a conversation but Stratton was as good at that as she was at getting away undetected. He'd always left the romancing technique to the other men in the Operatives. They were much better at it, especially Armando. His Latin charm made him a pro and the power of his appeal could be deadly. Literally.

He'd hung back until Jennifer had gone upstairs then he'd taken her seat in the bar. Five minutes ago, Stratton had noticed the maid. She'd shot out the elevator and practically run to the reception desk, her expression holding nothing but pure terror. The conversation that had followed between her and the desk clerk was frantic and whatever had upset the maid instantly infected the girl behind the counter, as well. She'd picked up the phone and a manager had just appeared. His face blanched as the clerk spoke rapidly. A moment later, the hotel's security chief dashed into the lobby from one of the corridors. Stratton knew the man although the former cop wouldn't recognize him. More years back than he cared to remember, they'd tangoed over a case Stratton would also like to forget. When the ex-policeman heard the maid's news, his lips went tight. Something bad had happened on his watch and he wasn't happy.

Their agitation floated across the lobby and into the bar. Two seats down from Stratton a young couple watched with curiosity and then said something to the bartender. He shrugged but his gaze remained on his co-workers even as he replaced the couple's drinks.

Stratton tapped his glass on the bar and the man in the white apron immediately came over.

"Big star checking in?" Stratton tilted his head toward the reception area. "Things look kinda busy over there all of a sudden."

"I wouldn't know, sir," the bartender replied. "Would you like a refill?"

Stratton nodded with a sigh. Just his luck to get a reticent bartender. Most of them you couldn't shut up.

Without being obvious, Stratton continued to watch but after a while, he dropped the pretense. Everyone else in the bar was looking and a few had even picked up their drinks and gone into the lobby to eavesdrop.

When the security chief headed for the elevator with the manager trailing behind him, Stratton stood up and dropped a handful of bills onto the bar, nodding once to the bartender as he walked out of the lounge. Turning to his right, he entered a deserted corridor and followed it to the service staircase he'd located when he'd first arrived. The door to the stairwell opened easily because he'd taped down the latch when he'd walked down from his own room earlier in the day. He ran up the stairs to the fourth floor, paused and regained his breath, then slowly opened this door, which he'd also taped.

"Shit." The curse came out softly. A crowd of people, housekeepers, security men, even other guests, stood before the entrance to Leonadov's suite, their faces all tight with the same expression. An elevator arrived with a ding and the two men he'd seen downstairs exited the lift.

In the States, the floor would already have been cleared and locked down, the police on their way. But this wasn't the States. The manager and security man jostled their way through the gawkers and stared, too. Faintly, so faintly Stratton wasn't sure at first that he was actually hearing it, the sound of someone's sobs reached his ears. He closed his eyes and cursed again, relief and annoyance mixing together to create a confused reaction inside him.

Jennifer Rodas was crying, which meant she was okay. He heard nothing that even remotely resembled Ami Leonadov's thick accent. Which meant he wasn't okay.

Taking the kind of chance he usually didn't, Stratton started down the hallway. So many people were in the corridor now, he would just be another spectator should anyone spot him. He had to push a bit to get closer to the door but when he drew even with it, he immediately wished he hadn't.

Ami Leonadov lay on the carpet, a stream of blood pooled beneath his head, his eyes wide open and staring.

JENNIFER COULDN'T stop shaking, a cold unlike any she'd ever experienced, chilling her completely. The policewoman who stood nearby seemed sympathetic enough but there was suspicion in her eyes, too.

The suite was full of policemen, some in uniform, some not, crime technicians milling around as well, taking samples and cutting pieces out of various things, like the carpet and the bedspreads. In one corner, the hotel manager waited, a pained expression on his face. Jennifer couldn't tell which bothered him more—having a murder take place in his establishment or having the police ruin the once luxurious furnishings.

She noted all these things through a haze of disbelief, her shock at finding Ami's body still reverberating inside her. The whole thing seemed unreal. She'd read a book once about a woman who'd had out-of-body experiences. The author had perfectly described how Jennifer felt right now. Later on, when she'd absorbed everything, she knew grief would follow but for the moment, she was as numb as she'd been from the moment she'd opened the door and saw him.

She realized someone was saying her name. She looked up to meet the curious gaze of a man she had yet to meet. He was in his late forties, maybe fifties, with dark hair and dark eyes. She couldn't read his expression as he extended his hand.

"Señorita Rodas? I am Detective Angelo with the police of Rio de Janeiro." He spoke English as he clasped her fingers and shook them gently. "May I have a word?"

She nodded and allowed him to lead her to the balcony off the living room.

"It has too much noise, the room," he said. "You do not mind, do you?"

"This is fine," she said distractedly.

"Tell me what happened," he asked.

She told him all she could, explaining about Ami's note and how she'd gone to eat at the café. She left out the part where she gotten scared—it made her sound stupid and it didn't matter anyway—then she continued. "I had a drink in the bar." She stopped and corrected herself. "No, I had two and then I came upstairs. When I opened the door and switched on the light, he was there. I screamed."

"The lights were off?"

"Yes."

"And the door? It was locked?"

"Yes."

"Did you touch him?"

She sucked in a breath and shook her head.

He pulled a package of cigarettes from his inside coat pocket and offered her one. Jennifer didn't smoke but suddenly she wished she did. She shook her head, but with nicotine-stained fingers, he took one out for himself, lighting it and inhaling deeply.

"Why were you and the *señor* in Rio?"

"He had business here and he'd asked me to come with him so I could translate."

"You speak Portuguese?" He seemed surprised.

"I had a Portuguese grandmother," she responded. "And I studied it in college."

"You were his secretary?"

He knew more than he'd let on, but the way he said the word was what drew her attention, even through her shock. "Yes," she said sharply. "I have been for two years. Before that, my mother worked for him."

"And what kind of business did he have?"

"Mr. Leonadov is a diamond broker." She realized what she'd said and stammered out "wa…was a diamond broker."

He raised his dark eyebrows. "An interesting business. Did he have diamonds on his person tonight? Is anything missing?"

She shook her head. "He said he'd put his inventory in the safe downstairs. As far as I know, it's still there. Nothing was taken from here."

She looked over the railing, her eyes filling with tears. "Nothing but his life."

A movement through the glass caught her eye and Jennifer looked back. They were taking out Ami's body. She started forward but the policeman put a hand on her arm and stopped her. "Don't worry," he said softly. "We will take care of him."

The silence built for a moment, then Jennifer managed to ask what she'd wondered from the very first. "What happened to him?" She stuttered to a stop then started over. "I mean, how was he—"

"Your employer was shot," the detective supplied.

"Most likely with a long-range rifle. You didn't see the glass?" He nodded to one of the windows.

Jennifer followed his motion and released an audible groan that she couldn't hold back. "Oh, my God, who would do such a thing? Why would this happen?"

"I do not have an answer for you," he said staring toward the beach. The traffic had finally slowed and the occasional sound of a wave echoed in the darkness. "But I will find one, that I promise."

From out of nowhere, she thought of Thomas. "I have to call his son," Jennifer said. "Back in Houston."

"There will be time for that later. You have your papers handy?"

She looked at him blankly.

"Your passport," he explained. "And Mr. Leonadov's, too. I'll need your return tickets, also."

She frowned. "I don't understand. Why do you need those?"

"For information's sake," he said smoothly. "Merely a technicality. After we release you, we may have to keep them but it will only be for a day or two."

She nodded, then his words soaked in. A giant band tightened around her chest and all at once she couldn't catch her breath. "After you release me? Wh-what are you talking about?"

"You will have to come with me to the *policia centrale, señorita.* There will be forms, paperwork, things like that." He shrugged apologetically then added, almost as an afterthought. "I will have some more questions for you, too, I think."

Anxiety blossomed like a rose inside her chest. "How long will this take?"

"I don't know."

His vagueness alarmed her and before she could stop them, the words slipped out, her voice rising suddenly. "Are you arresting me?"

"No, no, Señorita Rodas. It is nothing like that, I promise. We merely need to talk some more, that is all."

Jennifer didn't know what to do but her dilemma was short-lived. The detective took her arm—ever so gently— and led her away from the railing and back into the living room. Everyone seemed to freeze as they stepped inside. Only the detective's grip on her arm kept Jennifer going forward.

"Go get the passports and tickets," he suggested quietly. "I'll wait for you here then we will leave."

There was nothing she could do but follow his orders. Her heart in her throat, Jennifer walked toward her bedroom.

STRATTON WASN'T SURPRISED when the elevator doors closed on the detective and Jennifer Rodas. He was taking her to the central station for more questioning. Standard Operating Procedure. He knew that and so did the detective but what was going through Jennifer's head? She'd looked terrified but almost every amateur he'd ever seen being led off by the police wore the same deer-in-the-headlights expression, guilty or innocent.

He followed them in a cab to the station just to make sure, then he had the driver take him to a bar near Ribeiro Gomez's neighborhood. The area was a rougher part of Rio than the tourists ever saw, but it didn't come close to being one of the favelas. He'd called Gomez from the hotel and told him to meet him there.

Staring out the window of the cab, Stratton found himself wondering why nothing could ever be simple. His earlier theory that the old man and Jennifer Rodas could have planned C.J.'s murder was now just as dead as Leonadov himself, and to make things even more complicated, Jennifer had an airtight alibi. Stratton had been watching her eat while Leonadov was killed. Unless she had an accomplice Stratton didn't know about, there was no way Jennifer could have done in her boss.

But the two murders had to be linked. Even if Ami Leonadov wasn't behind C. J. Singh's death, the victims had been friends and business associates so that meant they were connected. Stratton's deduction went beyond just that simple fact, though. Something about both situations just didn't feel right to him. As the cab pulled up to the bar, he found himself wondering what else the two men must have shared.

The former *federale* was waiting for him. He shook Stratton's hand. "Trouble has found you," he said. "Why am I not surprised?"

Stratton shrugged. "I'm just lucky, I guess. I'm going to need some more help, though. Can you handle it?"

"You tell me what you want," Gomez replied, "And I will see that it gets done."

With as few words as possible, Stratton explained. He was through in ten minutes.

"No problem," the ex-cop said. "Anything else?"

Stratton finished the bottle of water he'd ordered. "That's it," he said. "Just be sure there are no mistakes."

Gomez nodded and a moment later he was gone.

JENNIFER HAD BEEN petrified. The idea of going to any police station, much less one outside the United States, sounded like a very bad idea to her. She'd seen the same movies everyone else had and visions of dank cells with torture chambers nearby immediately took control of her thoughts.

But the detective couldn't have been nicer. He took her to his office, listened to her story again, then asked more questions, mostly about Ami. After talking to the clerk who remembered directing her to the café and then the waiter who'd served her dinner, he seemed satisfied.

He left her alone, saying something about some paperwork he needed, and Jennifer let her shoulders slump, her eyes instantly filling.

Ami was dead.

How could this have happened?

She was in a state of shock, the chaos that had first come over her lifting to reveal disbelief. Who would want him dead? Especially in Rio? She'd given the detective some of the names of Ami's contacts in Rio—the few she knew—including the man he'd met tonight, Joaquim Ioao, but after that, she wasn't much help. They were searching for the cabbie who'd taken him to dinner but Rio was a huge city, and Angelo had explained that a lot of the drivers were unlicensed and illegal. Coming forward and contacting the police would be the last thing they'd be interested in doing, especially if murder was involved.

Before the questions had begun, Angelo had let her call Thomas. She closed her eyes and let her head fall to the wall behind her. The conversation had been horrible, absolutely horrible. Understandably, Ami's son had had a thousand questions but she'd had no answers. She'd told him what she could then promised to call him later. Her throat closed as the image of Ami's body re-entered her mind. She tried to catch the sob that came with it but she failed and it escaped. Angelo's voice made her open her eyes.

He stood by the edge of his desk, his features now sympathetic instead of suspicious.

"This has been a terrible introduction to our city for you, *señorita*. I am very, very sorry."

She fought for her composure. "I am, too," she replied. "I just can't believe it happened."

"We will do all we can to find who did this," he promised. "In the meantime, you are free to go. We have contacted the American Embassy for you and they will assist you from now on."

"What about…" she stumbled. "What about the body?"

"You shouldn't wait for the release," he said gently. "That may take a little longer."

She wiped her eyes and stood. He handed her an envelope.

"Those are your tickets," he explained.

"And the passports?"

His eyes shifted then came back to hers. "We need those a bit longer. You should have them in a few days."

"A few days?" A few hours would be fine, but days? "I can't wait that long to leave!" Horrified by the thought, Jennifer shook her head violently. "You don't understand. I have to get home. I can't stay here."

"You have been involved in a terrible crime, Señorita Rodas. Surely you understand the need for your presence."

"For a little while, yes, but days?"

"I am very sorry but I have no choice. Those are our laws. I will release your passport as soon as I'm allowed." He glanced at his watch then over her shoulder. "The night has passed, but I suggest you return to the Copa and try to rest."

Distracted by his comment—as he'd obviously planned—Jennifer followed his gaze to look out the window behind her. Daylight flooded the parking lot. Time had stopped for her, but the rest of the world had kept going. It didn't seem right.

She turned back to the detective to continue her argument then a wave of exhaustion hit her. She swayed slightly from the force of it, and Angelo reached for her elbow, an expression of alarm crossing his face.

"Are you all right?"

"I'm fine," she reassured him. "It's okay, really."

He didn't look convinced but he released her, albeit reluctantly.

"I'm fine," she repeated. "I just want to go back. I want to go home."

"I understand," he said. "As soon as possible, I will let you do that. In the meantime, my driver will return you to the Copa and I will personally deliver your passport the minute the magistrate releases it."

Jennifer nodded then followed the detective to a waiting car. Using his horn more than his brakes, the man behind the wheel wove in and out of the heavy traffic. In a blur, they passed slums and mansions, corner stores and boutiques, the vehicle finally shooting out thirty minutes later from the side road to the avenue that fronted the beach. Until that point, even though she'd probably taken the same route last night, none of it looked familiar to Jennifer.

The lobby fell silent when they entered. Escorting her to the reception desk, the young cop delivered her to the clerk behind the counter along with a spate of Portuguese instructions. The words were an even greater blur than the scenery had been. When he nodded goodbye and left, she turned to the clerk herself.

"I want a different room." Jennifer put her hands on the polished counter. "I can't go back to the suite."

"*Sí, señorita.*" The young woman was respectful despite her curious gaze. "We've already had your bags moved. The police have the suite restricted now regardless. They won't release it until they've inspected it more closely."

She tapped the bell to her right and a young boy appeared instantly. She handed him the key. "Take Ms. Rodas to Room 608."

Walking across the marble lobby, Jennifer felt many eyes on her. Only after she was alone inside the new room, much smaller and much less luxurious than the suite, did she relax but when she did, the tears came in a flood that seemed endless. Ami's murder was horrible, but knowing she had to stay here so much longer was all it took to overwhelm her.

The telephone rang five times before she managed to answer it. "Ye— Yes," she hiccupped.

"You have a call from the States. A Mr. Leonadov. Will you take it?"

For a single second, she thought the operator meant Ami, then she understood and her heart fell. Thomas was on the line.

She gripped the phone tightly. "Put it through."

Thomas sounded hoarse, and she wondered if he'd been crying. She couldn't conjure the image no matter how hard she tried.

"Jennifer! When did you get back?" he asked in a petulant voice. "I've been trying and trying to get you—"

"I just walked in," she answered.

"Well, would you please tell me what's going on? Should I come down there or what?"

The thought of putting up with Thomas as well as everything else almost sent her over the edge. "No, no. That's not necessary. But I don't know anything more. The detective said he'd try his best. Like I told you before, the shot came from outside the hotel and that's all they know right now."

"It must have been a random thing," he said brokenly. "He had no enemies, no reason to be killed."

Jennifer agreed. "I told the detective that, but who knows?" She paused. "You wouldn't know more about the people he had made appointments with down here, would you? The more details we can give the police, the better."

"I don't know any of them. He handled all the out-of-country stuff himself, you know that."

She tried not to notice how sharp and bitter his words were. Thomas's territory had been a real bone of contention between the two men, Ami feeling he wasn't ready for more, Thomas pushing for all he could get.

"I just thought I'd ask," she replied. "The detective wanted to know."

"Well, I can't help you there."

They discussed a few more details then Jennifer told him about the police keeping her passport.

"My God! They don't suspect you, do they?"

She'd been hoping for a little reassurance but Thomas's comment only gave her more anxiety. "Of course they don't think I did it." She spoke sharply even though it'd been obvious the police *had* suspected her at first. "Why would you even ask such a thing?"

"Don't get snippy with me, Jennifer, I was merely asking." He paused. "Where *were* you when this happened?"

Unbelievably his question held a tinge of suspicion. She told herself again that they were both on edge, but his question still rankled and she answered bluntly, his admonition ignored. "I was out having dinner," she answered. "They talked to the waiter who served me. Would you like his number, too?"

"That isn't necessary," he said quietly. "I was merely asking because I'm glad you weren't hurt yourself. I was concerned, that's all."

She instantly felt like a jerk. "I'm sorry, Thomas." She covered her eyes with her hands. "It's just been so horrible, though. I—I wasn't thinking when I said that. I didn't mean anything by it."

"Not to worry." He hesitated. "I have to ask you something else, though."

"What is it?" she asked bleakly.

"How much inventory did he have with him?"

"None," she answered. "Everything's in the safe downstairs."

"You checked it yourself?"

"Yes," she answered wearily. Detective Angelo had made her check before he'd taken her to the station. "It's all there."

The conversation finished after that. On wooden feet Jennifer walked into the bathroom and turned on the shower, peeling off Cissy's beautiful black dress and leaving it in a heap on the tile floor. But the water did nothing to wash away the terrible emptiness inside her. Feeling even worse, she went to the bed after she finished her shower and escaped into a sleep so deep, it felt endless. She didn't move and she didn't dream.

SHE PASSED THE FOUR DAYS that followed in a similar haze, her mind unfocused, her grief swelling. She got up every morning and dressed, then after that, the sadness set in. She spoke to Cissy twice and Thomas several more times but the conversations that really hurt were the ones she shared with her mother. Devastated by the news, Jennifer's mom had a hard time believing her former employer and friend was actually gone, much less that he'd been murdered. Every time they'd talked, she'd insisted on hearing every detail again. Understanding the need, Jennifer had accommodated her mother, but the wounds of her grief were reopened with each telling. She couldn't help but compare her mother's reaction to the official from the Embassy who'd come by to see her once. It was clear all he wanted was to be able to say he'd done his duty so he could move on. Detective Angelo showed up on the fifth day, and she met him in the lobby.

"I will bring your passport tonight," he announced, "when the court closes and has released it. There is no need for you to remain here any longer. The Embassy has made all the arrangements for the shipment, too."

Relief washed over her. "Have you arrested some-one—"

He interrupted her question by shaking his head. "We do not have a suspect yet. But we will find him, I promise."

They'd been sitting in a corner of the lobby, and he stood with that assurance, the interview apparently over. "I'm sorry this was your introduction to our country, Se-ñorita Rodas. Please come back another time and let us redeem ourselves."

Jennifer got to her feet, too. Returning to Brazil, or any other foreign country for that matter, was the last thing she would ever want to do. She didn't tell the de-tective that, however. A simple goodbye sufficed and then he was gone.

Crossing the lobby behind him, she went immedi-ately to the reception desk. The man behind the counter was the same one who'd flirted with her the night Ami had died. It seemed as if that had happened years ago. "I'll be checking out this evening," she said.

His dark gaze met hers. "Very well, *señorita*."

She said nothing else and he did the same. A few minutes later she was back in her room and calling the airline. Unbelievably they had a seat on a flight that left at ten that night. She booked it then called the States.

Thomas sounded strange when he picked up the phone and he'd sounded that way all week. But who wouldn't? He'd lost his father under the worst of circumstances.

"I've been released," she said without preamble, "and I have a reservation on a flight out tonight."

"Tonight? I'm surprised you could get one so fast."

"I am, too," she said, "but I took it and didn't look back." She paused. "The Embassy—"

"They've already called," he said curtly. "The body will arrive late tomorrow afternoon. I've made the arrangements."

"I'm surprised you could get that done so fast." She gripped the phone, wincing when she realized she'd just echoed his thought.

"I told the Embassy to handle it and they did everything."

His explanation left her cold and empty. "I understand," she said. But she didn't. Not really.

They hung up a few minutes later and the hours passed quickly after that. By seven she had paid the bill, retrieved the diamonds and was ready to leave.

But her passport had yet to arrive.

Pacing the lobby nervously, she looked out the revolving door every few minutes, her gaze going to her watch in between times. The lobby was unusually crowded, the guests louder than normal. Some kind of party, she assumed. By eight, she was getting panicky.

"You have a phone call, *señorita*." A bellhop appeared at her side, tilting his head toward a bank of telephones against one wall. "The desk will put it through over there."

She nodded, a bad feeling coming over her as she headed toward the phones. Snatching up the first one that rang, Jennifer felt her heart sink as Detective Angelo's voice said her name.

"I need my passport, Detective." She didn't give him time for an excuse. "I've checked out, I have my ticket. I need to go! You said—"

"There's been a problem."

"Then fix it."

"I cannot do that tonight. That is why I am calling you. To let you know. Tomorrow, I promise—"

"I don't want your promises, Detective. I want my passport."

"I understand that, but—"

She interrupted him a third time, not caring if she sounded rude, a sudden fear overcoming her. "What's the problem?"

"It is perfunctory, I assure you. The magistrate failed to sign all the necessary documents you will need to show at the airport."

"Then find him and have them signed."

The silence at the other end of the phone told her this was not an option. Growing desperate, she tried to force the issue. "I'm an American citizen, and you can't hold me against my will." Her words hung in the marble lobby for everyone to hear. Flushing at the realization, Jennifer lowered her voice. "You *promised*," she hissed.

He answered her coldly. "And now I am breaking that promise. Your passport will not be delivered tonight. If the magistrate signs the papers tomorrow, you will have it. If not, then you will wait until he does. Good night, *señorita*."

Jennifer dropped the receiver back into the cradle and moaned, cursing the detective under her breath with every epithet she could dredge up, in English and in Portuguese. When she finished, she made her way across the packed lobby and faced the clerk once more.

"I can't leave," she announced. "My passport has been delayed. Please check me back in."

"I am afraid that is not possible," he answered. "The rooms, they are all gone."

"What?"

"We're having a wedding." He pointed to the milling crowd behind her. "We have been booked for many months."

God, could anything else happen to her? "Surely you have something," she said. "You've got to! I don't know any other hotels here."

"It wouldn't matter if you did," he explained helpfully. "They are full, too. The bride is a local television star and the groom, he plays polo—"

Jennifer ignored his explanation. "What am I going to do? I can't sleep on the street!"

One of the younger girls tugged at the man's sleeve. When he bent down she said something in Portuguese and he nodded.

"There is one possibility," he said when he straightened, "but…"

"I don't care what it is. I'll take it."

"It is the suite," he replied solemnly. "The *policia* released it just today. The bride had wanted it but we have not finished the repairs."

Jennifer swallowed, her throat suddenly tight.

"It would be complimentary, of course," he assured her. "And we have had it cleaned."

They could have scrubbed down the silk-covered walls and burned the expensive leather furniture, and it wouldn't make one iota of difference. If she walked inside that living room, she'd see nothing but Ami's body.

"I can't do that."

"Then I am sorry." He shrugged, a movement she'd come to associate with defeat. "There is nothing else."

Jennifer simply looked at him, then she gave in.

"Let me back into the safety deposit box, then give me the key to the suite," she said quietly. "After everything else I've been through, I should be able to handle something that simple."

CHAPTER SIX

"She's checked out of the hotel."

"When did she leave?"

"Around seven. Her flight was at ten. We confirmed her reservations just to make sure."

"I can't have any screwups here, Gomez." Stratton rubbed his bloodshot eyes with the back of his hand. He was exhausted from waiting. Waiting for the cops to leave. Waiting for Jennifer to get out of Rio. Waiting for information. He'd forgotten how much of his job entailed waiting.

"There will not be any. My man is reliable. One hundred percent. The police are out of the hotel and so is the woman. I guarantee it."

"What the hell took so long?" Stratton's irritation with the whole situation leaked out. "Why did they have to quarantine the room for so long? I could have inspected it on my hands and knees three times by now."

"I have no idea," Gomez said. "These things take more time here."

The delay had put Stratton in a very bad mood. There was probably nothing in the suite that could tell him anything but he wasn't leaving until he could get in there and see for himself. He suspected the cops had been parked in the luxurious hotel room because the surroundings were a lot more pleasant than where they usually found themselves, but there had been nothing he could do about it. He'd kept an eye on Jennifer Rodas while he'd waited.

"Any arrests yet?" Stratton asked.

"No. My sources tell me the police suspect it was a random shot. A lot of crimes happen here that are never reported. Some of those include the use of firearms."

Gomez's voice seemed curt but Stratton decided he was probably hearing an echo of his own impatience. The ex-*federale* had worked with Stratton for years and never given him anything but the truth.

They discussed a few more details then said goodbye. They wouldn't see each other again, until the next time Stratton needed something illegal.

He pulled the curtains back and looked out the window. A soft rain was falling and the usual rowdiness was missing from the street. He settled in with a cup of coffee. The last few hours were always the hardest.

JENNIFER PULLED the blanket closer to her chin and closed her eyes with determination. She was grateful she had a bed, but walking into the suite's living area had been one of the most difficult things she'd ever done. Her eyes had gone immediately to the spot where Ami had lain. The rug was gone, of course, but she could still see the body. The desk where he'd sat, the bedroom where he'd hung his clothes, everywhere she looked the memory of him lingered.

A few years back Cissy had decided to buy a house, and she'd insisted Jennifer help her. Every property they viewed had had to pass her "energy" evaluation. She swore that places took on personalities, absorbing the forces of the people who'd passed through and the activities that had occurred there. If she felt any kind of negativity, they had to turn around and leave instantly.

Jennifer had dismissed the whole exercise, telling Cissy she was crazy.

Now, Jennifer wondered. There *was* a much different feel to the room than when she'd first seen it. She couldn't describe the change but it was definitely there.

Rolling to her side, she reached out for the clock on the bedside table. It was 3:15 a.m. She'd been in bed for hours and had only caught snatches of sleep. She flopped to her back and closed her eyes. Part of her problem was the nightgown she wore. Somehow in the confusion of changing rooms and packing things, her T-shirt had gotten misplaced. The only thing she'd had left was the ridiculous nightgown Cissy had given her. Jennifer fingered the soft silk and shook her head, remembering the way she'd laughed when she'd found it. Had that really happened to her? The whole incident seemed more like a dream.

She closed her eyes again and willed herself to sleep.

STRATTON EASED DOWN the deserted hallway and walked silently toward the door of the suite, the key Gomez had given him in one hand, his other on the Ruger automatic tucked inside his waistband. He didn't like to keep a weapon where anyone could see it but right now his need to have it handy had outweighed his concern. He felt uneasy and on edge. He attributed his anxiety to the fact that he hadn't worked in a while, and he was out of practice, but he also knew the feeling came from his gut, too. Something wasn't right, but he didn't disregard it. The police report Gomez had given him had told him little more than the bare facts. The killing shot had come through the window.

The key glided into the lock without a sound and Stratton turned it to the right. The door gave way and he stepped inside, closing it quietly behind him. The draperies were open and the room came into focus as his eyes adjusted to the darkness. He had a penlight with him, but it was better if he didn't use it.

Walking to the middle of the living room, Stratton paused then turned in a circle. The room was generous with two doors leading off it—to the bedrooms, he assumed. A set of French doors opened to a balcony, heavy velvet drapes tied back on either side.

He moved to the spot where Leonadov's body had lain, standing where he imagined the elderly man had been when the shot had hit him. The report had been vague—as they all were here—but Stratton had a pretty good idea of where he'd been positioned. He pivoted slowly until his back was to the French doors.

The living room stretched out before him. The carpet was obviously new, but the luxurious furnishings were the same ones he'd seen when he'd passed by the room the night of Ami's death. The largest and most ornate piece, a gilt console, caught his eye, the huge matching mirror above it a monstrosity from another age. Walking closer, Stratton realized the entire room, from one end to the other, was reflected in the glass. He looked to the place where Leonadov had stood, then at the French doors. He fixed the imaginary triangle inside his head. He was still thinking about what that meant when a glimmer in the mirror drew his attention. He looked closer and saw that someone had swept glass shards into a small pile beside the window then had failed to pick them up.

He crossed the room on silent feet then pulled the drapery back. The pane of new glass stood out from the others, the surface still clean and free of spots. Turning back to the heavy velvet, he ran his hand over the fabric until he found the hole where the bullet had passed. Glass was cheap but velvet wasn't. A fold in the curtain hid the damage and someone had decided to leave it alone.

Down on his knees, Stratton sighted a line through the tear. His gaze went directly across the side street to another hotel. Countless balconies were before him. The shooter could have used any of them, or he could have even been on the roof. It would have been a very simple shot with the right kind of weapon. For the right kind of shooter. It would *not* have been random.

Stratton rocked back on his heels, the murder of Ami Leonadov taking on a whole different feel. Singh's death had been sloppy and ill planned, or at least, set up to look that way. Leonadov's had been efficient and carefully developed.

Which told Stratton two things.

Someone had wanted the diamond dealer dead badly enough to hire a professional. And more importantly, whoever had been hired didn't give a damn if anyone knew.

Meredith had told him too many times to count that every detail was a message from the killer, conscious or otherwise. She'd explained this, of course, so he would be aware of his own tells, but he turned the advice around now and considered what this meant.

There were numerous ways a professional killer could make his work look like something else, but no effort had been made to do that by whoever had shot Ami Leonadov.

Stratton searched the rest of the living room with cursory interest. Learning what he just had, he knew he'd find out little else that was relevant, at least to the identity of the killer. The first bedroom revealed nothing, either. He opened the door to the second bedroom and slipped inside, closing it behind him.

His gaze swept over the room as he started forward, but when he reached the foot of the bed, he stopped and so did his heart.

SHE'D LEFT THE DRAPERIES open, the darkness too stifling otherwise. In the dim light that came from the streetlight outside, the man at the foot of the bed stilled. He said nothing but Jennifer wasn't sure she would have heard him if he *had* spoken—her pulse had begun to roar in her ears as soon as she'd opened her eyes and seen the shadowy figure in her bedroom.

She stared at him, her eyes wide with fear, the blanket clutched to her chest as if it could protect her.

"Who the hell are you?" she asked. "And what are you doing in my room?"

He maintained his silence, coming two steps closer.

"Stop right there," she said sharply. "I'll scream."

"Go ahead," he said. "No one will hear you and if they do, they'll ignore it."

Something told her he was right. With her eyes on

his face, she swung her feet off the bed and stood. He made no further moves yet his silence scared her more than a sudden lunge would have.

"There's money in my purse," she said, gesturing toward the chair behind him. "Take whatever you want then get out."

He moved to his right and the light fell across his face. He was muscular and wide shouldered under his black T-shirt, his blond hair cut close to his scalp, his face all angles and edges. She couldn't see his eyes for the shadows but she could feel their gaze.

There was a wall behind her and the balcony doors were to her left. Behind him was the bathroom and the door to the living room. The balcony didn't sound like a good idea but neither did trying to pass him.

"I have pearls," she said. "They're in my case in the bathroom. I'll get them for you if you'll just leave."

"I'm not here for your jewelry."

He spoke in English and his voice held no accent. Her mouth went dry and her initial fear deepened. His appearance was no coincidence, she thought suddenly. Whoever this man was, he was in her room because of what had happened to Ami.

Nausea threatened. She swallowed it back and made her voice tough. The only way she was getting out of this was to bluff. "If you're here for the stones, you're out of luck. I don't have them. They're in the safe downstairs."

She started to push her way past him but in the second that followed he grabbed her by both arms and threw her to the floor. Jennifer screamed as his body covered hers and he started them in a roll across the carpet; her breath jolted from her chest by his weight. Glass shattered and something whizzed through the air past the point where her head had been the moment before.

She screamed again and started to struggle but he put a hand over her mouth.

"Shut up!" he whispered in her ear. "And be still!"

Too scared to listen, Jennifer pounded the man's chest, but he squeezed her jaw with a painful strength, his other hand capturing her fists. "Be still!" he repeated, "and be quiet, for God's sake. There's someone outside shooting!"

Jennifer went motionless but only for a second, her fear overriding her brain. All she wanted to do was get away. She tried to pry his fingers off her face, but he held on.

There was the sound of a second hit on the wall behind them.

The man on top of her began to inch backward, pulling Jennifer with him. A third shot came through the window and then a fourth. He yanked her to her hands and knees and pressed his face next to hers, his breath hot against her skin.

"Crawl into the bathroom when I tell you to go," he ordered. "*Do not* go into the living room. They can see the whole room."

"Who are you?" she asked. "What are you doing—"

She felt his body tense, his legs going tight and hard. A gun appeared in his right hand. "Get ready," he said. "One, two, three—"

He pushed her forward as he said the last word, his

weapon firing with rapid succession, the muffled sound a cannon shot to Jennifer's ears but little more than a spit to anyone outside the room.

Jumping to her feet, Jennifer did exactly what he'd told her not to—she ran for the living room and headed straight for the door. He tackled her just past the edge of the couch and they fell together—once again—to the parquet floor. She struggled to get loose but he held her tightly against him, another shot whizzing past the back of the sofa.

"What's wrong with you?" he demanded hoarsely. "Didn't you hear me? Someone is shooting at you!"

She opened her mouth to scream again, then she stared into his eyes, fright overriding everything else as his features registered.

He was the man from the hallway, she thought dumbly. The one she'd seen in Houston.

The one with the cold dead eyes.

"I know you," she said with panic. "You're the guy I saw outside our office. What are you doing here?"

He lifted his gun. Catching her breath and holding it inside her chest, Jennifer blinked then braced for the shot. *This is it. This is how I'm going to go. Underneath a stranger in the middle of Rio.*

"Forget about me," he answered, confirming her fear. "The question that matters is, do you want to live or die?"

"I WANT TO LIVE," she said softly.

"Then shut up and do exactly what I say. *Exactly* what I say and nothing more. If you try anything else, I'll shoot you before the guy outside can even aim again." He paused. "Do you understand what I'm saying?"

She swallowed, the muscles in her neck moving convulsively, then nodded.

"The shooter can see this whole room because of the mirror over there." He tilted his head behind them. "The only reason we're not dead is this couch." He tilted his head again, this time to the massive piece of furniture on his right. He spoke slowly, an obvious effort to make sure she understood. "Do you get that?"

She nodded a second time.

"I'm going to cover you and you're going for the door. In return, you're going to hold it open till I get there, then we're both running down the hall to the stairway. After that, we're going to the second floor. I have a room there. I've got to get something out of it, then we're leaving this hotel. Together. Do you understand?" he repeated.

"Can't you just let me go?" she said in a small voice. "I won't tell—"

"You wouldn't make it to the end of the block. Whoever's behind that rifle wants you dead and I'm the only reason you're not."

"But that doesn't make any sense."

"It doesn't have to make sense. It's the truth."

"But—"

Her protest died when he tightened his grip on his pistol and raised it slowly. "No more *buts*."

Their gazes locked, then she nodded one last time.

"Good." He whispered the word softly. "Now, get ready."

He pushed himself upright, his pistol already firing.

He knew he wouldn't hit the shooter. His only goal was to distract him. Behind him, Stratton heard Jennifer grunt and then she was gone. A second later, he followed, his weapon discharging continuously as he ran backward for the door.

As soon as they were in the hall, he grabbed her hand and yanked her toward the exit, his pistol cocked and ready. They were halfway down the corridor when a door to their right opened. He swung the gun without thinking, and the gray-haired woman who stood on the threshold, clutched her robe and began to scream hysterically. They flew past her to the stairwell then clattered down the stairs, bursting out two floors later to race toward his room. His haste didn't lessen after they pushed through the door.

He grabbed the satchel that held his extra weapons then glanced around the room. He never set out anything personal but he had to make sure.

"Can't we just hide and call the police from here?" Jennifer stood in the middle of his room, her hand on her chest, her hair tumbling around her shoulders in disarray. "The hotel's huge. Surely he couldn't find us—"

Stratton had been looking under the bed. He jumped to his feet at her words, but the answer he'd had ready suddenly disappeared. Before this point, he hadn't noticed what she was wearing. Now he did.

"You can't go outside like that." He nodded at the scraps of lace and blue silk that barely covered her body. "You've got to put something else on."

She looked down, her eyes as surprised as his when her gaze came back up. "I...forgot. It was a gift. I don't normally—"

He yanked a white cotton shirt from his suitcase and threw it at her. "Put that on," he ordered. "It's not much, but it's better than that thing you're wearing."

She caught the shirt and pulled it over her head, rolling the sleeves up so her hands were free. Reaching over the bed, she pulled a tie from his case, as well, and made herself a belt.

Stratton blinked then returned to his search. "We can't stay here. The guy with the gun has inside help. If he knew where you were, he'll know about this room."

He ran into the bathroom, her voice following him. "But why would he want me dead? And why tonight? I've been stuck in this hotel for four days—"

Stratton came back into the room, a dripping plastic bag in one hand. He'd had an extra gun and ammo in the tank of the toilet. "He probably wants you dead for the same reason he wanted your boss dead."

"Which is?"

"I don't know," he admitted. "But I will."

She blinked. "Why tonight?"

"I would guess he couldn't get a clean shot into your other room. He was probably going to hit you on the way to the airport but when you had to stay in that room again he decided to go back to his original plan."

"How do you know all this?"

He sent her a look that made her abandon the question, just as he'd known it would. Checking the inside pocket of his bag for his passports and papers, he grabbed her elbow. "Let's go."

He managed two steps before he realized she was holding on to the edge of the mattress. He gave her arm a painful yank, but she only held on tighter. "What the hell are you doing?"

She looked at him with dark distrust. "I'm not leaving this hotel until you tell me who you are and what's going on. You can shoot me right here if you want to, but I'm not moving till you answer some of my questions."

For one brief second, he thought about leaving her. She wasn't his responsibility so what did he care? She could deal with the guy behind the rifle. But as quickly as the idea came, it left. He had enough blood on his hands to last a lifetime; he didn't need more.

Besides she could help Stratton. She knew more than she was letting on. And even if she didn't know she knew, Stratton would get the information out of her one way or another.

"Who are you?" she repeated.

The truth was something Stratton didn't generally share, but short of following her advice and shooting her, he wasn't sure he could come up with anything else.

"I'm an investigator. You can call me Stratton," he said, winging it. "Your boss hired me when C. J. Singh was shot."

"You were working for Ami?" Her brown eyes rounded with surprise then filled with suspicion. "Why didn't he tell me?"

"Beats me," he countered. "Now let's go—"

"What about the police in Houston? Aren't they investigating C.J.'s death?"

"Leonadov didn't think they were doing a good enough job. Now can we *please* get the hell out of here?"

"I can't go without the stones downstairs."

"Forget them," he said impatiently. "They're probably not even there anymore and if they are, then someone's down there, too, just waiting for you to show up. Do you want risk your life for a bag of diamonds?"

"How do I know you're not lying?"

"You don't," he said bluntly. "But I'm leaving now. You can come with me and live or you can stay here and die."

He opened the door, then suddenly she was at his side. Two minutes later, they stepped into the steamy night.

CHAPTER SEVEN

JENNIFER WAS NOT a hasty person. She always thought things through with a compulsive attention to detail. The most minor options were considered, evaluated, then selected or discarded.

Jumping into a waiting cab with call-me-Stratton, she tried to figure out what she was doing and why. Never in a thousand years would she have done something so crazy back home, but this wasn't home. And nothing was the same, including, apparently, her. She only hoped the man now sitting beside her didn't lie as well as he could shoot. If he *had* told her the truth, and Ami had hired him, her feelings of being watched could now be explained. She found a measure of relief in that, but it was a very small measure. Good guy or not, he frightened her.

Their taxi forced its way into the stream of traffic, the man behind the wheel spouting a string of Portuguese invectives as he yelled out the window at the other cars.

She tried to keep track but by the fifth or sixth turn Jennifer had no idea which direction they were heading. The streets narrowed the farther they went and the expensive shops and boutiques that had surrounded the hotel gave way to rundown bodegas and bars that were still open, their patrons spilling onto the sidewalks. Cursing even more loudly, their driver barely managed to miss two men who were fighting, but Jennifer didn't know how. She could have leaned out the window and thrown a punch herself, they'd been so close.

She held on to the seat with both hands, trying not to slide toward Stratton, but after a particularly hard turn, she was thrown against him.

He didn't seem to notice. He had a cell phone to his ear and was speaking rapidly.

She straightened and braced herself for the next turn. They entered a residential area, some homes large and elaborate, some little more than shacks. Ten minutes later, maybe more—she'd lost track of time—they stopped outside a walled compound. The place resembled a fortress. There were guards on either side of the gated drive with weapons cradled in their arms and as they pulled in, she caught a silhouette of someone on the roof, as well.

She turned to Stratton in confusion. "Where are we? What is this?"

He leaned over the seat and thrust a wad of bills into the driver's hand. She started to repeat her questions but swallowed them when she saw the man who opened Stratton's door.

Clearly Brazilian, he was well over six feet and muscular, his hair cut so short, she wondered if he were in the military. His cheeks were blotched with a series of small round scars, his eyes hard and dark. Menace pervaded him, making the man beside her look like a choirboy. Without a word, both of them headed for another set of gates, Stratton's grip on Jennifer's arm forcing her into a trot just to keep up with them.

When the solid mahogany doors closed behind them, they were in a courtyard, lush and tropical, the scent of plumeria and something richer filling the air around them. In another time and place, Jennifer might have been impressed, but not here. Most gardens soothed her but this one seemed to assault her senses, even threaten them. Without thinking about what she was doing, she drew nearer to Stratton in the breaking dawn's light.

The tall man held out his hand. "It's a pleasure to make your acquaintance. My name is Gomez," he said.

She dragged her eyes away from the foreboding greenery. "Jennifer Rodas."

His handshake was surprisingly gentle. "I know who you are."

The sentence chilled her, and she gripped Stratton's arm even tighter. Looking down at her, he let a small smile lift his lips and she stiffened, chagrin flooding her face.

Gomez released Jennifer's hand and tilted his head behind him. "Come inside and we'll talk."

He led them through the courtyard to another set of doors, the stalk of a dark green plant, sticky and sharp, pulling at Jennifer as they brushed past. She set her jaw and concentrated on the stream of Portuguese the two men were speaking. The conversation was rapid and low and Jennifer only caught a bit of it.

Two of the words stood out, though.

One was *diamantes*.

The other one was *assassinato*.

STRATTON STOPPED when they entered Gomez's house and turned to Jennifer. He pointed to a bench against the wall. "Wait there."

Gomez sent him a look that clearly said "Rude Americano" and contradicted him, taking Jennifer's elbow and guiding her into his living room. "You'll be more comfortable here, *señorita*. Please have a seat. I'll send in coffee."

Jennifer dropped soundlessly to the cushions of his leather sofa, her face blank, her cheeks without color. Her expression wasn't what Stratton would have expected, and he found his opinion of her possible involvement shifting. If she was connected to the murder of Singh, Jennifer Rodas hadn't counted on Leonadov dying or the possibility that she might, as well. The fright that had overtaken her was genuine and complete.

Gomez got her settled then he led Stratton to a small den off an adjoining hallway. Stratton had never been inside the man's home but he wasn't surprised at how nice it was. Federal cops were paid well in Brazil, not necessarily by the government, though.

Stratton spoke first, his anger barely contained as he glared at Gomez. "You told me she'd checked out. Why the hell was she still there?"

"She did check out," Gomez said calmly. "But Angelo held up her passport and the Copa comped her the suite since it was all they had. No money, no record. The whole thing wasn't put in the hotel's system so we didn't know. He still has her passport, by the way."

Stratton went quiet. This wasn't good news. "Why?"

"I have no idea." Gomez sat down behind a large desk. "I thought you might know."

Stratton shook his head, then turned to stare out the open door. Gomez followed his gaze back toward his living room and echoed Stratton's assessment of Jennifer Rodas. *"É espantada."*

"I know," Stratton answered. "And I intend to take full advantage of that fright in just a few minutes. In the meantime, you have to find out what the hell's going on. Whoever killed Leonadov is obviously not finished." He tilted his head toward Jennifer. "She's next. I don't want to be in line after her."

Gomez nodded, and Stratton explained what he'd found in the suite and what he needed next. The minute he was done, Gomez called for his car. He was on his cell phone before the car pulled out of the gates.

Stratton stood beside the window in the den and pondered how best to proceed. His usual techniques for gaining information seemed too harsh for this situation so he had to rethink his strategy.

He hadn't come up with an answer but he headed for the living room a few minutes later anyway. Time was short and even though Gomez had a virtual army protecting his home, Stratton didn't want to test it.

Jennifer rose to her feet as he walked into the living room and resumed the argument they'd had back at the hotel. "You have to tell me what's going on," she said. "I think we should call the police. And who is the man who lives here? Does he know I'm an American citizen?"

His expression a deliberate mask of intimidation, Stratton took a step closer and Jennifer instantly fell silent.

"He doesn't give a rat's ass if you're the Queen of England," he said softly. "And frankly, neither do I. I was hired to figure out who murdered C. J. Singh and that's what I'm doing." He paused. "You're going to help me, too."

"And if I don't?"

"I explained that back at the hotel and nothing's changed." He waved a hand to the door behind them. "Leave if that's what you want. You'll be dead before noon."

She paled at his blunt words, and like air leaking from a balloon, her bravado fled. Abruptly, she sat back down.

"I can't help you," she whispered, her dark eyes huge as she stared up at him. "What on earth could I do for you?"

He walked to the chair beside the couch and sat down. "Tell me the truth," he said. "I need to know why you're here and what you and Leonadov were doing. I need to know all the connections between Leonadov and Singh. I need information."

"Didn't Ami explain all that when he hired you?"

She might be scared but she wasn't stupid. "He told me what he wanted me to know," Stratton answered. "I want to hear it from you."

"There's not that much to tell," she said. "C.J. was killed a few months ago leaving his house. The police said it was a robbery. I guess Ami didn't believe that so he hired you. We came to Rio on business—"

"Why did he bring you?"

"I speak Portuguese," she said. "He didn't want to use the translator he'd used last time."

"Who was that?"

"I don't know his name."

"Did he come here often?"

"Maybe every three or four months. He'd started to come more often this past year."

"Why?"

"I don't know."

He paused and let his expression shift, his voice dropping. "Were you sleeping with him?"

She stared at him in confusion, her forehead furrowing. She was either a great actress or he had his answer. "Sleeping with who?"

"Leonadov."

Her eyes rounded, her hand flying to her neck. "My God, no! Of course not! I worked for Ami, that's all. We were close, but not like that."

Stratton nodded. There went one theory. "What was he doing in Rio?"

"He had clients here. Other dealers who wanted his stones."

"Why didn't he just mail them?"

"That's not how Ami did things. Most of his clients were his friends, too."

"Who was he seeing here?"

"A man I didn't know named Joaquim Ioao." She looked as if she wanted to cry but wouldn't allow herself the luxury. "I'd never met him but he was supposed to be an old friend of Ami's." She paused. "Just like C.J. had been. Just like Wilhem and Barragan."

Stratton made a mental note of the man's name. "Who are Wilhem and Barragan?"

She explained about the other two dealers. "One is in Buenos Aires," she said, "and the other one lives in Mexico City. They were in town last month—in Houston—having their usual meeting."

Stratton focused suddenly. "Their 'usual' meeting? What does that mean?"

"They were friends," she reiterated. "They got together every so often, either in Houston or Mexico or Argentina, and did business."

"How often?"

"Maybe two or three times a year." She paused and amended herself. "Actually that's not quite true. The last year they'd been seeing each other a little more. I teased Ami about the frequent flyer miles he was getting."

"Did Singh meet with them, too?"

"Yes."

Stratton leaned back in his chair and stared at Jennifer. Four men, regular meetings, two dead. Not good.

He said nothing for several moments. "Who was your boss eating with that night?"

"Joaquim Ioao, as far as I know."

"Anyone else with them? Think hard. Did you hear him on the phone before he went out? Did he say anything on the plane?"

She started to shake her head then she stopped. "He spoke Yiddish," she said slowly. "On the phone that night. Besides Wilhem, he didn't have that many customers who spoke that language."

Stratton nodded. "Anything else unusual? Think past the last few days."

She chewed her bottom lip. "He had been writing a few checks on his own. I usually did that, but he'd wanted some blank ones for himself. I didn't see who they went to." She stopped then narrowed her eyes. "There was something else, too."

"What?"

"On the plane we were talking about sitting in first class and having lots of money, just being silly, I thought. He said something like 'When this is all over and I'm rich I'll find you the perfect diamond.'" She shook her head, her eyes meeting Stratton's. "He'd told me a few minutes before that he had a 'secret' deal going, one he didn't even want his son to know about."

"He didn't tell you what this deal was?"

"We didn't talk about it again." Her eyes filled. "He was killed that night."

WHILE THE MAN with the scars was gone, his maid brought Stratton and Jennifer something to eat but Jennifer didn't touch the food, nausea hitting her at the mere sight of it. She did, however, change into the clothing the woman brought to her. The expensive linen slacks and matching blouse fit a little too snugly, but tight—and tighter—seemed to be the fashion norm in Rio.

After the housekeeper came back and collected the trays, Jennifer headed for the phone. She wanted to call Detective Angelo, but before she could dial, Stratton materialized at her side and took the receiver from her hand, returning it with a thud to its cradle.

"What are you doing?" she protested. "I have to try and get my passport back!"

He stood too close to her. "No, you don't," he replied coldly.

She froze, their dark eyes meeting in the still space between them, her mind going wild. There was only one reason she wouldn't need her passport and that was if she was dead.

He was going to kill her.

She'd told him everything he wanted to know and he was done with her. Ami hadn't hired him and he wasn't really named Stratton. She was in deep shit.

Panic swept through her, but before she could react the low purr of a car broke the silence of the room. She heard a car door slam. With relief, Jennifer stepped back from Stratton as Gomez strode into the living room.

He took in her change of clothes with a blink—did they belong to his wife?—but he said nothing about them.

"I have everything." He turned to Stratton. "I have some bad news, too."

Jennifer stood as Stratton crossed the room. He glanced back at her. "Stay here," he said.

She sat down as the two men disappeared down the hallway then she eased off the sofa and tiptoed in the direction they'd gone. Gomez's voice came from a door on the left.

"They are looking for her," he said bluntly. "You were right."

They spoke Portuguese but the adrenaline that rushed into her veins helped her translation skills, and Jennifer understood every word.

"The police think she set the whole thing up so she could take the diamonds Leonadov brought into the country. They are not in the safe like she told you."

She caught her gasp before it could escape but just barely. She'd put those stones back inside the box herself. How could they be gone?

"And the shooter?"

"They have no idea."

"Is that the bad news?"

Gomez laughed, but it wasn't pleasant. "No. The bad news is that a dead engineer was found last night, too. It took a while to put the parts back together and identify him. I doubt there's a connection but—"

"His name wasn't Joaquim Ioao, was it?"

Gomez made a whistling sound. "I'm impressed, my friend. How did you know his name?"

Moaning silently, Jennifer closed her eyes.

"ESP," Stratton answered. "What happened?"

"Not enough left to say for sure. He was tortured first. I would surmise he had some kind of information that someone wanted rather badly."

"He supplied Leonadov's location. They'd met earlier."

"Why?"

"I don't know."

She heard the click of a lock, a small one like a briefcase might have, then Gomez spoke again. "I got these for you. They're not too bad."

Stratton grunted. "Maybe so, if you're blind."

Gomez laughed again. "That is the best that I could do, my friend. In fact, I have done all I can for now. You need to find a hole." He fell silent for a moment, then said, "Do you want me to take care of the woman?"

Jennifer's heart began to pound so loudly she was afraid they might actually hear it. She put her fingers against her chest to muffle the sound, but the action did no good.

"I appreciate the help and everything that you have done," Stratton said formally. "But I'm not finished with her yet. I'll handle things when it's time."

Her mouth went dry, fear sucking out every drop of moisture and replacing it with the taste of copper.

Gomez chuckled but the sound held as much humor as his garden held beauty. "I am sure that you will, *señor*. I am sure that you will."

HE WANTED TO LEAVE immediately, but Stratton knew they'd be better off if they waited until dark. The decision hardly mattered, though, because Stratton had no idea where they were going or what he should do next. All he did know was that he and Jennifer couldn't stay at Gomez's. It was too risky—for them and for him.

They finished up their business, which consisted of Stratton giving Gomez the rest of the money he had on him and Stratton promising the ex-cop they'd be gone by the time he came home that evening. Gomez had nodded once, shook his hand then walked out the front door, leaving Stratton to figure out the rest on his own.

He watched Gomez's car pull out of the gate, turned and went back into the living room. He'd known she was listening to their whole conversation but Jennifer was sitting on the sofa as if she'd never moved.

"Who *is* he?" she asked as Stratton returned to the living room.

"You don't want to know," Stratton answered. "Señor Gomez isn't someone you should tell anyone you've met."

"Why not?"

"He isn't a nice man. The police would probably drop the charges against you if they could pin them on Gomez." He shook his head. "But you don't want that, believe me. Gomez isn't someone you'd want mad at you."

Jennifer stood and moved to the massive stone fireplace that took up one wall of the living room. For a full minute, maybe more, she looked at the blackened brick lining the inner hearth, then finally she turned. Her eyes were filled with mistrust. "What happens now?"

"Give me what I want and I'll help you get out of here."

"Tell me what you want then I'll see if the price is right."

Stratton found himself struck by her determination. Considering everything that had happened to her, most women—and even more men—would have caved by now, but Jennifer Rodas refused to be cowed.

"I need more information," he replied.

"Ami's dead," she said bluntly. "Why do you even care now?"

"Let's just say I don't like to leave things unfinished."

"You told me you were supposed to figure out who killed C. J. Singh. What does Ami's death have to do with that?"

He said nothing and she stared at him. After a moment, she turned pale. "Oh, shit."

"You didn't think you were just running into a string of bad luck, did you? These murders are not coincidences."

She came back to the sofa and sat down. "But why and who?"

"I don't know," he said, "but you do."

She started shaking her head. "I don't know anything—"

"You know the business," he said. "You know the people. You know all the connections." He paused. "You may not know you know, but the truth is in there somewhere."

Her hands were in her lap. She held them open, palm up. "I wouldn't even have a clue as to where to start."

"You don't have to," he said. "I'll figure that out."

"And how are you going to do that?"

He smiled coldly. "You don't want me giving away all my trade secrets, do you?"

"I'd just as soon know what's ahead of me."

She stared at him until she couldn't stand it anymore, then her gaze slipped away from his. He felt a flash of guilt at intimidating her, but a job was a job.

He leaned forward and her gaze flew back to his. "Talk to me," he ordered in a quiet voice. "Repeat everything you've already told me, then tell it to me again. Start at the beginning and keep going until I stop you."

CHAPTER EIGHT

THE SUN HAD SHIFTED well into the west by the time Jennifer fell silent. Stratton had interrupted her only once and that was to ask a question about Thomas. She stared at him from where she sat—they'd moved at some point to the patio off the living room—and waited for him to speak.

He stood instead and walked to the edge of the tile, keeping his back to her. Lined up in a row near where he paused, five stone pillars carried the weight of the roof. They were massive but he made them look small. Not because of his size, Jennifer realized slowly, but because of his attitude.

He'd save her life but at what cost?

A knot of apprehension formed inside her chest and made it difficult for her to breathe. The feeling didn't contain the pure terror she'd experienced when he'd told Gomez that he would "take care of her," but it was bad enough because she was pretty sure that whatever he had in mind wouldn't be something she was going to like.

She couldn't stand the silence. "What do you think is going on?"

He didn't speak for so long she thought he might not have heard her. Just as she started to repeat herself, he answered, his back still to her. "I think your boss and his buddies probably got into something they shouldn't have and whoever killed them thinks you're part of it, too." He turned to her, his eyes piercing. "Are you?"

She answered quickly, her nervousness fueling her anxiety. "If I am, I don't know about it."

"What about the diamonds?"

She shrugged helplessly. "I have no idea. Before I went to the suite, I put them in the safety deposit box and that's the last I saw of them."

"Who was with you?"

"No one," she said. "The night clerk let me in, then she stepped out. I was alone when I opened the box and when I put it back."

"So no one knew where the diamonds were, but you?"

His suspicion was obvious. "Did you see me take anything from the room when we left?"

"No, I didn't. But you could have already taken them out of the hotel."

"I could have," she conceded. "But I didn't. I don't know where they are and the only person I told about the safety deposit box was Thomas. Since he's a few thousand miles from here, I don't see him as a suspect. He owns them anyway."

"Are they insured?"

"Yes, they are."

He said nothing.

"Thomas isn't a thief," she said.

"But you don't like him much, do you?"

His perception shocked her. "No, I don't. He wouldn't engineer his father's death for a handful of diamonds, though."

"You can't be sure of that."

"That's true, but even if I were wrong, he couldn't have done it. I talked to him that night on the phone. He was in Houston and he sounded genuinely upset."

"This was a professional job. When you pay for murder, your hands don't get dirty. It's easy to pretend you aren't involved."

His confidence on the subject sent a second wave of unease over her, this one even stronger. She wanted to ask "How do you know that?" but she didn't and she knew why. She couldn't afford to hear his answer right now.

She swallowed and changed the subject. "Well, if you're right, won't the police know that, too? And if they do, then wouldn't they let me go?"

"I doubt they've figured it out," he answered, "but if they have, they'll assume you paid for the hit. You're all they have and as far as they're concerned, that's good enough. Why keep looking?"

"But it wouldn't be the truth."

"In South America, the truth is relative."

Jennifer had been scared since this nightmare had begun, but his words made things worse. The situation Stratton outlined sounded impossible, hopeless even. Her voice slipped an octave higher. "What am I going to do?"

"If I were you," he said, "I'd head for the border."

HER EYES TURNED into pools of complete distrust. "What does that mean?"

He pushed himself away from the column at his back. "I'd hit the road," he said. "Vamoose, skedaddle, get the hell out of Dodge. Do you need another cliché to understand?"

"I can't do that." Her fingers slipped to her throat. He'd come to recognize the gesture; it was a dead give-away she was getting scared. "It'd be illegal! It'd make me look guilty, too."

"Trust me," he said, "you can't look any more guilty than you already do."

"You might have a point." Her concession surprised him, then she went a step further. "But frankly that option doesn't exist because I wouldn't even know how to start. As you've so eloquently explained, there are more than one or two hurdles facing me, not the least of which is that I have no money and no passport."

Stratton hadn't thought it'd be this easy but she was right where he'd wanted her. And she'd gotten there a hell of a lot faster than he'd ever expected. He moved toward her. "But I have both."

"I'm sure you do," she replied, "for yourself."

He reached behind his back, pulled out a small dark green book and threw it to her. She caught it easily. Flipping to the first page, she studied it, then looked up at him in amazement. "My God, that's the photo from my driver's license! How on earth did you get a Brazilian passport for me?"

"Gomez. And hang onto this one, for God's sake, because it cost a bloody fortune."

"But what about the photograph? My hair isn't this dark…"

He reached into a small paper bag that was sitting on the coffee table and pulled something out. Her eyes went from the sack to the plastic bottle in his hand. *Morena Elegante* was spelled out in bright orange letters down the side. It was hair coloring.

"It will be shortly. And you don't want to know how Gomez got the photo. Let's just say he has access to things that others don't and leave it at that. As for the hair, I guess the color didn't come through right."

She looked at the fake passport again, reading the name. "'Maria Santiago?' Couldn't he have done better than that?"

"He probably didn't have a choice," Stratton said. "In this business, beggars can never be choosers."

She stared at the photograph a little longer, then closed the booklet. She transferred her scrutiny to him, the intensity of her gaze making him wish he could turn away.

"And what business would that be?" Her question was softly spoken, almost politely. "Don't give me the investigator line again, either."

Stratton gave as good as he got, his gaze never wavering from hers. "You have a lot of questions for someone who's not in a position to ask."

"I don't like surprises," she said. "In my experience, they're never good. I'd rather have the truth, straight up."

Stratton wondered briefly why she felt that way—as far as he knew, Jennifer Rodas had lived the quiet life of a secretary. No husband. No children, no involvements, no crises. If she wanted to know about bad experiences, he thought, she ought to ask him.

"All right," he said. "I'll tell you what I can."

Surprise swept across her face, then he spoke again. "As soon as we get to Buenos Aires."

GOMEZ'S HOUSEKEEPER handed Stratton the leather suitcase she'd pulled out of her bedroom closet and pocketed his reals in return, her expression so blank Jennifer could tell she'd been asked to do much stranger things than sell her used luggage to a pair of weird Americans. Jennifer didn't want to speculate on what those things might be. She concentrated, instead, on the curve Stratton had thrown her a few minutes earlier.

"Buenos Aires?" She'd shaken her head. "No way. I told you everything I know and now I want out of here. I want to go back to the States. You said if I helped you, you'd help me."

"I said I'd get you out of here," he'd answered bluntly. "I didn't say where I'd take you. You're going to get me in to see Joseph Wilhem. It'll make my life a lot easier—and possibly save his."

She'd argued for another twenty minutes without even making a dent in his resolution. Finally, when the silence between them had turned as cold as his eyes, she'd given up. That was when he'd led her down to the maid's quarters.

The woman went out of the room then reappeared a second later, her arms full of clothing. Clearly not her own, the slacks and tops were all as expensive and new as what she'd already given Jennifer to wear. She pointed to Jennifer then pointed to the suitcase, making folding motions with her hands.

"She wants to pack for you," Stratton instructed. "I'd let her. She can do it faster—and better—than you."

Jennifer nodded and Stratton spoke to the maid in a harsh language that sounded Latin-like but clearly wasn't. She made some more motions with her hands and he said something else before they left, Stratton turning to Jennifer as they walked down the hallway.

"When she finishes with the packing, she'll help you put the rinse in your hair."

Jennifer nodded, then when they were out of earshot, she spoke, tilting her head behind her. "What were you speaking back there?"

"An Indian dialect. It's from her part of the country."

"She understands it but she doesn't speak it?"

"She did speak it at one time." Stratton kept his eyes straight ahead. "But a few years back some of Gomez's 'associates' kidnapped her to get some information about Gomez out of her. When she didn't cooperate, they cut out her tongue and sent it to Gomez."

Jennifer's stomach rolled over. She wasn't conscious of it, but she must have made a sound of distress. Stratton glanced at her.

"Don't worry," he said. "Gomez found where they were holding her and he took care of a few of their extremities, too." He smiled. "He chose body parts they needed more than their tongues."

Jennifer gagged but she tried to hide it with a cough.

"Like what, you ask?" Stratton spoke as if she'd questioned him. "Well, their heads, for one. But he didn't start there."

She held up her hand at that and he stopped.

They were in a taxi and on their way to the airport half an hour later, Jennifer's newly darkened hair still damp. As they sped through the crowded streets, Stratton told her their tickets were waiting for them at the counter, but before they reached that point, their passports would be checked by security, then once again by the airline employees, as well.

"Let me do the talking," he instructed, "unless they ask you something directly, which they probably won't."

She felt really queasy—over his earlier story or everything that had happened, she didn't know which—but Jennifer kept it to herself. "In other words," she said smartly, "let you be the macho man of the household while I pretend to be the little woman?"

"It works for me." He glanced at her. "Let's hope it does the same for you."

The possibility that his plan might not be successful made her silent after that. What if someone spotted her? What if the fake passport was discovered? What if this was all some kind of horrible trick on Stratton's part? Would "associates" of *his* come after *her?*

She'd considered the latter possibility ever since Stratton had brought up the idea of Buenos Aires but with no other option, she'd gone along. What else could she do? She'd never done anything illegal before, much less something like this. As soon as she got to B.A. she'd slip away from him and call Thomas. He could help her get home from there. Working out the situation from a country other than Brazil seemed like a much better thing to do in the long run. Or so she told herself.

Stratton stepped out of the taxi at Galeão then turned and held out his hand to Jennifer, carefully assisting her from the back of the car.

She scooted across the seat, and then paused, staring at him in surprise. She'd noticed earlier that he hadn't shaved and that he'd darkened his hair, too. His suit had caught her eye as well. Especially the pants. They fit so tightly they looked as if a tailor had hand stitched them in place that morning.

Somewhere between Gomez's compound and the airport, though, the changes had gone deeper, past the surface and into his personality. Stratton had turned himself into a man like the ones she'd seen cruising the Copa, a suave Latino businessman with money to burn. Even the way he held his body struck her, a loose kind of natural grace replacing his determined head-on approach from before. The transformation was uncanny.

Taking his hand, she stepped out of the cab. He tucked her arm into the crook of his elbow then signaled for the porter behind them to follow, his lips brushing her ear as he leaned over to speak. "Could you please smile and act as if you like me just a little? It might make our honeymoon story more believable."

She'd already lifted the corner of her mouth but at his words, her expression faltered. "Honeymoon? That's even worse than the name on the passport. Couldn't you have come up with something a little more original?"

"I didn't have a choice—the passports matched." He touched her cheek with the tip of his finger then kissed her nose lightly, smiling as he spoke. "If I were in your position, I'd be a little more grateful and a lot less fussy. Unless, of course, you'd like to stay here and face the police. I'm doing you a favor."

She glanced at him with what she hoped was a flirtatious look. "Joseph Wilhem would never agree to see you without my intervention and you know it. That's not exactly what I'd call a favor. Blackmail, maybe, a favor, no."

"Oh, he'd see me," Stratton contradicted confidently, "but he wouldn't trust me. And *that's* why I need you."

What he said was the truth, but her stubbornness wouldn't allow her to turn the subject loose. "We could have called him," she said.

He didn't bother to reply. Instead, Stratton shifted his shoulders and seemed to grow even taller, putting his hand over her fingers and squeezing them. "We're almost to security," he warned. "Are you ready?"

She wanted to scream "no" and run away but when she looked up at Stratton, his eyes stopped her. They were suddenly so warm and reassuring that she felt the weight of her fear lift for the first time since seeing Ami's body. She had no idea if his expression was part of his ploy or if it was genuine. She could have even been imagining the look. Either way, it didn't matter because suddenly she felt better.

THE FEMALE GUARD watched warily as Stratton and Jennifer walked her way. Stratton sized her up quickly. Twenty-something with a clean uniform and nicely done nails, but scuffed heels and no wedding band. She needed her poorly paid job but it was so boring, some days she thought she'd already died and gone to Hell.

He cursed under his breath. Where was Armando, the lady-killer, when you needed him?

Knowing he had no other choice, Stratton started to smooth the way even before they reached the small podium where she waited, his smile lifting his lips, his eyes rippling over her tight skirt and even tighter blouse in an appreciative appraisal. By the time his gaze reached her face, she was pursing her lips, her expression growing warm in return.

He spoke English to impress her, but used a local accent. "Good evening, *señorita*." He handed her their passports, his eyes dipping to her neckline before coming back up. "The officials must be changing the security process at Galeão. If all the *guadas de segurnça* look like you, the bad guys have no chance." He held out his hands, turning his wrists over. "Do you have handcuffs? Take me now, if you do."

She giggled at Stratton's corny approach, but his gaze held enough heat to make up for it. A light blush covered her cheeks.

"I have no handcuffs today, *señor,* but I do have questions for you," she said primly.

His expression full of disappointment, he made a tsk-tsking sound. "Ask away then."

As the woman rhymed off the queries, he glanced down at Jennifer. She looked completely bored, a frosty mask of indifference on her face.

Stratton answered for both of them. The guard slapped the passports shut and handed them back to Stratton, her hand brushing his in the process.

"Have a nice day, *señor,*" she purred. "And a safe journey, too."

He sent Jennifer a sidelong glance, then captured one of the woman's fingers and held it for a moment, the ploy hidden by the passport. "The same for you," he replied warmly. "Perhaps I will see you when we return?"

She smiled. "Perhaps you will."

He took Jennifer's elbow and led her away from the stand, directing her to the first-class line.

She looked up at him through her eyelashes. "'Do you have handcuffs?'" she mocked under her breath. "How cheesy is that?"

He eased a black curl away from her temple and smoothed it over one ear. The action was tender but the look in his eyes made her fall silent. He didn't need any critiques, especially from her.

At the airline counter where a much older woman was in charge, he changed tactics, using deference as well as his obvious status. To his great relief, she handed over the tickets quickly and moved them along. They got over the final hurdle of metal detectors without incident then walked toward their gate, Stratton's tension easing slightly.

He felt Jennifer relax, too. Her newfound calm evaporated a moment later, though, when two *federalas,* complete with weapons and boots, turned a corner and strode toward them. Two more men, not in uniform— which was even worse—came into view behind them. Jennifer's hand tightened on his arm.

Stratton looked down and smiled reassuringly, but panic had already sculpted her features into a mask of guilt. She looked so suspicious, they'd be stopped by the guards just to find out what the hell was going on with her.

He cursed then brought them to a stop and pulled her into his arms. Caught by surprise, Jennifer stumbled against the wall behind her, and he followed, pressing his body into the length of hers.

What followed next was pretty damn convincing, even by Brazilian standards.

JENNIFER DIDN'T HAVE TIME to prepare before Stratton's mouth covered hers. She didn't protest, though, because she knew exactly what he was doing. Pushed against the wall, with his hands cupped around her face, Jennifer's entire body was hidden from the view of the men coming toward them.

Wrapping her arms around his waist, she kissed Stratton back and melted into him, their two forms molding together as closely as possible. Through the silk of her blouse, his body felt hot and persuasive, his lips even more so. After a very long moment, he tore his mouth from hers and slid his lips down her neck, tipping his head to see past her as he spoke.

"Maria, por favor, meu namorado encantadora."

She pulled back slightly, but he stilled her movement with a thrust of his hips. Startled but compliant, she stayed within his embrace and clung to him, her heart banging with fear against her chest.

Stratton turned his head to stare at her; his eyes coolly appraised her, his gaze sweeping over her face and hair as a real lover's would, his lips a breath away.

"Do you see them anymore?" she whispered. "Please tell me they didn't stop."

Instead of answering, he kissed her once more, his "passion" clearly unsatisfied as their lips met a second time, his hands trailing up and down the side of her body. After another few seconds, he took away his mouth then glanced down the hallway again. Jennifer's pulse continued to thunder, but underneath her hands, now on his chest, his heartbeat was steady and slow. Finally he pulled back, dropping his arms with what looked like reluctance. "They're gone."

Her relief was palpable. Sneaking a glance, Jennifer surveyed the stream of people passing by as she straightened her clothing. In the States their action might have garnered a few curious stares, but not here. No one looked even remotely interested in them or the public display of affection they'd just engaged in so flagrantly. She felt a momentary surprise, then she remembered the couples she'd seen on the beach the night she'd eaten at the outdoor café. They'd done more and no one had seemed to notice. Except her.

Which seemed to be the case right now.

Without another word, Stratton took her hand and they continued on their way.

HE DIDN'T ALLOW HIMSELF to relax again until they were in the plane and it was lifting off. Seeing the cops had rattled Stratton, especially since he'd dumped his weapons at Gomez's house. He wouldn't have been able to carry them, of course, but knowing they were in his luggage had always bought him a small sense of false security. He hadn't even had the luxury of that, but the kiss had been a good ploy, enjoyable, too. If it hadn't worked, and he'd been forced to do something else, he would have done it with a smile on his face.

He glanced across the seat in Jennifer's direction, then blinked in surprise. Her eyes were closed and her face was pale, a slight sheen of perspiration gleaming on her forehead. She was gripping the armrests so tightly her hands were knotted into a rigor that looked as if it could be permanent.

With a curse, he leaned over to speak. The last thing he needed was a sick accomplice, willing or otherwise. "Are you all right? You look like crap."

She didn't open her eyes but her throat moved as she swallowed. "I don't like to fly."

She'd found a body, escaped death and fled a foreign country but she was scared of flying? He started to chuckle but squelched it. She'd done pretty damn well for an amateur and who the hell was he to laugh? There were things that scared him, too, like thinking about his past and wondering about his future. He tried to get her mind off the problem.

"Well, that's fine," he replied with obvious relief.

She opened one eye and glared at him. "You're happy it scares me to fly?"

"Hell, yes," he answered. "For a minute there, I thought my kiss might have done you in."

She didn't laugh but she did make a sound he interpreted as amusement. "It wasn't the kiss," she said finally. "The handcuff comment really got to me, though."

"I have other talents." He shrugged carelessly. "Charming women isn't one of my strong points."

After a second, she lifted her head from the headrest, his attempt at diversion obviously working. "I'm not sure I'd agree."

He leaned back in his seat and stretched out his legs, sending her a sideways glance. "Then I assume I don't have to apologize for the kiss?"

"I didn't say that."

"Wouldn't matter if you did." He paused. "I still wouldn't say I'm sorry."

"Because the men kept going?"

He stared at her for a second too long. She blinked then looked away, her eyes returning to his only when he spoke again.

"That's as good a reason as any," he said quietly. "Let's leave it at that."

CHAPTER NINE

THE FLIGHT FROM Rio to Buenos Aires took twelve hours. They stopped twice, once in Porto Alegre and once again in Montevideo. Jennifer suffered through each landing and takeoff, her mouth dry, her stomach threatening to revolt. She managed to live through the ordeal, but barely. By the time the jet touched down in Buenos Aires at eight the following morning, she felt as if she'd been to Hell and back. Having Stratton at her side, studying her face for signs of panic, didn't help, either. She decided she must have imagined his sympathetic expression right before they'd gone through the security checkpoint in Rio because she'd seen nothing else from him since then that even remotely resembled any kind of reassurance.

As they waited for their luggage, Jennifer thought back to their kiss. She'd pushed the incident from her mind, but after their conversation in the plane, when he'd offered not to apologize, she'd started her usual second-by-second critique. Why had he chosen to kiss her? Couldn't he have thought of another way to handle the problem? Had he *wanted* to kiss her? Considering the fact that he'd just gotten her out of a country where she was about to be arrested for murder, a kiss was a pretty small toll to pay. His actions weren't what bothered her, though. What bothered her was how *she* had responded when his body had pressed into hers. Being aware of a man was the last thing she would have expected from herself considering everything that had happened to her in the past twenty-four hours.

But she'd definitely been aware of Stratton. Very aware. Past aware.

Her eyes swept the crowd until she located him. She wasn't surprised to see that he had a porter at his side. There had been only three of them to meet the incoming plane but he'd snagged one. The two men were talking easily, Stratton pumping the redcap for information, his expression concentrated and intent. She shivered lightly. When he focused like that, a person couldn't do anything but respond. He didn't allow any other reaction. She told herself that's why she'd felt the way she had during their kiss—he'd willed her to make it look authentic so she had—but deep down she wasn't too sure about that theory.

Stratton pointed at something and the porter jumped toward the revolving belt. His action startled her from her thoughts and she dropped them with relief. Nothing could be gained continuing in that vein.

HIDING IN PLAIN SIGHT had never been one of Stratton's mottoes. He liked to stay underground as much as possible and being at the Copa had driven him nuts. He was glad to be in charge of the accommodations in B.A.

When they pulled up to the Hotel *Palacio,* Jennifer sent him a curious look but she didn't say anything. In fact, she hadn't said two words after their conversation on the plane had ended, which suited him just fine. Regardless of how much he might have enjoyed it, they'd communicated enough already. He had plenty to worry about without being distracted by her.

Like how soon they could hook up with Joseph Wilhem, for one.

Stratton checked them in and requested a suite, which wasn't as good as it sounded at the *Palacio,* then the bellboy took them up. The elevator, like most in B.A., measured approximately three feet by three feet and it was made for one person, or two friendly ones at the most. Stratton and Jennifer stepped inside the lift then the porter squeezed in their luggage and himself. Stratton stood rigidly as they jolted upward. He refused to use the word claustrophobic but there was nothing he hated more than being stuck in small spaces. An eternity went by as they went past the second floor and then the third. Somewhere between the sixth and the tenth, he felt Jennifer tug at his sleeve. He looked down.

"Now I understand how you knew I was afraid to fly," she said. "It takes one to know one."

"What are you talking about?" he asked gruffly.

She didn't answer because she didn't have to—they both knew full well what she meant.

They finally reached their floor and then their room. Tipping the porter, Stratton sent him on his way then he checked out the room. When he'd gone through the entire suite and was sure they were alone, he returned to Jennifer's side. She was right where he'd left her.

"I want to catch Wilhem off guard. You know where his office is, don't you? Would he be there this early?"

"I'm not leaving until I can clean up," she said

wearily. "And I have to call Ami's son. He's probably going crazy by now."

"No phone calls. He'll be contacted by the airline. You've been bumped."

"But my mother will be worried…"

"She'll get the same message. I don't want you calling anyone," he repeated. "We need to figure out what's going on first. For all you know Thomas Leonadov could be behind everything. I want him thinking you're still in Rio."

"I already told you I don't think—"

"What you think doesn't matter," Stratton said coldly. "That's the way it's going to be unless you dislike Thomas Leonadov enough to get him killed, and in the process, probably do us in, too. The people behind this aren't dumb."

Her expression shifted to fear but she tried to hide the reaction from him for some reason. "All right," she said haughtily, "for now. But I have to have something to eat first."

Her bargaining didn't sit well with him. "You should have eaten on the plane."

"And you should have breathed while we came up in the elevator," she shot back, "but we don't always do what we're supposed to, do we?"

He wanted to grab her elbow and drag her out the door, but he held up his hands in defeat, her pale face and shaky demeanor giving him second thoughts. Having her pass out on the street would not be a good thing.

"I'll order room service. You can shower. Then we go."

She grabbed the suitcase they'd bought from Gomez's maid and walked toward the bathroom as he picked up the phone and ordered them something to eat.

When Jennifer came back into the room twenty minutes later, the food had just arrived. Standing beside the service cart, Stratton glanced up. She was wrapped in a robe two sizes too large and had washed her hair. The strands, now chestnut-brown again, hung wetly around her scrubbed face and he found himself startled at how young she looked without her makeup.

"How old are you?" he asked without thinking.

"I'm thirty," she said, surprising him further. "But I think the past few days have added a few more wrinkles than they should have." She sat down on the sofa and seemed to be studying her bare feet, her head hanging down. Only when he saw her shoulders shaking, did he realize that she was crying. He cursed without thinking.

"I—I'm sorry," she said in a broken voice. "I usually don't do this, but everything just hit me again in the shower." She lifted her tear-streaked face. "I can't believe he's gone. I can't believe Ami's dead."

Once again Stratton found himself wanting one thing, but doing something else. Instead of leaving her alone, as he would have liked, he went to where she sat and lowered himself to the cushion beside her. He stayed silent because he didn't know what to say, but the arm he found himself putting around her shoulder was apparently all she needed.

Faster than he expected, she pulled herself together. "I'm sorry," she sniffed. "I'm not a person who cries easily but I think all this is getting to me."

"You wouldn't want to be the kind of person it didn't affect."

She blinked as she raised her head, her brown eyes still swimming in tears. "You are."

"I didn't know your boss." Stratton sidestepped the question. "You did."

"I'm upset about Ami, but there's more to my reaction than just that." She shook her head, the strands of wet hair sending off droplets of water. "It's getting shot at and leaving like I did and everything that's ahead of me."

"You're alive, you escaped, and you don't know what's ahead of you. Don't go where you don't have to until it's necessary."

She considered his words, then looked at him again, this time with speculation. "Is that how you survive?"

"Partly," he answered.

"What's the rest?"

He removed his arm. "A Rutger automatic and a steady hand."

She fell silent once more, her eyes focused on the wall across from where they sat. "Where's this going to end?" Her voice was soft. "After Wilhem, then what?"

"I don't know."

"I just want this to be over," she said.

"I know you do. But that's not going to happen any time soon."

"Why not?"

"Because these kinds of things never end quickly or neatly. When you start unraveling situations like this, you always end up with an even bigger mess than you had before." He paused but he couldn't think of a better way to say it. "In fact, you'd better get ready because I think the real shit's about to hit the fan."

JOSEPH WILHEM'S office was in a section of Buenos Aires known as the *Microcentro*. Bounded by two of the largest avenues in the city and central to everywhere, the high-rise buildings looked both contemporary and ancient. Some appeared as if they were one step away from falling apart while others still gleamed with their newness. Ami had described the area to Jennifer after a visit once, saying it was a strange juxtaposition of the past and the future, but she'd thought that he was exaggerating. As their car swung onto the crowded *Avenida 9 de Julio,* she stared out the window and realized his comments had been bang on. She couldn't have described the district any better herself.

A cyclist, weaving between the lanes of traffic, whizzed by the car window startling her and she pulled back abruptly, bumping into Stratton. She murmured an apology but he said nothing, his face unreadable behind a pair of dark sunglasses he'd pulled from somewhere. She was still wishing she hadn't let him see her cry. She wanted to seem strong in front of him for reasons she didn't understand, but her predicament had hit her full force. It'd worked out all right, though. In the end, he'd fled the hotel and left her alone for an hour. An overwhelming need to connect with someone familiar had assailed her and she'd immediately picked up the phone to call Cissy. But she'd put it back with great reluctance, remembering Stratton's words of caution about Thomas. The last thing in the world Jennifer wanted to do was lead danger to Cissy's door but God, she felt so alone. Murder, missing diamonds and fleeing a country—these weren't subjects with which she was familiar. The fact that Stratton *was* wasn't as comforting as she would have expected.

The car inched its way up the street, horn blaring, to

Avenida Córdoba. When a line of snarled traffic came into view ahead of them, Stratton grunted then threw a wad of pesos over the front seat. "We'll walk from here."

Pulling Jennifer with him, he started out briskly. "*Avenida Florida*'s only four blocks ahead. We can get there quicker this way."

She looked at him in surprise. He'd said nothing about knowing the city so she'd assumed he'd never been to Buenos Aires before. She was probably better off not assuming anything about Stratton, though. Something told her that even the people who did know him probably didn't really *know* him.

He held her hand as they wove in and out of the heavy foot traffic and they reached Joseph Wilhem's office building a few minutes later. Twenty stories of glass and metal, it was one of the newer-looking high-rises. They stepped through the revolving door and into a marble-floored lobby where a uniformed guard, sitting behind a circular table made of more marble, eyed them with little interest.

"You handle this one." Stratton spoke under his breath, then pressured her forward, his hand on the small of her back.

Jennifer swallowed nervously as she approached the desk. "We're here to see Sr. Wilhem." She spoke in Spanish and tried to smile. "He's on the fourth floor."

"Los visitantes no permitieron."

"But I'm his niece," she said. "And this—" she turned to Stratton "—this is my husband."

The guard just shook his head, his bored expression

blank as he pointed toward the bank of phones behind them. *"Llámelo primero."*

It took her a second to understand, then she made the translation, his slurred pronunciation of the words totally different from the Spanish she knew.

She turned to Stratton but he was already walking toward the phones. Dodging two businessmen and a woman in an incredibly short skirt, she caught up with him quickly.

"I wanted to surprise him," Stratton said, looking at her sideways. "But this is going to have to do. There are too many doors to this place and I can't watch them all. He could slip out of here and we'd never know." He picked up one of the receivers and held it out to her.

She looked at him blankly. "What do I say?"

"Tell him Ami's dead and he might be next. That ought to get his attention."

The German diamond dealer answered on the first ring and when she heard his voice, Jennifer knew she didn't have to tell him about Ami. His quivering hello and shaky "Who is this?" gave him away.

"Mr. Wilhem, this is Jennifer Rodas, Ami's secretary—"

"Ach verdammt! Why are you calling on this line?" His voice was filled with panic. "Are you downstairs? *Mein Gott,* please tell me you are not downstairs in my office building!"

He had caller ID, she realized suddenly. "That's exactly where I am," she said. "And I need to talk to you—"

He interrupted before she could say more. "What are you doing here? I don't want you near me! They're looking for you! You killed Ami—"

"That's not true," she cried. "I *found* Ami. I didn't kill him. You know I couldn't do something like that."

"Leave here and leave me!" he screeched. "I don't want anyone knowing I had anything to do with you or Ami's crazy scheme. Get out of here!"

His words sent a chill straight to her heart. Gripping the phone with both hands, she forced herself to continue. "Look, I'm here to help you, Mr. Wilhem. You have to talk to me, though. I need more information."

"I'm not telling to you anything!"

She lowered her voice. "Ami hired an investigator to look into Mr. Singh's death and he's with me now. He can protect you. But you have to talk to us."

He fell silent and she could feel his fear.

"Let us come up," she pushed. "You can tell us—"

"Not here," he interrupted. "Meet me at the *Plaza de Mayo*. Tonight, at one o'clock by the bench on the west side, the angle that faces the *Casa Rosada*. I'll be waiting."

He hung up before she could say anything else.

STRATTON COULD TELL by her expression the conversation had not gone well. But there was more than disappointment on her face. There was fear, too.

He took her by the arm and led her from the building, their pace steady but not hurried. Walking across the street, they entered one of the hundreds of small plazas that filled the city. Jennifer started to speak but he held up a hand and made her wait until he found an isolated bench with its back against a brick wall. Scanning the area, he finally turned to her.

"What's wrong?"

"He didn't want to see us at the office."

"Why?"

She licked her lips. "He knew they're looking for me in Rio. He thinks I killed Ami."

"And that's why he wouldn't meet us?"

"No." She took a deep breath, her eyes so huge they dominated her face. "He was terrified that someone might see me and assume he was involved in Ami's 'crazy scheme' as he put it."

Stratton's gut tightened. "What crazy scheme?"

"I have no idea," she answered, "but whatever he was talking about, it's got to be related to what Ami said on the plane."

Stratton watched a flock of bright green parrots lift off from a huge jacaranda tree, their feathers glowing in the afternoon light.

"What do you think he was talking about?"

Stratton looked at her. "You could answer that better than me."

She shook her head in silence.

"Are you sure?" His voice cut through the stillness with a grating harshness.

"Don't you think I'd tell you if I could?" In a practiced, but nervous, gesture she reached down and massaged her right calf, her fingers knotting as they went deep, her forehead lined with concentration. After a few seconds of kneading, she raised her eyes to his. "You still don't believe me, do you? You think I was involved in Ami's death."

Her accusation didn't faze him. "I think it makes sense," he said slowly, almost conversationally. "You have the most to lose."

She frowned. "I have no idea what you're talking about."

Stratton leaned forward, his arms on his knees, his hands clasped together in front of him. "Secretaries know all their boss's secrets. Whatever his 'crazy scheme' was, you'd be the logical one to be in on it and you wouldn't want it revealed, either. Maybe Wilhem was right to be scared."

"That's ridiculous."

"Not from where I sit." He tried to measure her reaction. "Ami was clearly concerned, or he wouldn't have hired me. Maybe he was worried about you double-crossing him."

She shook her head at the possibility. "You're not making sense. If Ami and I were 'in' on something, he wouldn't hire you to investigate it. He wouldn't want to risk you finding out what it was."

Stratton smiled. "Good try. I'm impressed."

She frowned again. "What?"

"Ever heard of a thing called an 'alibi'?" Stratton glanced at her, his gaze catching hers and holding it. "Maybe Leonadov wanted to make sure you weren't double-crossing him. Hiring me, he could maintain his own innocence in case you turned on him."

"That's even crazier! Ami wasn't that kind of man! He'd never do anything illegal to begin with, but even if he did, he wouldn't be that clever about covering it up. He didn't think that way." She paused, then stared at Stratton strangely. "What kind of person does think that way?"

Stratton didn't reply. The answer was obvious.

CHAPTER TEN

STRATTON TOOK his usual precautions. Returning to the hotel using an aimless path no one could have possibly followed, he checked the room then told Jennifer to take advantage of the break and rest. He went to work.

His first phone call was to Lucy Wisner. He should have contacted her before he had ever left Brazil, but he'd run out of options then he'd run out of time. The woman who'd hired him picked up on the first ring and barked out her name, the dulcet tones she'd previously used now gone.

"Wisner here."

"I've got trouble."

He heard a moment's silence then she spoke, confirming his supposition. She wasn't happy with Stratton. And she knew about Ami. "Where are you?"

"Forget about me," he said. "What's important is that you've got another dead man on your hands."

"I'm aware of that. The question is, how do *you* know?"

"Let's just say I was in the neighborhood when it happened. I'm assuming you've made the logical leap that there's a connection between the two?"

"You're in Brazil?" Her voice rose in disbelief but

she tempered it. "I don't believe we authorized any kind of travel like that. You might be responsible for the ticket costs yourself, Mr. O'Neil—"

"Do you think there's a connection?"

"Why should I think that? One man died in Houston during a robbery. The other murder took place thousands of miles away."

"How do you know it was a murder?"

"We have a modern invention here called the television. We get the news on it. Maybe you should consider watching one yourself now and then."

"You're not concerned?"

"No, not a bit. I do think the assistant of the man in question should be, though. The Brazilian authorities are searching for her. You wouldn't know anything about that, would you?"

"No." He echoed her earlier answer. "Why should I?"

"If you were 'in the neighborhood' as you put it, I thought you might have seen her. Which brings to mind the question, why are you there?"

"I like to travel."

"I thought you were working for us."

"I am. I like to travel while I work. It saves time. Combining business and pleasure is always a good idea. You should consider it now and then."

"I have," she said with an acidity that told him she didn't appreciate his parroting her. "It hasn't quite worked out that way for me."

"I'm sorry. Maybe you combined the wrong ingredients of each."

"That's possible. Before I give the idea any more

thought, though, I need to know what your plans are, Mr. O'Neil."

"I don't have plans," he said. "I just do the job."

"I think you're a little far away from the scene of the crime for that. Mr. Singh's murder was in Houston. That's what you're supposed to be investigating. And that's why we're paying you."

Her message was crystal clear, which made Stratton all the more suspicious.

"I'll keep your advice in mind. In the meantime, you work on that business-play thing and I'll work on my case."

She was still talking when he hung up the phone.

LUCY WISNER SLAMMED DOWN the telephone and cursed loudly. What in the hell was Stratton O'Neil doing in South America? She fumed silently for a few more moments then she rolled her chair back from her desk and looked out at the darkening skyline. The hard lines of the skyscrapers reminded her of the man she'd just spoken with. Like those buildings, there was nothing soft about him and something told her he'd be just as hard to move as one of them. He made his own decisions and once they were made, they weren't reconsidered.

What did he think of the IDDA? Did he even have the slightest clue as to what was really going on?

Her eyes followed the path of a solitary pigeon as it glided in the emptiness between two buildings, its wings backlit by the orange tinge of the sunset. He didn't know, she decided. If he did, he wouldn't be in South America. He'd be standing in front of her desk, demanding some answers. She imagined his anger and how it would feel to have it directed at her. It would be a cold anger, she thought, and the punishment that would follow wouldn't quickly be forgotten. If it ever was.

She'd known all along that Stratton O'Neil was going to be trouble. She'd tried to warn Ian, but as usual, he hadn't listened to her. In his eyes, she was just another piece of office equipment. A useful piece, she conceded, but a piece all the same. He was naive, naive *and* stupid. She'd known men like Stratton and danger always accompanied them, an evil hanging over their heads that frequently expanded to include everyone nearby. When she'd tried to explain that to Ian he'd blown her off then pulled her into his lap.

She picked up a pen and tapped it lightly against her desktop, her reflection in the window thoughtful and serious. Maybe it was time for her to move on. Maybe Ian Forney had reached the end of *his* usefulness to her. She'd grown bored with him a long time ago but she'd stayed because, well, because nothing better had come along. He had money and an interesting career—a man who worked in the diamond industry had some cachet—but he was a lousy lover and he had a wife. She'd hung around for all those reasons and although they were still present, so were some other opportunities. Another man's face came into her mind. He was probably worse than Ian but she was comfortable with his kind and she'd be able to manipulate him more easily. Men on the edge were like that.

STRATTON WALKED to the bedroom where Jennifer was sleeping. For long moments, he watched her breathe and thought about his conversation with Lucy Wisner. During their original contact, she'd been perfectly confident and assured. This time, she'd been nervous during the entire call. He'd been suspicious of the IDDA, but his radar was really going off now. He needed to ask Jennifer what she knew about the company.

He let her rest another few hours then they left. After a thirty-minute taxi ride, they ended up in a part of B.A. few Porteneos themselves even knew about, at a tiny Lebanese grill squeezed between a bicycle shop and a used-book store. The grubby diner was the only place Stratton felt safe in Buenos Aires and after talking to Lucy Wisner, he'd felt the need for some extra security. Something hadn't felt right about that conversation.

Stratton held the door open for Jennifer as they paused on the sidewalk. "We'll eat here, then sit until it's time to go to the plaza. Maybe the details of Ami's 'crazy scheme' will come to you." He added the last with a raised eyebrow.

Jennifer pressed her lips together, keeping whatever retort she'd been about to unleash to herself.

The Lebanese who owned the grill, Ali Hassam, greeted them with a quick *Marhaba* but said nothing more, his piercing eyes meeting Stratton's briefly, a simple nod of recognition his only acknowledgment they knew each other. Several years had gone by since their last encounter but in the past they shared, time wasn't measured with a calendar. They were both still alive and that was the only thing that counted.

Hassam took them to a low table tucked in the rear corner where once seated, Stratton could see the front of the restaurant *and* the back door through the drapes that led to the kitchen. He didn't order but a bottle of arrack appeared on the table shortly, along with glasses and ice. The mezza quickly followed. Baba ghanoush, hummus, pickled black olives, feta cheese, tomatoes, pickles, Khiyar bi Laban and taboula. Jennifer stared at the array of food in disbelief.

Stratton poured her a drink, the liquor turning milky as it hit the ice. Jennifer took one sip and began to cough violently.

Stratton sent a look over her shoulder to Hassam. The Lebanese shrugged then went into the kitchen, reappearing a moment later with a pot of tea and a fresh glass in his hands. Stratton thanked him in Arabic then filled Jennifer's glass. "Careful," he warned as she reached for it. "It's very hot."

He took a triangle of pita bread and scooped up some of the baba ghanoush, waving the bread at the food. "Eat," he commanded. "You don't know when you might get another chance."

"I think my throat has a hole in it," she croaked. "Why didn't you warn me about that stuff?"

"What's to warn? It's only grape juice."

"I see you didn't drink any of it."

"It's not my favorite drink," was all he said.

She took a piece of bread and followed his lead, her face finally clearing as she chewed on the laden pita.

Stratton picked up her glass of arrack and turned it in the light, his tone deceptively conversational. Despite what he'd just said, the temptation to down the drink was almost more than he could handle. "Did you know an Arab alchemist discovered distillation?"

"I thought Muslims don't drink."

"They don't," he said. "He used the process to make perfume and cosmetics. Every heard of kohl?"

She made a circling motion in front of her face. "The black eyeliner that goes on your eyes?"

He nodded. "'Al-kohl' turned into 'alcohol.'" He held the glass out to her, but she shook her head quickly and he set it down once more.

His segue to the topic he really wanted to discuss wasn't smooth, but Stratton wasn't interested in smooth. He didn't have the time for smooth.

"Tell me about the IDDA," he said abruptly. "What do you know about the organization?"

She blinked at his bluntness, but answered. "They run the diamond industry. They control the mines, they control the distribution, they control the price. Nothing gets done in this business without the cooperation of the IDDA."

Stratton waited as Hassam cleared the table. When he started bringing in the first course, Jennifer looked at Stratton and frowned. "What's he doing now?"

"That was just the mezze," Stratton explained. "Starters. This is the main course." A plate of shish tawouq, grilled chicken, was followed by kibbeh, balls of ground lamb and wheat. The table was soon covered again.

"Capitalism doesn't generally allow that kind of setup." Stratton filled a fresh plate and handed it to her, returning the conversation to the topic he was interested in. "What's the deal?"

"The company has always been owned and operated by one family, the Badenheimers. They were Swiss who happened to be in the right place, South Africa, at the right time, when diamonds were just becoming popular. They owned the largest mine and had the foresight to buy all the others as they came onto the market. It didn't take long. They offered a lot of money and the people who sat on most of the property were farmers and they were thrilled to sell out."

Stratton picked up a piece of chicken, his eyes on her face. "The Badenheimers still control the company?"

She nodded. "It's a privately owned corporation, run out of Zurich. They write all the rules, including who gets to buy what."

He arched an eyebrow. "How does that work?"

"Every five weeks, the company holds what they call a 'sight' in London. Only 'sightholders' are allowed to come. There were a lot more of them but the company's cut back. Last I heard they were down to eighty. These are people who've been in the business for years and years, some of them are even third or fourth generation holders." She made a square with her hands. "They each receive a box that contains a single parcel of rough that's been selected from the stockpile they have squirreled away."

He stopped her with a raised hand. "Are you saying they don't sell everything that's mined?"

"Good grief, no." She turned her thumbs toward the table and spoke. "The market would collapse and prices would go in the toilet. Diamonds are parceled out to maintain their value."

"I didn't know that."

"Most buyers don't," she said. "But it gets better. The holders have to accept what they get or reject the whole packet—they can't pick and choose. If they complain or make waves, then worst case, they lose their place at the table and aren't invited back for a few years. Best case, they get junk in their box the following year and can't make any money.

"From there, the holders distribute their goods to the wholesalers and/or manufacturers where the stones are cut and polished then made into jewelry. After that, the final product goes to the retailer where it ends up on the consumer."

"That's an unusual way of doing business, to say the least."

"It is," she agreed, "but how else are you going to control the price of something that's basically worthless?"

"And the monopoly laws?"

"The parent company operates out of Europe."

He nodded. "Was Leonadov a holder?"

"Oh, no. Ami was nowhere close to that level of the business. He bought his stones from dealers in New York or Tel Aviv, sometimes India if he needed a large lot of melee."

"Melly?"

"Melee." She spelled it out. "That's a term for small diamonds, generally less than twenty points, give or take. They're not always the finest quality, although they can be, and they're usually put in less expensive pieces of jewelry."

"Why India?"

"Different parts of the world supply different kinds of stones," she explained. "You have a client who wants something nice and big, you go to New York or maybe Antwerp, sometimes Tel Aviv. Smaller stones, go to Bombay. For years if you wanted very fine goods, you looked to Russia. The diamonds from their mines were always beautiful, but the Russians didn't play right."

Stratton leaned closer. "What do you mean?"

"They would put their stones on the open market without going through the IDDA."

"What happened?"

"Dealers who bought from them were cut off from the sights. If they needed anything other than those very high quality stones—and everyone does—then they were out of luck. And eventually, out of business, too." She stabbed a piece of chicken with her fork. "Not surprisingly, the market eventually dried up for the Russians and they gave in. Now their stones are sold through IDDA, too."

Stratton leaned back against the cushions. "It's all controlled."

"Absolutely. Even down to the advertising." She dabbed at her mouth with a napkin. "Haven't you ever wondered about the ads you see? One year at Christmas all the jewelers are pushing diamond bracelets, then the next year, they might be selling three-stone rings. Didn't you ever wonder why?"

"Not really," he said dryly. "Diamond jewelry isn't something I'm interested in."

"The market is driven by the IDDA's inventory. If the mines produce a lot of melee one year, then everyone gets melee so the stockpile mix stays even. You have to work with what you get so the manufacturers make diamond bracelets with tiny diamonds. Next year they might have a quantity of larger goods, caraters or just under for example." She explained at his frown of confusion, "One-carat stones. If that happens then everyone tries to sell solitaires or these three-stone rings that were popular a few years back."

Hassam interrupted again, clearing the table and replacing their plates with fresh fruit and coffee.

Stratton let the information settle into his brain, his stare alternating between Jennifer and the front door. Jennifer took a small taste of the coffee and coughed again, her eyes filling as she put the small gold-rimmed cup down with a rattle.

"My God, that's strong! Are you trying to kill me yourself? Couldn't we have just gone to McDonald's or something?"

He answered her with distraction, his mind still on the IDDA. "I brought us here because I knew we'd be safe and because we had to eat." He lifted his chin toward the back of the building. "I've known the owner for a long time."

"And you speak Arabic."

He nodded.

She linked her fingers around her cup, the delicate china more appropriate for her hands than it was for his. "You're a man of many talents."

Stratton considered his answer carefully, then turned around her obvious ploy to gain information.

"Maybe," he conceded, "but right now, I'm missing a skill I'd really like to have."

"And that would be?"

"Mind reading." He leaned closer to her and tapped her temple. "Wilhem better give me something to work with."

"He's an old man, Stratton. Give him a break."

His name rolled softly off her tongue, startling him. She'd used it before, but something about the way she'd said it stopped him. He stayed exactly where he was, but in his mind, he pulled back, the implied familiarity making him uncomfortable. Somehow sensing this, she bent to nervously massage her calf, just as she had in the park.

"What's wrong with your leg?" His words were colder than he meant for them to be, an effort to distance himself even more.

"I was involved in a car wreck in high school. I broke my leg and sometimes it hurts. I think it's stress more than anything else."

"Sounds like a serious accident."

"It was," she said. "But my injuries were nothing compared to my twin sister's."

Her expression morphed into a guilt-laden frown that she didn't even realize she wore. Stratton found himself suddenly intrigued. Whatever had happened, it'd been her fault. Or so she thought.

"Tell me about it."

She continued but reluctantly. "We were hit by a guy who was high on PCP. He never even touched his brakes. Julie was completely paralyzed afterward. It was bad. She lived another twelve years, but it wasn't a good life."

He spoke flatly, without any kind of clue to give away his feelings. "You were driving."

Her eyes jerked to his but before she could ask, he answered her unspoken question.

"Your face is an open book, Jennifer. I've never seen anyone less capable of hiding their thoughts."

Chagrin washed over her, leaving a wry smile in its place. "That's what my friend Cissy says. I'd like to have a few secrets, though."

"Secrets aren't all they're cracked up to be."

"You have yours."

"That's true," he sidestepped again. "But they aren't good ones. I'd just as soon forget them myself."

She started to say something then paused and turned at a sound from the kitchen, brushing a lock of dark hair away from her face.

He wasn't sure what it was, but something about the way she moved made him suddenly remember her comment in the elevator.

It takes one to know one....

She had recognized his fear of closed places because she had a fear of her own, flying. But they shared something that went much deeper than run-of-the-mill phobias.

Something much stronger than fright and more acidic than hate.

They shared guilt. Overwhelming, impossible-to-ignore, gut-wrenching guilt.

Keeping his face a mask, Stratton considered Jennifer from across the table, an unexpected ripple of sympathy rising despite himself for who she was and what she carried. Like a lover he could never abandon, guilt was an old friend of Stratton's and he was accustomed to its presence. It would be part of him forever and he knew that. Jennifer's burden seemed fresh, and her understanding of its impact had yet to arrive.

He felt sorry for her. She didn't yet know how deep the pain could go. Or how long it could live in your soul.

STRATTON'S DARK MOOD seemed to grow after dinner. Jennifer didn't know if his attitude was due to something she'd said or simply how he felt, but the quieter he became, the more nervous she got. He finished a second round of coffee, this one shared with the proprietor over a steady stream of Arabic and then they were gone, taking a taxi back to the central part of town. The car let them out on the edge of a huge park.

She looked for a sign but couldn't spot one. "Is this the *Plaza de Mayo?*"

"No." Stratton paid the driver then turned back to her. "This is *San Martín.* We'll wait here for a while then we'll head for *Plaza de Mayo.* It's not that far away. We'll walk."

As they started toward the middle of the well-lit grounds, Jennifer glanced at her watch. It was almost midnight, but the sidewalks were busy and crowded. The packed bistros and restaurants that ringed the area were still serving dinner as bundled-up children scrambled over the park's grassy rises. Young lovers, their arms closely entwined, huddled nearby.

Stratton pointed out several of the buildings and explained their function. Jennifer was nervous and edgy thinking about the meeting ahead of them, but she could almost imagine the two of them as carefree tourists, which, she realized a bit later, was exactly how he wanted them to appear.

"That's the Plaza Hotel." He nodded toward an elegant, European-style building with dozens of blue-and-white Argentinian flags flying along its ornamental parapets. "And over there is the Blessed Sacrament Church."

She followed his gaze to an equally elaborate building, topped by three spires.

"And of course, we have the requisite monuments." Smiling down at her, he tucked her hand into his arm as they strolled down the sidewalk. His attitude was casual, his expression easy. In contrast, though, his eyes never stopped moving. Under her fingers, the muscles of his arm felt equally tense. He was ready for anything.

"In that direction you'll find the *San Martín* statue." He gestured toward a multifigured sculpture. "And over there, is the memorial to the Malvinas' Soldiers."

Distracted and scared, Jennifer would have asked him to explain more but frankly she kept expecting a bullet to fly over her head at any moment.

"We'll wait over there," he said.

She followed his gaze to an isolated bench and once again, they found themselves waiting.

For a long time, neither of them said anything, Jennifer too nervous, Stratton too focused. She watched him watch the people until she couldn't stand the silence any longer. She spoke just to break the quiet, turning on the bench to look at him directly. "Why did you want to know about the IDDA?"

He tried to make light of it. "I'm a curious kind of guy."

"And a liar, too."

He glanced at her. "That's not a nice thing to say."

"Maybe so," she conceded, "but it's the truth."

He didn't reply so she tried a different tactic. "Tell me again how Ami found you."

"I didn't tell you the first time." He wouldn't look at her.

"Humor me," she said softly. "I told you what you wanted to know and you promised that you'd answer some of my questions, too. How did a guy like Ami find someone like you?"

His profile was stony but he answered. "I came recommended."

"By whom?"

"I didn't ask."

"Didn't you want to know? If I were you, I'd have to find out—"

Slowly but with purpose, he draped his arm across the back of the bench and laid his fingers on her shoulder, his smile superficially warm as he stared into her eyes. "You might as well stop trying, Jennifer."

"What do you mean?"

"Don't act dense. It's not your style."

"But—"

"But nothing. I've told you everything you need to know about who I am and what I do. I'm not saying more."

"You told me who you want me to *think* you are. I bet I don't know a single thing about you that isn't a lie."

His eyes came back to her face and a spark of electricity sizzled between them. The response caught her off guard and for the second time that evening, Jennifer found herself reacting to Stratton in a way she wasn't expecting. The first had been in the restaurant when he'd asked if she'd been driving the night Julie was hurt.

His arm still around her, he returned to his survey of the park. But he spoke as he did so, his voice flat and mechanical. "I grew up in Los Angeles and I have a degree from UCLA in chemical engineering. My parents live in San Diego. My dad's a retired Marine, my mother taught school, and I have three brothers. They're all Marines, too. So was I for ten years."

"Then what?"

He gave the area a thorough look then turned to her, pulling her closer. Their thighs were pressing against each other, Jennifer's awareness of the situation turning it into a connection than seemed larger than it actually was. He touched her cheek in a seemingly gentle gesture. Anyone watching would have thought them sweethearts unless they heard him speak. His voice could have cut glass.

"I've said all I'm going to, Jennifer. Don't ask me any more personal questions because I'm not going to answer them, no matter how hard you try or how cleverly you pose them."

At that, he kissed her again, his lips pressing against hers with a fierceness that shouldn't have surprised her but did.

Just when she thought she couldn't take a second more, he pulled back and let his gaze lock on hers, the intensity in his eyes a perfect match to the searing kiss they'd just shared.

"Don't ask again," he repeated.

She shivered, the cold wind—or maybe his words—finally getting to her, her desperation building. "We've shared so much during the past few days, though. I'm not used to this, Stratton. I have to know—"

He cut her off once more. "I'm not the kind of guy you'd take home to meet the folks, Jennifer. You don't even *want* to hear the rest of the story and if you did—" he paused "—you wouldn't believe it."

THEY SAT IN THE PARK another thirty minutes before Stratton stood and brought Jennifer to her feet. "We need to get going." He looked down at her. "Are you ready?"

Her brown eyes were cool. She didn't like the way he'd spoken to her or the fact that he wouldn't reveal all his secrets but what was he supposed to do? Tell her about the Operatives? The organization he'd been a part of was so far removed from Jennifer's sphere of understanding, she'd scream and run the other way if he even attempted to explain.

Any normal person would.

And that wasn't the worst of it.

They moved out from the park where the streets were quieter. The taxis and buses continued to run but a ribbon of fog was crawling in and it muffled the traffic's constant rumble. The smell of diesel and the taste of oil hung in the droplets of moisture that hit their faces, and the steady stream of pedestrians began to dwindle the farther they got from *San Martín*. They'd see more people as they approached *Plaza de Mayo* but it was a good ten blocks away.

He put his arm around Jennifer, and she didn't protest. She might be stubborn, he decided as they walked, but she wasn't stupid. In fact, just the opposite. She understood too much and her questions were getting way too pointed. When they finished with Joseph Wilhem, Stratton was going to have to cut her loose and send her back to the States. She hadn't had anything to do with Ami Leonadov's death and Stratton had been stretching to even think so. But he'd had to look somewhere. Whatever the dealer's "crazy scheme" had been, Jennifer clearly didn't know a thing about it, either. If she had, her face would have given her away.

The faint sound of footsteps came to him. Someone was approaching from behind. Stratton slowed then stepped into the nearest doorway, bringing Jennifer with him. She started to say something but he laid his finger across over her lips and shook his head. Hugging her tightly, he waited until the person he'd heard—a woman with her arms full of groceries—hurried past. He stayed where he was another minute, Jennifer's body warm against him, then he opened his arms. They moved back to the sidewalk without a word and resumed their trek, the curves of her body a memory and nothing more.

Five minutes later, the lights of the plaza glowed straight ahead of them. Beside him, Jennifer tensed just as she had at the airport. He tried to distract her.

"Do you know about this park?" he asked. "*Plaza de Mayo?* Sometimes it's called *Madres de la Plaza de Mayo.*"

She frowned. "The Mother's Plaza? Why is that?"

"Every Thursday at three, the mothers gather. They're women who want justice. They lost children during the military rule in the eighties. *Los desparedcidos,*" he added. "The Disappeared."

"What happened to their children?"

"That's what they want to find out, although most of them know already." He paused, a heaviness in his words. "In most of South America, adoptions are almost impossible. If you don't have children and you want them, you're out of luck. During the eighties, when a lot of political prisoners were tossed in jail—or killed—

their children were taken away and given to military families who had none."

Her eyes rounded in shock. "Their children were taken? Just like that? No one stopped them?"

"The military was completely in charge. They threw people out of helicopters for fun. How would someone have rescued their children from people like that?"

Jennifer shivered and drew the jacket Gomez's maid had given her closer to her throat. "I don't think I like this part of the world."

"It's not all bad. South America can be a good place to live, you just have to pick the right spot and the right time."

They had reached the edge of the park and Stratton turned his attention to his next problem. He didn't want Jennifer near when he and Wilhem talked, but he had to have her there to start the conversation. They headed for the side where the presidential palace was located.

The fog was getting thicker. Stratton glanced around, the rattle of a can in the gutter, the only muffled sound he could hear. The weather had scattered the park's visitors, and it was growing emptier by the moment.

His low voice seemed hollow in the silence. "I want you to go to that spot over there and sit down." She followed his nod to a park seat on the edge of the plaza. The wooden bench was surrounded by dense, green underbrush with only a small clearing right before it. "When Wilhem comes up to you, show him where I am, then leave. Don't look back, don't stick around, just leave. See that dark green car over there? The Falcon?"

She glanced across the street.

"He's waiting for you," Stratton explained. "Don't

get in any other vehicle. He'll take you back to the hotel and I'll meet you there."

She frowned. "Who is—"

"He's the nephew of Ali Hassam, the guy who owns the restaurant where we ate. Don't ask him any questions because he won't know the answer anyway. Just get in the car and go."

She started shaking her head. "I don't like this. I think I should stay with you. You might need me for something—"

"The only thing I need is for you to stay away from here," Stratton answered. "I don't want to have to worry about you while I'm trying to get information from Wilhem."

"You don't have to worry about me," she said stiffly.

"All right," he countered. "Then let's put it this way—I also don't want to have to worry about the guy with the gun who shot *at* you in Rio."

She swallowed and he nodded. "I thought that might clarify things."

He untangled her hand from the crook of his arm and took it in his. Her fingers were frigid as she clasped his with a frantic grip. She looked pale and washed-out under the streetlights, the tension of the past day etched across her face in furrows and shadows. He wondered if he was doing the right thing, then he wondered about wondering. He'd never experienced second thoughts before; it wasn't a comfortable sensation.

"Are you okay?" It was the only thing he could think of to ask.

"I will be," she said shakily, "if I make it past this."

Telling himself it was all part of the plan, he cradled

her cheek with his hand. Her skin was smooth and soft, incredibly soft, and knowing better but doing it anyway, he kissed her once more then he gave her a push and sent her toward the bench.

CHAPTER ELEVEN

JENNIFER APPROACHED the bench with grateful appreciation. She wasn't too sure she would have made it much farther. Her legs were so shaky she felt as if she were still on the airplane, her stomach roiling in distress. Her nervousness was due in part to the situation, but also to Stratton's attitude. The closer they'd gotten to their meeting with Joseph Wilhem, the smoother Stratton had become. His kiss had proved the point. He'd kissed her better than she'd ever been kissed before. It was strange how he seemed to be enjoying the situation, his every move calculated.

What kind of man was he?

A scary one, she decided, but oh, so intriguing. She sank to the bench and crossed her legs, the moisture in the air brushing her face with whispery fingers as soft as Stratton's had been. His touch had felt strangely reassuring. The quick changes—in his personality *and* demeanor—were making her dizzy. She wondered if they represented his true nature or if the chameleon-like behavior was something he'd learned during the years he wouldn't explain. If he'd made up a lie about that time in his life, she would have accepted it unknowingly, but

An Important Message from the Editors

Dear Reader,

Because you've chosen to read one of our fine romance novels, we'd like to say "thank you"! And, as a special way to thank you, we're offering you two more of the books you love so well, and a surprise gift to send you — absolutely FREE!

Please enjoy them with our compliments...

Pam Powers

Peel off Seal and Place Inside...

EDITOR'S FREE GIFT SEAL THANK YOU

How to validate your Editor's
"Thank You"
FREE GIFT

1. Peel off gift seal from front cover. Place it in space provided at right. This automatically entitles you to receive 2 FREE BOOKS and a fabulous mystery gift.

2. Send back this card and you'll get 2 brand-new *Romance* novels. These books have a cover price of $5.99 or more each in the U.S. and $6.99 or more each in Canada, but they are yours to keep absolutely free.

3. There's no catch. You're under no obligation to buy anything. We charge nothing—ZERO—for your first shipment. And you don't have to make any minimum number of purchases—not even one!

4. The fact is, thousands of readers enjoy receiving their books by mail from The Reader Service. They enjoy the convenience of home delivery...they like getting the best new novels at discount prices BEFORE they're available in stores... and they love their Heart to Heart subscriber newsletter featuring author news, special book offers, book reviews and much more!

5. We hope that after receiving your free books you'll want to remain a subscriber. But the choice is yours— to continue or cancel, any time at all! So why not take us up on our invitation, with no risk of any kind. You'll be glad you did!

GET A *Free* MYSTERY GIFT...

*SURPRISE MYSTERY GIFT COULD BE YOURS **FREE** AS A SPECIAL "THANK YOU" FROM THE EDITORS*

THE EDITOR'S "THANK YOU" FREE GIFTS INCLUDE:

▶ Two BRAND-NEW Romance Novels

▶ An exciting surprise gift

YES! I have placed my Editor's "thank you" Free Gifts seal in the space provided at right. Please send me 2 FREE books, and my FREE Mystery Gift. I understand that I am under no obligation to purchase anything further, as explained on the back and opposite page.

PLACE
FREE GIFTS
SEAL
HERE

193 MDL D37Q   393 MDL D37R

FIRST NAME	LAST NAME

ADDRESS

APT.#	CITY

STATE/PROV.	ZIP/POSTAL CODE

Thank You!

The Reader Service — Here's How It Works:

Accepting your 2 free books and gift places you under no obligation to buy anything. You may keep the books and gift and return the shipping statement marked "cancel." If you do not cancel, about a month later we'll send you 3 additional books and bill you just $4.99 each in the U.S., or $5.49 each in Canada, plus 25¢ shipping & handling per book and applicable taxes if any.* That's the complete price and — compared to cover prices starting from $5.99 each in the U.S. and $6.99 each in Canada — it's quite a bargain! You may cancel at any time, but if you choose to continue, every month we'll send you 3 more books, which you may either purchase at the discount price or return to us and cancel your subscription.

*Terms and prices subject to change without notice. Sales tax applicable in N.Y. Canadian residents will be charged applicable provincial taxes and GST.

If offer card is missing write to: The Reader Service, 3010 Walden Ave., P.O. Box 1867, Buffalo, NY 14240-1867

BUSINESS REPLY MAIL

FIRST-CLASS MAIL   PERMIT NO. 717-003   BUFFALO, NY

POSTAGE WILL BE PAID BY ADDRESSEE

THE READER SERVICE
3010 WALDEN AVE
PO BOX 1341
BUFFALO NY 14240-8571

NO POSTAGE
NECESSARY
IF MAILED
IN THE
UNITED STATES

he'd snapped himself shut so completely and tightly, she'd been instantly curious.

She stared into the growing emptiness of the park and shook her head. When this was all over, their paths would diverge. Why did she even care?

Shivering, Jennifer pulled her jacket closer and peered into the darkness. Stratton had melted into the shadows and Joseph Wilhem was nowhere to be seen. A few couples strolled down the sidewalk that bordered the *Avenue Rividavia* but the earlier crowd had now dissipated. A vehicle rumbled past and a horn honked in the distance, but the ordinary noise only served to emphasize her solitude. She felt as if she were the last person left in the world and the feeling wasn't a good one.

A second later, the noise of someone running broke the creepy silence. The rapid approach quickened her pulse so drastically, Jennifer felt as if her heart and whoever was drawing near were in a race. She gripped the edge of the bench and tried to stay put but in the end, she couldn't. Jumping to her feet, she caught her breath just as a blur of movement burst into her peripheral vision.

She swallowed her scream but barely. The person who'd exploded out of the bushes was only a small boy. Nine, maybe ten at the most, he was so thin she could almost see through him and so intense he seemed to be vibrating. Spanish spewed from his mouth in a rapid-fire delivery, his arms and legs moving, it seemed to her, in sync with his words.

She put her hands on his shoulders to quiet him. Beneath her fingers and the rags that he wore, his bones felt like a bird's. He yanked himself out of her grasp, but he didn't fall silent. Instead, the opposite occurred—the flow of information seemed to increase until it became a river that even he couldn't control. Only when he paused to grab a breath was Jennifer able to speak.

"Slow down! Slow down! What is it? What's wrong?"

"Are you the Señorita Diamante?"

His question threw her off, then she understood.

"A man, *la officina aya,* he sent me. He said to find you and tell you to come. Now! He has the south door open. Find the fourth floor and follow the hall to the back. He'll be waiting."

Behind his street-savvy bravado, the boy moved nervously as he spoke, his eyes lit with fear. She couldn't imagine Joseph Wilhem scaring a child, but the boy had been frightened by someone.

Jennifer grew suspicious as the message sank in. Had Wilhem just planned this diversion or had he never intended on showing up? "When did he tell you to do this?" she asked. "Did you just come from there?"

His expression turned cagey. "What do you care?"

Once again, it took her a second to get the message. Digging into her purse, she pulled out a ten-peso note and thrust it at the child.

"He grabbed me this afternoon. On the square in the back. He told me you'd be here tonight, when the church bell rang once."

She glanced up and anxiously searched the park with her eyes but Stratton was nowhere to be seen. The boy tugged at her arm so violently, that for a moment, she thought he was trying to snatch her bag. She jerked back.

"*Señorita?* You want I should take you there now?"

"No," she said firmly. "I know where the office is. You go home. Go home and go to bed. Forget you heard any of this, okay?"

He nodded, his eyes too old for his face, then he ran off, the dark swallowing him as efficiently as it had Stratton. More likely than not, the child didn't even have a home to go to, she thought as she watched him flee, but there was little she could do about that right now. Maybe her money—and Wilhem's—would help.

She waited uncertainly. Five minutes passed, then another five. She looked around the park with growing concern. Had something happened to Stratton? What was going on? Finally giving up on him, she started down the empty sidewalk.

Then she heard the footsteps behind her.

THE MINUTE HE'D SEEN the kid, Stratton had known what the old man had done. He wasn't surprised at Wilhem's caution, though. The German hadn't lived as he had all these years without picking up some tricks of survival.

Concentrating on what to do next, Stratton wasn't thinking when he grabbed Jennifer's arm. With a gasp, she jerked away from him, pivoting on one foot then pushing against him, using his own weight to force him back. He was so surprised by her reaction, he almost went down.

Twisting sideways, he broke free and immediately stepped closer, pinning her arms to her side, his breath coming almost as fast as hers. "What the hell are you doing?"

"What am *I* doing?" she cried. "What are *you* doing?

You scared the crap out of me! Why didn't you say something?"

"I wasn't thinking about you," he said hotly. "But if I'd known you were going to attack me, I would have let you know, believe me!"

Her eyes had been wide with fright but at his words, her expression turned angry. When he spoke again, though, it softened instantly.

"You're fast," he said. "And good. That was a slick move, I'm impressed."

She straightened her sweater self-consciously. "Cissy and I took self-defense classes. And knitting and target shooting and painting and—"

"Okay, I get the message." He switched topics. Time was passing. "The kid told you Wilhem wants to meet somewhere else, right?"

She nodded and explained. "So what do we do now?"

"We do exactly what he said for us to do," Stratton answered with a grim expression. "You go first. I'll be right behind you. If I follow you, I'll have a better chance of seeing anyone who might be tailing you."

She agreed, although there was reluctance in her eyes. Stratton put his hand on her arm and held her still. "Listen—" He paused until she lifted her eyes to his. "I'll be right behind you, okay? Don't worry."

Stratton watched her walk away and for one short moment, he thought about calling her back. What the hell was he doing? Who knew what was going to happen up there. If anything, he should go first. Realizing he was beginning to get too protective of her, he forced himself to put distance between his growing feelings for

Jennifer and the job he needed to do. He scanned the street and its doorways.

In a matter of minutes, Jennifer was on *Avenue Florida,* Stratton trailing too far back for anyone to connect them. When a man approached her unexpectedly from one of the side streets, Stratton tensed and thrust his hand into his jacket for the gun Ali had provided him, but the guy hurried past and kept going. A moment after that, she reached the corner nearest the office they'd visited earlier that day. Crossing the street, she walked beside the high-rise, using the shadows and avoiding the front entrance completely. She continued toward the back, then all at once, she was gone.

Stratton cursed and ran across the street, his footsteps quick as he tried to figure out what had happened. Where had she gone? He studied the side of the building until he spotted a thin shaft of light lying across the sidewalk. It was coming from the threshold. Wilhem must have had the door propped open and Jennifer had gone through it.

Stratton slipped inside, the sound of Jennifer's footsteps ringing on the metal stairs as she climbed to the floor above. He tracked her eight flights, to the fourth floor, then everything went silent again. He ran lightly up the stairs and paused beside the doorway to free his weapon from its holster. Closing his eyes, he exhaled softly then opened the door and eased into the hallway.

JENNIFER LISTENED intently, her heart lodging itself in her throat. For the second time since she'd entered the building, she was sure she'd heard Stratton in the hallway behind her, but just like before, when she'd stopped and held her breath, nothing but silence had reached her ears. The building was eerily empty and felt totally abandoned, its daily inhabitants obviously long gone for home and hearth. Giving herself an extra few seconds, Jennifer let her pulse slow, then she started forward again, following the signs to Wilhem's suite.

Ami had always teased Jennifer about her memory. Jennifer didn't believe her skill was such a big deal, but people—her mother and Julie included—were always impressed by her ability to remember numbers. She kept them in her head with no effort. After hearing or reading them once she could see them in her mind as clearly as if they were written on a blackboard in front of her.

She rounded the corner and found the office right in front of her. She looked over her shoulder once, then paused. If someone other than Stratton was behind her she had nowhere to hide. She hesitated, her pulse thumping painfully, then tapped the door. It'd be safer to wait for Stratton inside the office. The heavy mahogany gave way under her knuckles and swung forward slightly. The door was not only unlocked, it'd been left open. She pushed it back and peered inside.

"Sr. Wilhem? Are you here?"

No one answered. She went two strides farther into the room, then paused again. "Sr. Wilhem? It's me— Jennifer. Are you back there?"

Again she heard nothing. She bit her bottom lip and paused then gave it one last attempt. "Hello? Sr. Wilhem? *¿Qué pasa, señor?*"

Again, he didn't answer, but deep down, Jennifer didn't expect to hear his voice. There was no one in the office and she'd known that the minute she'd walked into the reception area. The suite held the steady quietness that only an empty room can produce, the air still and leaden because no one's breath disturbed it.

Go forward, turn back or wait?

Jennifer looked around and tried to decide what to do, her eyes noting the furniture. A small desk shoved against one wall, a line of chairs beside it, a sad-looking plastic tree in one corner. An area the size of a large closet opened off to her left, a desk in it as well. Wilhem's trade was strictly wholesale and the sterility of his office reflected that.

The faintest noise sounded behind her. Stuck in the center of the room, Jennifer's whole body went cold, her fingers curling into fists at her side. She knew she'd heard something, dammit, and this time she was sure, a step, a sigh, a word? She couldn't tell what it was, but she didn't care, either. A rush of fear washed over her, leaving behind a salty taste in her mouth. If Stratton had somehow slipped past her and was back there, he would have called her name.

She tensed, then started to pivot.

But she was too late. Before she could complete the turn, a hand stole over her mouth and a muscular arm went around her midsection, yanking her backward. The grip was like a steel bar, the impact jarring Jennifer's teeth as her back collided with someone. Whoever held her jerked her into the office she'd noted off the reception area. Just as they crossed the threshold her assailant tripped on the edge of the carpet. All the instructions from the self-defense classes Cissy had dragged her to came back in a flash. Jennifer lashed out but missed. All she could do next was spin around and face her attacker.

He instantly tightened his grip and pulled her against him. Jennifer managed a single grunt, then she was silenced, his embrace cutting off her shock.

The attacker wore a mask, was strong and wasn't a man.

Beneath a hood that completely covered her head, the woman was betrayed by her figure. In the dark, her gender would have gone undetected. She was dressed in a loose black turtleneck with a black coat on top of it and she wore jeans with boots, but Jennifer could feel her breasts pushing into her own. Her body might have held the strength of a man's but there was no mistaking the full softness under the sweater. They were eye to eye, as well. Jennifer could see through the slits in the mask. She had dark eyes that were ringed in eyeliner—Stratton's comment about "kohl" came to mind—and lashes that had been curled and mascaraed.

The petty detail broke Jennifer's trance. She screamed loudly and began to pound the woman's shoulders. She silenced Jennifer instantly by slapping a hand across her lips but Jennifer bit her. Hard. Jerking her hand back, the woman yelped in surprise. Jennifer got in another "Help!" then her attacker clamped her fingers back over Jennifer's mouth, this time making sure it was closed. Grabbing both Jennifer's wrists with her other hand, she kneed Jennifer and lifted her off the floor, carrying her farther into the smaller office.

Using her weight as leverage, Jennifer kicked backward and managed a solid hit against her attacker's legs. Distracted and in pain, the woman let Jennifer go.

Before she could take a single step, though, she was caught and dragged backward once again. This time when they collided it was different. The tip of something sharp and cold was pressed into the bottom of her throat, just beneath her chin. Jennifer stilled and gasped, her chest rising and falling rapidly.

"Shut up and don't move." The woman's voice was harsh, but unlike Jennifer she was cool and calm, the fight a mere inconvenience. "You've been a shitload of trouble already. All I need is one good excuse to get rid of you."

Jennifer tried to speak but the woman pressed the knife closer. The tip sliced into her skin.

"Try that again," she taunted. "I'm not too good with this puny little knife. It might slip accidentally—" she twitched and the tip went in deeper, a white-hot pain coming with it "—and do something bad."

Jennifer swallowed and a warm trickle slid down her neck. The woman waited but Jennifer didn't move.

"That's it?" she asked in a sulky voice. "No more fun?"

"I'm afraid not."

The voice came from the reception area and both women looked at the doorway.

"Playtime's over," Stratton said with a smile, his pistol in his hand. "Drop the knife and move away from the girl."

HE DIDN'T EXPECT the woman to do what he ordered but he didn't expect what happened next, either.

In the space of one heartbeat, she cocked her arm back and threw the knife at Stratton's head. The blade sailed close enough to nick his ear but if he hadn't ducked at the last moment, it would have pierced his eyeball instead. His shock at seeing her disappeared in a rush of adrenaline. Had the miss been deliberate?

She was out the door before he could even straighten. He tried to grab her as she went by, but he missed. Yelling at Jennifer to stay put, Stratton raced into the hallway. Looking both ways, he saw nothing, then the door to the stairs whispered shut. Throwing himself against the door, he fell into the stairwell and aimed his pistol at the metal stairs over his head. They were empty and he swept the gun to the ones below to find the same. He headed down the staircase, his feet clattering loudly as he took the steps two at a time.

The woman was nowhere to be seen when he reached the bottom and yanked open the door. Closing the doorway, he headed back up the stairs as fast as he could, his mind considering the possibilities as quickly as his feet moved up the steps. The only woman he knew who could throw a knife like that was Meredith Santera, but why would she be involved in this? Lucy Wisner? He doubted it. She was too polished, too cool. It took a certain kind of woman to handle a blade and she hadn't struck him as that kind.

When he reentered the office, Jennifer was exactly where he'd left her, the only difference being the fact that she was now sitting on the floor instead of standing, a thin red scratch bisecting her throat.

Looking up at him, she swallowed and the line moved. "What was that? Who was that?"

In the pale oval of her face, her eyes were huge and dark and filled with emotion. Stratton began to curse himself for not stopping her when he could have. Then he realized he was misreading her expression. She wasn't frightened. She was pissed.

"Who was that?" she repeated angrily. "She damn near slit my throat!"

"I don't know who she was," he answered, "but I *will* find out. Eventually." His hand slipped up to his ear. "Have you seen Wilhem?"

She shook her head.

"Stay here," he ordered. "I'm going to check out the rest of the office then we're getting the hell out of here."

She nodded and lifted a hand to her throat, her fingers smudging the blood. He tried not to notice but the image registered with a jolt that opened a gate he wanted to keep shut, a second image joining it. The picture was one he fought to keep at bay, but in that split second, he saw everything again as clearly as if it lay before him on the carpet of the office. The sprawled bodies of a woman and a child, a man on his knees beside them, his expression one of disbelief before it morphed into panicked fear. Blood everywhere. Smeared blood.

He came to with Jennifer touching his arm, her face puzzled as she spoke his name. She stood right beside him and he hadn't even realized she'd moved. "Are you okay?"

The bloody memory dissipated at the sound of her voice. He shook his head to clear it then gripped her arm so tightly she winced. What was going on? He'd never had a flashback in his life.

"Stay here," he commanded again. "And don't move until I call you. I'm not letting you out of my sight again."

With that, he stepped back into the reception area, his weapon at his side. Four silent steps took him closer to the inner office. The door that led to it was cracked open, as well.

He touched the bottom of the wood with the toe of his boot and swung it back gently, his eyes darting across the room as it was slowly revealed.

There was nothing in the room but a desk and a chair.

Stratton stayed where he was and reached around to the hinged side of the door, pushing the heavy mahogany until it rested flat against the wall. He doubted the woman had had help, but he wasn't willing to bet his life on it. A single small window was behind the desk, but there were no other openings. He concentrated on the desk. The only spot left where anyone could possibly hide was beneath it, in the kneehole.

He made his way toward the piece of furniture, his pistol extended in a double-fisted grip. If someone was concealed underneath, they would have the advantage. They knew he was coming and it'd just be a matter of blasting away when he got within range. Short of shooting through the desk skirt first, Stratton's only approach was a direct one.

A second later, the odor hit him. The smell was faint because it was fresh but it wouldn't be for long, the slightly sweet mixture of blood and other things he didn't want to think about combining in a perfume he'd experienced too many times not to recognize.

He stepped around the edge of the desk, then swung his gun before him, his eyes following his weapon's line of sight just in case he was mistaken.

He wasn't.

He relaxed his stance with a sigh to stare at the body—he assumed of Joseph Wilhem—lying beneath the desk in a pool of blood.

Death had caught the diamond dealer by surprise. His face still wore a look of disbelief. Stratton bent to look closer and quickly figured out why. The woman had taken him from behind and he'd never seen her coming.

The old man's throat had been slit from one side to the other.

WHEN JENNIFER HEARD Stratton call her name, she tensed. He spoke as he usually did, with a low, gravelly tone, but something else lingered beneath the surface. He repeated her name two more times before she could set her feet into motion.

Stratton was squatting behind the desk when she came into the office and she realized that they'd come too late. Moving even slower than before, she rounded the piece of cheap wooden furniture and looked down.

In the back of her mind, she'd expected it. Still, there was a Grand Canyon's worth of difference between anticipation and reality, especially where death was concerned. Confronted with the blood and the violence of Wilhem's motionless form, she felt nausea rise inside her throat. Tamping down the response with a determination she didn't know she had, Jennifer lifted her eyes to Stratton's. "How long has he been dead?"

With a casualness that spoke of experience, Stratton picked up the dead man's hand, then let it drop. Jennifer recoiled.

Stratton looked up. "Not long. He's cooling off but he's nowhere close to getting stiff. She must have just finished when you came in."

Stratton stood, and Jennifer made a sound of distress. He looked at her, his eyes narrowing.

She waved him off and he pulled a handkerchief from his pocket then dabbed it at her throat. "We need to get the hell out of here. You didn't touch anything did you?"

"Only the doorknob, but—" Shocked by his words, she resisted his attempt to clean her up and pushed away his hand. "We can't just leave him like that, Stratton."

He stopped. "Do you really want to be around when the Argentine police show up? It'd be your second appearance in a foreign country with a dead guy close by. I wouldn't recommend it, personally."

"But—"

"But nothing." Stuffing the square of cotton back into the pocket of his jacket, he tugged her toward the reception area where he wiped the doorknob then grabbed her hand. "Stay behind me," he said. "And don't look back."

Ten minutes later, they were in the park again. It was completely empty with no sign of anyone about, including the car that should have been waiting for Jennifer. A certain kind of numbness had begun to seep into her while they'd been in Joseph Wilhem's office, and now, in the eerie stillness that surrounded them, Jennifer felt it sink deeper, until it settled into her bones. She wasn't sure if the sensation was good or bad. It muffled the shock, but it also added to her sense of chaos.

"We should let someone know." She stumbled after Stratton, her mind refusing to let go of the conventions to which she was accustomed. "It's not right to just leave him like that."

"He's not worried about it, so you shouldn't be, either." Stratton sent her a glance. "Forget Wilhem."

His coldness shook her. "But, Stratton—"

He stopped abruptly, their progress down the darkened sidewalk halted. "Jennifer, he's dead, okay? Nothing we do will matter to him now. He's out of the picture. If we don't put as much distance between him and us as possible, your friend is going to come back and finish the job I interrupted. Will that bring him back?" He didn't wait for an answer. "No, it won't. So we have to take care of ourselves. Nothing else matters."

"It's not the right thing to do," she said stubbornly.

"You can't afford to do the right thing anymore."

Jennifer stared at him, a sudden revelation coming to her through his words and by his demeanor.

"I don't believe that," she said quietly. "And you don't, either. We're the *good* guys. We have to do the right thing."

A shadow of emotion crossed his face and then it was gone. Jennifer felt as if she'd caught a glimpse of the man he truly was but the window opened and closed so fast that all she was got was an impression. An impression that she had clearly misinterpreted.

Because no one could carry around that kind of regret. A load that heavy would kill you.

CHAPTER TWELVE

JENNIFER LET STRATTON pull her along in his wake. She had no idea where they were going and for just a bit she had no recollection of where they'd been. It all came back in a rush.

Half an hour later, they entered the lobby of what looked like a small hotel. She wasn't too sure that's what it really was, but the building had the air of a place where people came and went. She caught a glimpse of two large sitting rooms on either side of the main hall then a woman took her hand and guided her gently into a luxurious bathroom off the entrance.

Clicking her tongue with distress, she cleaned Jennifer up and put a butterfly bandage on the cut, her touch sure and gentle. As she worked, the icy stupor that had encased Jennifer began to melt and she started to analyze what had happened in Wilhem's office. The first thing that came into her mind—the only thing, really—was the expression on Stratton's face when he'd seen the woman with the knife. Jennifer had assumed at the time that he'd been surprised to see anyone there but the more she thought about it, the more ridiculous she realized it was. Stratton was prepared for anything and everything.

No, he'd looked strange for another reason. He'd been surprised because he'd recognized the woman.

Somehow, somewhere, they'd met before.

Thinking back on the moment, Jennifer remembered a detail that convinced her of that. Her attacker had jerked when Stratton had first spoken then she'd tensed, her body pressed so closely to Jennifer's she'd been able to feel it. She'd been shocked to see him, but not *that* shocked.

The woman finished her ministrations and patted Jennifer on the shoulder with sympathy. She took her back into the lobby and for some reason sent Stratton a dark look. Ignoring her displeasure, he led Jennifer upstairs, to a bedroom with a small bath. In Jennifer's state of mind, the place seemed fine. It was clean, it was quiet, and there were no dead people anywhere. If she'd been a little less shell-shocked and a little more alert, she might have noticed the scented candles and array of massage oils on the nightstand. If she'd opened the drawer, she might have seen the condoms, too. But she didn't do any of those things. She simply sat down on the bed and watched Stratton.

He went into the bathroom. She heard what sounded like the shower curtain rustling, then he came back and checked the window on the other side of the mattress to see if it was locked. When she saw him drop to his knees and search under the bed, she spoke. "What are you doing?"

"What does it look like I'm doing?" He glanced around the room, obviously checking to see if he'd left anything out. "I'm making sure we're alone."

"Do you always do that when you go into a hotel room?"

"Only when I think there's a possibility someone might be looking for me." He stood up. "And this isn't a hotel. It's a whorehouse."

"Whorehouses are illegal," she said by rote.

"So is murder. But it obviously happens, doesn't it?"

She winced at his bluntness but it served to break her torpor.

"Who was that woman? The one who killed Wilhem?" she demanded. "Did you know her?"

He looked at Jennifer with an indifference that completely contradicted the feeling his earlier kiss had produced inside her. "Why would you think I'd know her? She might be the same person who killed your boss," Stratton said. "And Singh, too. If I knew who the hell she was, I would have taken her out."

The chilling words brought Jennifer to her feet. "And that's exactly why we need to stop this crazy running and contact the authorities." She grabbed Stratton's arm. "We *have* to call the police and let them handle this."

"The authorities *were* called in Rio, Jennifer. Have you already forgotten that?"

"No, but have you forgotten Mr. Barragan in Mexico City?" she cried, "Obviously, he's next in whatever the hell is going on here! We have to let him know."

"And what exactly would you tell him? Someone's killed three diamond dealers and you might be next?" Stratton shook his head with an air of disgust. "That won't help us, Jennifer. He'll run and we'll never find out what's happening."

"You'd rather have him dead?"

"No. I'd rather have him talking—to us. That's the only way we're going to figure this out. We have to talk to someone who was involved in your boss's scheme, whatever the hell it was. Barragan's the only one left. You're going to call and find out if he's in town, then we're heading for Mexico City."

She should have expected this, she told herself. She should have seen what was coming. "I'll call him," she said. "But that's it. I'm going back to the States. I'm *not* going to Mexico with you."

"The man won't see me without you."

"That's your problem."

"No," he said softly, "it would be Barragan's problem and he'll pay for it with his life. Do you want that on your conscience? It seems to me you're carrying enough guilt already. I wouldn't think you'd want to add to the burden."

His words stung, and Jennifer felt the last of her strength give way. She sat down heavily on the mattress, the springs squeaking noisily. "This is too much," she whispered hoarsely. "I'm not used to seeing corpses and being shot at and running from the police. I'm not like you. I don't know how to handle things like knives at my throat and I don't *want* to know how to handle them." She lifted her eyes as her voice rose in an unintentional wail. "I just want to go home, Stratton. I want to go back to Houston and back to my life and back to the way things were."

He crossed the space between them, knelt at her feet and brought her to him with a rough jerk, wrapping his arms around her. "Lower your voice, Jennifer! For God's sake! Hassam runs this place but cops push their way in here all the time. There could be one next door to us right now!" He shook her slightly. "Do you understand me?"

She blinked and he loosened his grip. "I want to go home," she whispered.

"I know that," he said quietly. "This isn't your world and you're scared. But you're here regardless and what's happened, has happened. It can't be changed. You have to deal with it. We can't leave Barragan hanging in the wind." He touched her chin. "We're the good guys, remember?"

Her throat seemed to close and she found herself unable to speak.

"You aren't going to be alone, okay?" His lips were inches from hers. "I live in this place where you don't want to be. It's where I'm from. If you let me, I'll get you out of here and safely back into *your* world without anyone else getting killed—including yourself—but I can't do that if you fight me."

She had no other choice. He was telling her the truth. She could see it in his eyes just as he had read it in hers.

"Do you promise?" The question seemed silly but she had to ask.

"I promise." He answered. "Cross my heart."

Then he kissed her and this time it was for real.

JENNIFER DIDN'T resist him. Her hands went around his neck as she pressed her body into his, her mouth opening beneath his own.

Her response should have shocked him, Stratton thought, as he tasted her, but everything about this case had been bizarre from the beginning.

What *did* shock him was his promise to her. What was he thinking? Promises were for fools. Only the most naive believed that something happened just because someone had promised that it would. And God knew, he wasn't a "good guy."

He was far, far from it, proving the point by kissing her. If he'd been the man she thought he was, he would have pushed her away right now. Instead of doing that, he let his hands skim over her hips to the swell of her buttocks. He imagined pushing her down on the bed, their clothes disappearing, their lips never parting. He could tell her body was firm and muscular but she still had all the softness that women were supposed to have. He thought about running his palms and then his lips over those soft places. She would smell good, he already knew, and taste even better.

The telephone sounded, the shrill ring shattering his fantasy and saving his sanity.

Stratton let his arms fall to his side but still he didn't move, his eyes on Jennifer's.

"Aren't you going to answer that?" she asked.

Her question cut the last thread holding them together. Stratton turned with a curse and picked up the phone, his greeting spoken in Arabic because he knew who was calling.

"Your time has run out," Ali Hassam said.

Stratton's gut tightened. "Already?"

"I am afraid so. It was probably gone before you even arrived, but that hardly matters now. You must leave. Your presence was noticed and the *policia* are on the way."

"Did you have enough time to set everything up?"

The Lebanese hesitated. "Not everything was done but your transportation is ready. You know where."

"It'd better be ready. The arrangements you made be-

fore did not work out. You might need to check on that
situation."

Ali swore in Arabic and Stratton knew the man's
nephew would be paying for his desertion.

When the curses died out, Stratton let the silence
build as he thought.

"There was a woman," Stratton started in Arabic.
"Tonight at the office."

"A woman?" Hassam's voice held doubt.

Stratton touched his ear. "She had a knife and she
was good with it."

Hassam sucked in his breath. "The only woman I
know who uses a knife is Mere—" He stopped all at
once, the name of Stratton's former boss dying on his
lips.

Stratton stared at a crack in the plaster on the wall
beside him. The fracture reminded him of his shock
when he'd entered the office tonight and seen what he'd
seen.

He thought about Meredith for a while then he finally
spoke. "This had better work."

Hassam took his turn at thinking, then he answered
quietly. "It will, my friend. If it doesn't, come back and
haunt me."

The line went dead and Stratton turned back to Jennifer. She was where he'd left her, her lips slightly swollen, her hair in disarray. He could have finished things,
but Stratton stopped himself.

"Get your stuff," he ordered. "We're out of here."

THEY WENT TO THE AIRPORT but not the same one at
which they'd arrived. Stratton explained tersely. "We
flew into Newberry. This is Ezeiza."

Once inside the terminal, Stratton stopped at a small gift shop. He bought a variety of magazines and toiletries, T-shirts and souvenirs. The last thing he selected was a roll of tape. Disappearing into the men's room, he stayed long enough for Jennifer to get even more nervous than she already was. She fingered the scarf at her neck. The silk carried the scent of the woman who had cleaned Jennifer up at the bordello. Stratton had handed over several pesos then taken the bright square and wrapped it around Jennifer's neck to hide the bandage.

She wasn't sure how much more she could handle. Between everything that had happened *and* the kiss they'd shared, her head was twirling. Her distrust had given way under the promise he'd made her but in the end, Jennifer wasn't accustomed to depending on someone else. *She* was the one others depended on.

Stratton sat down beside her. "We won't be here long and the plane we're taking out isn't well equipped." He nodded toward the ladies' room. "This might be your last chance for a while. When we're on the plane, we'll call Mexico City."

She nodded automatically, stood up and walked away from Stratton, wishing she could do the same with everything that had happened to her since she left the States. When she came back out, he was waiting for her. He took her arm and they headed out to the tarmac.

The jet was white and sleek. The only decoration it wore was a seal on the side with the name of a well-known corporation. Jennifer stared at it in surprise then glanced at Stratton as they walked up the stairs that had been rolled to its hatch.

"Don't ask," he said.

She lifted her eyebrows and followed him up the stairs and then onto the plane. They were the only passengers. They settled into their leather seats and a uniformed attendant brought them drinks. When she walked back to the galley, Stratton pulled a cell phone from his pocket.

It didn't look like any mobile phone she'd ever seen before and Jennifer found herself wondering why nothing was ever what it appeared to be with Stratton, not even his tools. He punched a series of buttons, then asked her for Barragan's number.

She repeated it from memory.

He entered the fourteen-digit code then handed the phone to her. The unit felt heavier than a regular cell and somehow seemed ominous, as well.

As the phone rang, the plane lifted into the air. No announcements here about turning off anything, she noted, then she realized something else. She could hardly tell they'd taken off. Either she was getting accustomed to flying or private jets were the way to go.

Joseph Barragan's secretary answered on the fourth ring, her laid-back *"Bueno?"* as smooth as always. Jennifer felt herself relax slightly.

"Crystal, this is Jennifer Rodas," she said in Spanish. "How are you?"

"Perfecto," the young girl replied. *"Usted?"*

Jennifer took a deep breath. Crystal obviously hadn't heard about Ami or Wilhem, but she was young and beautiful. When she left work, nothing entered her mind but having a good time. Bad news was for old people.

"I need to speak to the *señor.* Is he there?"

"No, he's not. He's in…" Jennifer heard some papers rustling then Crystal spoke. "He's in Tel Aviv this week. Antwerp next week."

"Antwerp and Tel Aviv?" Jennifer repeated the cities for Stratton. "Do you have numbers where I can reach him?"

The girl hesitated. She was young but she wasn't stupid. "I don't have numbers," she said. "But if you give me yours, I'll pass it on next time he calls in."

"It's important," Jennifer pressed.

"I understand."

She didn't but Jennifer couldn't tell her that. She put her hand over the phone and explained to Stratton. "Should I give her this number?"

"You can't call that phone," he said cryptically. "Ask her when he'll be back."

"I'm not sure," Crystal said when Jennifer posed the question. "You know how they are, these men. They go on business then something else pops up and they don't come back when they're supposed to." She lowered her voice. "Sometimes I think he sees a woman over there. He can disappear, you know."

Her mind on the problem, Jennifer stared at Stratton and shook her head, replying automatically to the girl. "That's nice."

She made a sound Jennifer couldn't interpret. "I don't think Mrs. Barragan would agree with you on that but who's to say, eh?"

Jennifer tried to recover. "Oh, right, yes." She held her hand out to Stratton as if to say what next?

He shook his head then pantomimed making another call. Jennifer nodded.

"I'll try you again later," she said. "Maybe you can get his number next time he calls in and give it to me?"

"Maybe," the girl said. "Adios."

Jennifer handed the phone back to Stratton. "She doesn't know where he is or when he'll be back. She wouldn't give me a number."

He frowned. "What the hell kind of game is she play—"

Jennifer stopped him. "No, it's not like that," she said. "Dealers always keep their travel plans fluid. They don't want anyone to be able to track them. It's a security thing. Crystal was probably telling the truth. She may not even know where he's staying, and she wouldn't have that number anyway. She'd have his cell phone number, but the dealers call in for messages. You don't call them."

"But she mentioned Tel Aviv and Antwerp?"

Jennifer nodded then she watched Stratton think. He believed he could hide his thoughts, but he was wrong, she was learning. The longer she knew him, the easier it became for her to interpret his looks. And she didn't like what she saw crossing his face now.

"We're going to Mexico anyway, aren't we?"

Her question seemed to make up his mind.

"It's the only thing we *can* do," he said cryptically. "I have a friend who has a friend who has a boat in Veracruz. We'll go there, hide and wait. Maybe in the meantime, I can figure out what the hell's going on."

Cutting off the conversation with that, Stratton pulled out the cheap carry-on he'd bought at the airport. Tossing out all the junk that he'd purchased, he pulled out an ingenious false bottom he'd made using tape, two empty rolls of toilet paper and a piece of cardboard that had apparently come with the bag. Jennifer watched in amazement as he lifted out his pistol. It was in fourteen pieces, each one wrapped in newspaper and plastic bags.

The move was clever but hardly good enough for security, even in South America. "You wouldn't have gotten that through security," she said.

"I wasn't going to," he answered. "You were."

Her eyes went wide. "I don't have enough problems already?"

"You would have checked it," he said confidently. "And it would have passed."

"I don't think so."

He shot her a dark glance. "Stick to diamonds and trust me on this one."

Stung by his attitude, she paused then asked what she wanted to. "Why did you bother? We didn't even go through security."

"I didn't know what kind of arrangements had been made. I had to cover my bases just in case."

"Did Ali Hassam do this, too?"

He kept his gaze on the weapon he was reassembling, but she had the feeling he could have done it with his eyes closed. "Ali who?"

"Ali Hassam," she repeated impatiently. "You know, the guy at the restaurant."

"I don't know who you're talking about." He glanced up then his eyes darted away, the nervous energy she'd seen in him earlier returning. When they were safe, he was anxious; when they were in danger, he was smooth. "You must be confused."

She started to argue, then she caught on.

He finished with the weapon and slipped it back into the bag at his feet. When he turned to her, his expression had softened, a relative term, she decided, as if he'd realized how wound up he was.

"Get some sleep," he advised. He reached out and smoothed a lock of her hair behind her ear, his finger resting for a second on the bottom of her jaw. "You need it."

His touch sent a ripple down her spine and like a rock tossed into a lake, she felt it spread to the rest of her body. Once again, confused by his action and the swift change in his expression, she spoke without thinking. "You do, too."

"Close your eyes," he said rather than answer her. "I'll wake you when we get there."

CHAPTER THIRTEEN

HIS GROWING FEELINGS FOR THE WOMAN sitting beside him were beginning to worry Stratton. He found himself anxious to keep her safe, a bad sign, and concerned about her future, an even worse sign. He didn't know how to handle his reaction because it'd been so damn long since he'd felt that way about a woman he'd forgotten how to deal with it. He'd been a young Marine the last time he'd fallen in love—not that that was what he was doing here—and it'd ended badly. Very badly. Huddled on a bare-ass ridge somewhere in the Middle East, freezing cold and under fire, he'd opened a thick envelope anticipating photos and love letters. He'd found a note from a lawyer and divorce papers instead.

Jennifer wasn't like anyone he'd ever met, though. She combined neediness and independence in a way that intrigued him, her guilt over her sister another element thrown into the mix. She was a very complex woman and obviously thought things through. The comment she'd made about them being good guys had floored him. It'd been years since he'd thought of himself in those terms, although considering it now, he realized that had been exactly why he'd joined the Operatives. He'd wanted to do the right thing and save the world. He'd ended up doing something much different.

The irony didn't escape him but he chose not to acknowledge it, his mind returning to the possibility that Meredith Santera might have been the woman in Joseph Wilhem's office.

Stratton had worked around violence and death for years but in all that time he'd never known anyone, man or woman, who could handle a knife like Meredith. It had been her specialty. Cruz had used his hands and Armando had used his knowledge of drugs and medicine. Could Meredith have been the woman in that office? If she had been, things had drastically changed in her world or there was a hell of a lot more going on in the diamond business than he suspected.

Terrorists funded some of their activities with diamonds, and he knew the civil wars in Africa were financed by what were called "blood" diamonds. Had Ami Leonadov been mixed up with one of those crowds? For Meredith to be involved, that seemed like the only answer, but it didn't feel right to Stratton. He let the possibilities roll around in his head some more, then he gave up and drifted into the state of semiawareness that was as close to sleep as he ever got.

After several stops for fuel, they landed in Veracruz as the sun was rising over the bay. The trip had taken a little more than twenty-four hours and for most of them, Jennifer had slept. Stratton reached out and woke her gently. Sometime during the flight, he'd covered her with a blanket and she had pulled it up to just beneath her chin. Now, it slipped down as he touched her, revealing the curve of her neck. He wondered what it would feel like to bury his face against her throat.

She opened her eyes and smiled sweetly at him, then she seemed to remember where she was.

He wasn't surprised to see her gaze flare in alarm and he squeezed her arm in reassurance. "It's okay," he said. "We've landed."

They took a taxi from the airport, a breeze traveling with them through the open windows, the warmth it carried a welcome change from the chill of Buenos Aires. The smells that came with it were the ones he always identified with ocean-front places—salt and sand and something that made him think of slow, lazy sex. He looked over at Jennifer in reflex. She was staring out the windows, the wind ruffling her hair, her eyes half-closed. He wanted to kiss her the way he had in the brothel and then take it even further, but the taxi pulled to a stop before the docks and disrupted his thinking, thank God.

Stratton found the boat quickly because he'd used it once before when things had turned complicated. He'd gotten a loan from Ali as well as a gun and fishing a handful of dollar bills from his pocket, he handed it to Jennifer, nodding toward the small bodega at the end of the dock. "Why don't you go buy us some supplies?"

She looked at the money. "Like what?"

"Food, liquor, anything you think you might need for a week or so. Maybe two weeks."

"Two weeks? Are you kidding?"

He shrugged. "You never know. Best to be prepared."

In a daze, she turned around and headed for the store. He watched her for a minute then he shed his shirt and began to check out the boat.

She came back with two scruffy kids she'd paid to haul her purchases. Plastic sacks in hand, they scampered on board as if they knew the craft, which they probably did, then they returned for another load. After two more trips, she tipped them. "I hope I got enough."

He looked over his shoulder at the galley. Groceries completely covered the countertop and the pass through that led toward the bunks. "I think you did. The question is, was there anything left in the store?"

"You said to be prepared."

She brushed past him and he smelled her shampoo. He was noticing too many details. Another bad sign.

The engine started on the first try, the motor smooth and quiet. At his nod, the kids, who were still waiting on the dock, slipped the ropes and threw them to the deck. He turned the wheel and they headed into the bay.

ONCE SHE GOT her sea legs, Jennifer went below deck. She put away the supplies then dug around the cabin for something to wear, chastising herself for not picking up a cheap T-shirt or pair of shorts at the *groceria*. The wool jacket, silk scarf and pants that had felt so good in Argentina were like lead weights now. She was about to give up when she uncovered a pair of grease-stained overalls so stiff with grime they could stand by themselves and the top of a hot-pink bikini, two sizes too small.

She held the halter in one hand and the overalls in the other but there really was no contest. She'd pass out if she stayed in the getup she had on and the jumpsuit was revolting. Rummaging around a bit more, she found a pair of men's boxers. Squeezing into the head, she struggled out of her clothing and into the top and shorts. She fastened the shorts at the waist with the scarf she'd had on her neck and the outfit was complete. Thank God there was no mirror, she thought when she'd finished.

Stepping on to the deck, though, she had second thoughts about her choice. Stratton's eyes widened when he saw her and she could have sworn he paled. She either looked so bad he wanted to jump overboard or she looked so good, he couldn't believe it. Whichever it was, she'd made a mistake.

She hesitated then started back down. His voice stopped her.

"Where are you going?"

She turned. "I think I need to find something else to wear."

"What's wrong with what you have on?"

"Judging from your face, I'd say just about everything."

His lips thinned. "Do me a favor and don't try to read my mind. People with much more experience than you in that department have tried and failed."

She came to where he stood, the wheel turning slowly beneath his hands, the turquoise water slipping past them in a blur. "I don't need experience," she said. "I'm a woman. And I think I can read you pretty well."

"You think wrong."

"I read your face in Wilhem's office well enough to realize you knew the woman with the knife," she said, repeating the accusation she'd made at the brothel. "That's something I know for sure."

"You're wrong."

"I watched you," Jennifer insisted. "You knew her."

He turned then. "So what if I did?"

"So what? She tried to kill me, that's what. I would think if you knew her, you might do something about it, like at least tell me who she is."

He seemed to weigh her question, then come to some kind of conclusion. "As soon as we get where we're going, I'll tell you what I know." He paused, staring at her shocked face. "But it's a pointless exercise because you won't believe me."

"Do me a favor," Jennifer mocked. "Tell me first, then I'll decide for myself."

HASSAM HAD BEEN TOLD to get maps, but he hadn't had time. Luckily, Stratton knew the area fairly well and he found the cay without too much trouble. Two hours after they left the dock, they anchored in sight of the fishing lodge he'd half expected not to be there but still was. By all rights the hurricane before last should have done it in, but someone had patched the roof and repaired the dock and it was still hanging on, just like the people who lived there. Scruffy and past disreputable, they wouldn't bother Stratton and Jennifer because they were there for the same reason the two of them were—they wanted to hide. From life, the *policia*, an addiction or a combination of those things. Name it and they were running from it. There would be fuel at the tiny store, though, and as far as Stratton could tell, Jennifer hadn't been able to bring extra diesel.

To his surprise, and relief, she'd accepted his promise to tell her more and she'd left him alone since they'd motored away from Veracruz. Stratton had no intention of telling her anything but when he'd seen her come out on deck in that getup, he'd momentarily lost his place in the universe. After giving the idea some more thought, however, he decided that telling her a few selected details might not be such a bad idea. She was sharp and she obviously knew Leonadov's business. Maybe she could connect a few of the dots.

Whatever details he gave her would have to be very carefully selected, though.

They ate lunch and afterward Stratton tended to the diesel engine, the boat moving gently in crystal waters. The motor had started with the first turn but he wanted to make sure it would do the same thing again if needed. He checked it thoroughly then patched a minor leak in one of the lines. The work was therapeutic and by the time he had finished, dusk was falling.

Wiping his hands with a greasy rag, he stood up and stretched and when he did, he realized a mouthwatering smell was coming from the galley. Jennifer's face appeared in the opening that led to the engine room.

"I threw something together for dinner," she said. "Are you hungry?"

"I wasn't until I smelled it," he answered.

"Don't get excited," she warned. "I'm not a cook by any stretch of the imagination."

She disappeared, and he put away the tools he'd used before pulling himself out of the engine compartment. He cleaned up by jumping overboard and swimming around the boat twice. Jennifer met him at the ladder with a plate. "Here you go."

He shook the water from his hair and a thought came

to him without warning. He couldn't remember the last time a woman had cooked for him. A vague memory came to him of a tribal woman in Rwanda handing him a wooden platter but he wasn't too sure goat stew qualified.

He took the offering from Jennifer, their fingers brushing. She jerked back as if she'd touched a hot poker then seemed embarrassed by her reaction, hurriedly returning to the galley. For a moment, he wondered if she was even going to come back, then she reappeared, another plate in one hand, two cold soft drinks in the other.

They ate in silence, the sound of water slapping against the hull the only break in the heavy quiet. When she finished, she pushed aside her plate and propped her feet up on the bench they'd used as a table.

She looked at him expectantly. "So who was she?"

"Who was who?"

She didn't smile. "The woman with the knife."

He tapped his can against the railing. "I don't know."

Jennifer shook her head. "Wrong answer. Try again."

"I really don't," he repeated. "For sure. But I worked with someone once who was quite talented with a knife. I wondered if it might be her."

"I saw her eyes. They were dark," Jennifer said. "She wore black eyeliner."

He shrugged. Meredith was half-Argentine and her eyes were dark, but that wasn't enough information to make a call.

"She had curves, too." Jennifer's cheeks darkened. "When she pulled me against her, I could tell."

Stratton raised an eyebrow at this, an image forming

that made him break into a sweat. "How big were these 'curves'?"

"Bigger than mine," she confessed, "but not over the top."

"'Over the top?' What does that mean?"

It was her turn to shrug. "You know—not tacky big. In proportion but not outrageous."

He smiled in the growing darkness. "You're obviously not a man or you'd know in that department, there's no such thing as too big."

She rolled her eyes.

Turning serious, he leaned forward. "Do you think you've ever seen her before?"

"Not that I can remember. I wasn't really trying to place her, though. At the time I was more worried about my throat getting sliced than anything else."

"Did she have any scars? Anything on her hands?"

"I didn't notice. All I could see were her eyes."

"Was she wearing contacts?"

"I couldn't tell, I'm sorry."

"Nothing to be sorry about. It's not like you were trying to memorize her face or anything."

"Do you have it memorized?"

Her question caught him off guard.

"You seem to know her quite well for someone you just 'worked' with."

"I did," he said brusquely, "but not like that. The business we shared was intense. We knew each other because we had to. Our lives depended on it."

"And what did you and this woman do?"

Stratton answered her. In his mind.

We killed people for money. Mainly people who de-

served it but a few who probably didn't. We played God, but then I made the kind of mistake God never does.

"We were in the trash business," he said flatly. "We collected it and took it away so it wouldn't stink up any place."

She stared at him until she realized he wasn't going to say anything else. "Ami wasn't a piece of trash," she said softly. "And neither was Mr. Singh or Mr. Wilhem. They were businessmen, just trying to earn a living. They weren't doing anything that should have gotten them dead."

"They were doing something," Stratton answered. "But whatever it was, it wouldn't have attracted the attention of someone like Meredith. That's why I don't think it was her." He paused. "Besides, she can't shoot that well. It would've had to have been a damn lucky shot for her to hit Leonadov through that window. And she's too smart to have tried the same thing again with you."

He leaned back against the cushions and gazed out over the water. From the fishing camp, a necklace of lights sparkled along the curve of the island. At night the place looked romantic, but during the day, it looked like hell. The faint strains of a song drifted on the waves. "Margaritaville"? He wasn't sure but it would have been appropriate since most of the inhabitants were probably well soused by now.

"Tell me about your work," he said, turning back to Jennifer. "What did you do on a typical day?"

"Boring stuff," she answered. "Get the mail, take care of the inventory. Note the stones that came in and went out. Answer the phone."

"Leonadov ever bring clients to the office?"

"He was a wholesaler. We didn't actually have customers come in unless they were personal friends of his. Sometimes he might get a stone for someone's nephew who was getting married but that was it."

"He wasn't a high roller, then? His crazy scheme or secret deal wasn't something you'd heard him talk about before you left for South America?"

She shook her head. "Ami was a straight arrow. I wouldn't put something crooked past Thomas, but he didn't have free access to the inventory."

"You never told me why you don't like him."

"There's nothing to tell," she said. "He's just creepy, that's all." Her expression shifted. "I haven't liked him since I was a kid."

He asked her why and she told him.

"Did your sister notice him looking at her?"

"She never said anything about it, but men were always staring at her. It wasn't unusual."

"How did that make you feel?"

She looked at him sharply. "What kind of question is that? Now all of a sudden you're a shrink?"

He laughed out loud. "No, I'm not a shrink but what you said just struck me. Since you were twins and everything."

"I didn't care," she said, her expression gentling. "Julie was beautiful, and I was happy to stay in the shadows. She liked the attention. I didn't."

"No jealousy or envy? No sibling rivalry?"

"Not between us," she replied. "We were sisters but we were friends, too."

"You miss her."

"Horribly."

"I'm sorry," he said. "It must be tough."

Her eyes glistened in the dark. "It was but it wasn't. By the time she finally died, her life had dwindled until only the bad parts were left." Turning her head she looked out toward the fishing camp.

Stratton stared at her profile. Once again, he wanted to pull her against him and say the right things. He wanted to comfort her and make her feel better. But he'd forgotten how to do those kinds of things. And maybe— probably—he'd never known how to do them in the first place.

Rising silently, he left her alone with her thoughts. It was all he could do.

JENNIFER NOTICED when Stratton got up but she didn't call him back. She didn't think she should——he'd had as bad a day as she had and all she'd done was dump on him about Julie. She would have liked to have asked him more about his so-called career. Had she really understood what he'd meant by "taking out the trash"? Ami had had need of protection on occasion so she knew more than the average person about security and bodyguards and people like that. But she had the feeling that Stratton's work was different. She wondered all at once if Ami had known who—and what—he was getting when he hired him. Considering everything they'd been through, Stratton's skills had definitely come in handy yet she wondered what the final price might be. Something told her it was going to be costly.

He was drawing her closer and closer to him without even trying. The sideways glances, the steady strength, the rocklike resolve. Stratton O'Neil reminded her of the heroes in the old Westerns she and Julie had liked to watch together. Never upset, always cool under fire.

But he reminded her of the villain, too, because underneath the quiet exterior, a very sharp edge waited, and she knew he wouldn't hesitate to use it.

She shivered lightly and tried to put those thoughts aside, choosing instead to let her mind go back to the days right before she and Ami had left. The urgency of resolving that problem had to take precedence over her growing fascination with Stratton, whether she liked it or not. Had Ami said something unusual before they'd left? Done anything strange? Surely she could figure out what had happened if she tried hard enough. She gave it another hour but nothing came to mind then suddenly she remembered that Ami had kept a locked cabinet in his office. She'd assumed he'd stored personal papers in it but now she wondered. Rising slowly from her deck chair, she went below, dumping their dirty plates into the galley sink then continuing toward the aft of the boat. Maybe something more would come to her while she slept.

Then again, maybe it wouldn't.

She took a single step into the cabin then stopped, the thought of sleep fleeing. Stratton had taken the bunk on the left and he was already there. Wearing a pair of shorts and nothing more. Cleaning his gun. Polishing it, actually, with long slow strokes, the oil glistening in the low light of the overhead lamp.

He glanced up. "I took this side but if you want it—"

"No," she said quickly. "It's fine. Don't move."

He nodded once then returned to his task. She stood awkwardly, too many thoughts making their way through her head to make sense out of any of them. What was wrong with her? She'd seen shirtless men before. She'd even seen Stratton shirtless before. But there was something different about seeing him that way this close and in a bed and rubbing that damn gun so precisely. A huge lump formed in her throat, and she didn't think she could swallow. Or speak. Or think.

He looked up again. "Something wrong?"

She shook her head and took cover in the head, her shower quick, her mind emptying. Regaining some of her equilibrium underneath the icy stream, she came out a few minutes later.

Without looking in Stratton's direction, she walked toward the bed on the right-hand side and climbed in. Pretending to be asleep, she lay stiff and still until he finally turned off the light an hour later. At that point, she took a deep breath and relaxed.

Then she heard the rustle of sheets as he climbed out of his bunk and came toward hers.

Her whole body tensed and suddenly she didn't know what she wanted. Stratton had come to mean something to her, something she didn't yet understand. Praying he'd turn away then hoping he wouldn't, she twisted the edge of the sheet in her fingers and waited.

He took another step toward her. She could hear him breathing and she could feel her heart beating.

Something whispered in the darkness and she felt his hand brush her cheek. He walked away a moment later.

CHAPTER FOURTEEN

THE TWO WOMEN stared at each other from across the booth. They were in the kind of sleazy diner that neither of them liked nor frequented, but meetings like they were having didn't take place in high traffic hot spots.

Trying to avoid touching the top of the table, Lucy Wisner leaned forward, her eyes pinned to the other woman's, her voice cold and brusque. "You had a job to do and you screwed it up. How are you going to fix this?"

"I didn't screw up anything," her dining companion replied in an unruffled manner. "You did. You told me they were in Rio. I went to Buenos Aires to take care of things and there they were. What was I supposed to do? Say hello, how you doing? I was lucky as hell to make it out of there."

"I was told you wouldn't have any problems. You're supposed to be a professional."

"I am." The woman's voice was crisp. "But so is Stratton O'Neil."

Lucy stilled. "That's not what I heard."

"I don't know what you heard—or who you heard it from—but O'Neil is a legend. Anyone who does what we do knows him. He's pulled off some impossible jobs. If he'd worked on my side of the street, he'd be worth a bloody fortune by now but he had ethics. They cost a lot." She paused and looked at Lucy with a thoughtful expression. "I guess that's why I was surprised to see him. If he's working for you, he's come down in the world."

Lucy ignored the insult.

The other woman's expression shifted slightly. "Of course, if *you* did the hiring, I could understand why you'd pick him. There's something very frightening about the man, but at the same time—"

"I know what you're trying to say. But professionally he was supposed to be washed up, a has-been. *That's* why he was hired."

The woman on the other side of the booth smiled. "Well, you got screwed, my dear. He made a mistake, yes, and he dropped out, true. But he's far from a failure. Just the opposite, in fact. He has skills I can't even begin to explain to someone like you. And those skills are as sharp as ever. If I'd known I was going against him, I would have turned down your crappy little job. It's not worth my life."

Leaning back, Lucy tapped a finger against the vinyl seat of the booth. "I think you're overreacting."

"I wouldn't tell that to all the people he's killed. They might not appreciate your opinion."

Disbelief washed over Lucy, and she felt herself blanch. She knew who Stratton was—and what—but hearing it put in those terms stopped her cold. "You're lying."

"I don't waste my time lying, Ms. Wisner. I've got more important things to do. Is there anything else?"

Lucy took a sip from the soda she'd ordered. She'd

vowed not to touch the glass but her throat was suddenly parched. She emptied the tumbler then put it back down on the table. "What's the plan?"

"*My* plan is to get the hell out of here and pray he never finds out I was the one who threw that knife. I don't know—or care—what yours is."

"What about the job we hired you to do?" Lucy asked in alarm.

The woman reached into her leather backpack, removed something and pushed it across the sticky table-top with one finger. "I took out what I needed for expenses and for the work I already did. Consider the remainder of the contract canceled."

Lucy looked at the brown envelope at the woman. "You can't do that," she said smugly. "I know who you are. I know what we paid you to do. If you don't finish this job, you're going to be in real trouble."

The woman laughed out loud and her amusement was genuine. "That's not how it works, Lucy, dear."

The use of her first name was a warning, but Lucy didn't notice.

The woman mimicked Lucy's earlier move and leaned closer, her voice softer, pleasant even. "*I* know who *you* are," she said. "I also know where you live and which taxi service you use and where you take your dry cleaning. I know your maid's first name as well as your hairdresser's and I'm good friends with the doorman of your building. I even know where your dog poops every morning." She smiled slowly. "*You're* the one who needs to be worried. Not me."

As Lucy gaped at her, the woman stood then snapped her fingers as if she'd just recalled something. "By the way, there's one more thing I know. Your boyfriend has another girlfriend in addition to you and his wife. You might want to ask him about that when you get back to the office."

While Lucy was still reeling, the woman pulled a card from her backpack and threw it on the table. "That's someone I know who needs money. He'll do anything. Send him to do your dirty work. I heard Stratton and the girl were headed for Mexico." She turned on her heel and left.

Her actions delayed by shock, Lucy finally jumped up, too. Running to the door, she looked up and down the street but the woman had already vanished.

"Shit," Lucy muttered. "If you want something done right, I guess you *do* have to do it yourself."

THEY'D BEEN ON THE BOAT for three days, and Jennifer's only accomplishment had been to call Luis Barragan's office again. And again. And again. Finally, his secretary had told Jennifer, in a slightly irritated voice, that her boss had not called in since "the last time" Jennifer had phoned. When he did, she assured Jennifer, she'd pass on the message.

Other than that, Jennifer felt as if she was in a state of suspended animation, but with one big exception. She was aware of where she was and what she was doing and, most of all, who was in the same state as her. In fact, every day she became more and more aware of Stratton. She knew when he went for his morning swim and she knew what he looked like coming out of the water. (Good.) She knew when he went to bed and how he looked when he slept. (Good.) She knew what he liked to have for breakfast and how he looked when he ate it. (Good.) In fact, she hadn't seen him do anything he didn't look good doing.

In contrast, she looked like a refugee from a used clothing store. Scouring the boat a second time for something to wear, she'd managed to find a few ratty T-shirts and two more pairs of boxer shorts but washing them had only made them smell better—nothing could have improved the way they looked. The only piece of women's clothing, besides the bikini top, she'd located was a teddy made from silk camouflage fabric. Who would buy something like that? Better question still, who would wear it? She'd tucked it back into the drawer where she'd found it and pretended she didn't know such things existed.

To distract herself one evening, she mentioned Ami's private files. "There might be something in those records that we could use."

Stratton nodded and asked a few questions and then they fell back into their usual silence. Anxious and growing more so, Jennifer let her thoughts return to something that had been bothering her more and more. Stratton's lecture about Thomas being in danger. Had he been telling the truth or was he simply afraid Thomas—and in turn, Cissy—might reveal their whereabouts?

Jennifer wouldn't want Ami's son hurt but she cared more about Cissy.

If that *was* the case, there was no way Jennifer could let her friend go about her life without being made aware of the situation. If she knew what was going on, she could at least be more vigilant, or even leave town for a few days. No one else Jennifer loved was going to be hurt because of her, no matter how remote the possibility, and she'd do anything she could to make sure of that.

She started to ask Stratton to tell her more, then she stopped herself. Why alert him?

As soon as he left on the Zodiac the next morning to get engine parts at the fishing lodge, Jennifer went into the wheelhouse with steady determination. She'd tossed and turned all night thinking about Cissy and now it was time for action. Stratton had taken his cell phone, of course, but there was still the radio. Short of yanking it from the console, there had been little he could do about it.

Fifteen minutes later, Jennifer had gotten no further than staring at the unit, the digital display a mystery, the settings and controls an even greater puzzle.

Nervous about his return, Jennifer gave up trying to understand the thing and simply picked up the receiver, punching buttons randomly. The process couldn't be too complicated, she thought, after all, it was just a radio.

To her amazement, a voice, speaking Spanish, responded to her instantly.

"Oh, my gosh! I need to call the United States," she answered excitedly. "Can you help me?"

"Is this an emergency?"

"Yes, it is." She gripped the mike in both hands. "It's definitely an emergency."

There was a pause so long her heart skipped a beat in fear she'd lost the connection, then the man spoke again. "This is the *Guardia de los Guardacostas.* We

will assist you. Describe your location and the nature
of your emergency."

"I'm—" She paused abruptly and amended what
she'd been about to say, refusing to answer the first part
of his question. "…in need of help. The emergency is
that I need to make a phone call! Can't you patch me
through to an American operator?"

He said yes and Jennifer gave him Cissy's number.

An interminable amount of time passed then Cissy
actually picked up. Jennifer wanted to cry but she didn't
let herself. "Cissy! It's me, Jenni—"

"Oh, my God, Jenn!" Cissy cried. "Are you okay?
What's going on? We've heard all kinds of things—"

"I'm all right. It's you I'm worried about. I'm calling to warn you." Jennifer rushed on before Cissy could
say anything else. "Listen, before he was killed Ami
hired this guy to look into Mr. Singh's death. He came
to Rio when we did and then Ami was shot and he was
there and he saved me.…"

She hurried to get out as much information as possible but after a few seconds Jennifer's flow of words
slowed then quit. Something didn't feel right. Cissy
never let her talk that long without interrupting. Something was definitely wrong.

"Cissy?" Jennifer asked. "Are you there?"

Silence answered her.

"Cissy? Cissy? Please tell me you're there."

Staring at the receiver in disbelief, Jennifer shook her
head. "Cissy?"

The radio made no sound at all and her heart sank.
She continued to punch buttons but without success.
Had Cissy understood the importance of what Jennifer

had been trying to tell her? Finally, with overwhelming disappointment, she hung the mike back on the hook by the dials. She didn't even know how she'd managed to pick up the Coast Guard's attention in the first place; she had no idea how to do it again. Her shoulders slumped and a tear fell before she could stop it.

A few minutes later, she heard the faint sound of the Zodiac puttering back. She wiped her face, put on a smile and walked to the railing to pitch Stratton the rope.

His shirt flapping open, he climbed over the side of the boat then grabbed her arm and held on tightly, his voice rough with anger.

"Just what in the bloody hell do you think you're doing?"

JENNIFER'S EYES WIDENED. Her expression could have been interpreted as innocence but Stratton knew better. It was fright and he was glad. He wanted her scared. She *should* be scared.

She licked her lips, the motion drawing his gaze. "What are you talking about?"

His slowly building frustration—sexual *and* otherwise—spilled over. "Do you have a death wish I don't know about? You must, because that's the only reason I can think of to explain what you did." He threw down the sack of spare engine parts he'd gone to pick up and glared at her in disgust.

"I don't know what you're talking about—"

He shook his head. "Don't even try, Jennifer. I was in the marine shop when your transmission came over the radio."

Under the tan she was beginning to acquire, her face lost its color, but she stood her ground. "I had to warn Cissy to get out of town. And I didn't tell her where we are. But even if I had, she knows how to keep her mouth shut."

He took a step toward her. "She might know how but I can guarantee you she'll forget real quick when she has wires attached to her in places you don't want to think about."

He'd thought she was pale before but at his words, Jennifer's cheeks went completely white.

"We're not dealing with amateurs, Jennifer. I thought you understood that by now. The people who killed Singh and Ami and Wilhem, the same people who also want to kill *you,* might have your friend's house wired, as well as where she works. They probably have Leonadov's office and his house bugged, too. I brought us here so we'd be safe while we waited for Barragan. If they trace that call, you've just handed them her head on a platter. And possibly ours, too."

Looking out over the water, Jennifer exhaled slowly, her eyes returning to his. "I assumed you were just afraid she might accidentally tell someone where we are."

"Don't ever—*ever*—assume anything about me, Jennifer."

She sat down abruptly on the padded bench that ran along the perimeter of the boat and suddenly Stratton's anger evaporated. Just like that. He'd never let go of it so quickly and he didn't understand what had happened but he came to her side and sat down, too.

"All I want to do is keep you safe. If you don't think

that's necessary, then go back to Houston." Taking her chin between his thumb and forefinger, he turned her head until she faced him. "I'm not holding you hostage, Jennifer. I'll see that you get to the airport if you think that's what you want."

"I don't know what I want."

"Then why did you call?"

"If you *were* telling the truth, I couldn't let Cissy be in danger because of me. I just couldn't."

He looked at her face and found himself studying parts of it. The way her eyebrows arched. The ridge of her cheekbones. The freckles she'd gotten since they'd come onto the boat. The story she'd told him about people staring at Julie suddenly came into his mind, and he couldn't imagine anyone being able to look past Jennifer. She had the kind of beauty that went far deeper than the surface—and she seemed perfect to him. But Julie's accident had left her scarred on the inside.

To prevent the possibility she might cause anyone else pain, Jennifer was willing to risk her own life. She'd *had* to call Cissy because the idea of her friend being hurt because of her was not an option. The burden of guilt she carried over her sister's accident was already too heavy to risk adding to.

And he understood that in a way no one else would have.

"Your friend's a smart lady." He spoke slowly, trying to think of something that might make Jennifer feel better. That was all his words would do, though. The damage had already been done. "Didn't you tell me that you both took self-defense classes?"

"We did. But Cissy didn't do well. She got a certificate but only because the teacher felt sorry for her."

She could have taught the damn class herself, but it wouldn't have made a peso's worth of difference. Not with these people. They were pros.

"So what do we do next?" Jennifer looked at him with a miserable expression.

"We wait and see what happens." His grimness returned. "I managed to cut the transmission right after she said hello and no one will know the call was from you. I couldn't tell exactly when the signal dropped."

"And if we're not lucky?"

"If we're not lucky, then somebody's gonna die." He stood but another sweep of sympathy hit him squarely in his chest, and all he wanted was to make Jennifer feel better. Because he was a man, there was only one way he knew how to do that.

Truth be told, every night since they'd come on this damn boat, his desire for her had done nothing but grow, yet he knew Jennifer wasn't the kind of person who took sex lightly and neither was he. He liked long, slow relationships that built gradually and lasted, or at least that's what he'd always thought he would like. He'd never stayed in one place long enough to find out for sure. Even his marriage had been hasty.

All these thoughts ran through his head, but Stratton still found himself reaching for Jennifer. Tugging her to her feet, he brought her closer to him and looked into her eyes.

She read his intent but she didn't pull away. To his surprise, instead, she pressed herself against him then looped her arms around his neck.

"You're going to kiss me, aren't you?" Her voice was husky and it made him want her even more.

"I was thinking about it," he confessed.

"Well, you should," she said. "We need to get it over with and clear the air."

He lifted one eyebrow. "Clear the air? I wasn't aware it was murky."

"Don't lie," she said. "It doesn't become you. And you don't do it very well, either."

At this, Stratton arched both eyebrows. "I was telling lies before you were even born. If I know how to do anything, I know how to lie."

"Maybe," she conceded. "But I know when you're doing it."

He cupped her face with his hand and ran his thumb along her jaw. Her skin felt softer than anything he'd touched in a very long time.

"I don't care if you know or not," he whispered, "as long as you let me do it."

STRATTON'S LIPS CLOSED over Jennifer's with a gentleness she didn't expect. Their previous kisses had sent her spinning but the restraint in this one was even more powerful. He wanted her but he was holding back. Because of that, nothing could have made her desire him more.

She felt as if her whole body was charged with an energy that overrode everything else, including her good sense. Nothing existed beyond Stratton's arms. Should he open them and release her, she wasn't sure she'd continue to live. Her heart might stop, she thought, and deprived of that, her body would shut down, as well.

Luckily for her, he didn't turn her loose.

He did just the opposite, his hands sliding down her back with a sensual slowness, his lips teasing her mouth to open to his tongue. She responded because she had no other option.

He moaned and tightened his grip now on her buttocks. Jennifer reciprocated by unlocking her arms from his neck and gliding them down his unbuttoned shirt. A moment later, her hands were on his bare skin. She spread her palms as wide as she could against his chest and held them there to feel his heart beating. Over the past few days they'd shared some anxious moments, but she'd never seen him even breathe hard. That wasn't the case now and she smiled to herself.

When he brought his hands up under the T-shirt she wore, however, her amusement fled and the hum she'd first felt became a buzz of confusion. But the thought of not feeling it was even worse. He moved his mouth from her lips to the tender spot behind her ear. Licking it slowly, he murmured something unintelligible. She had no idea what he said, but she could feel his intent.

Paralyzed with desire but unsure of what to do about it, Jennifer settled for hanging on to Stratton and letting the sensations wash over her. When he lifted his lips from her throat and looked her in the eye, the need she felt was reflected in his gaze. Stratton wanted her as much as she wanted him. She tightened her fingers against his chest and parted her lips to speak. They were two adults, unattached and free to do as they chose. Why not?

Apparently, he had a reason. A moment later, he let go and took a step back.

WHAT IN THE HELL did he think he was he doing? Stratton had lost his mind. Kissing Jennifer was the last thing he needed to be doing and even more importantly, was the last thing he *should* be doing. He'd seen more than one distracted person die in the arms of their lover so he ought to know better. You couldn't have sex with someone and stay alert at the very same time.

Besides that, he didn't deserve a moment in Jennifer's arms, much less a night.

Her hands still in the air where he'd stood a second before, Jennifer stared at him in disbelief. "What's wrong?"

"We can't do this," he said. "*I* can't do this."

Her face changed from confusion to concern and everything in between. Finally, her expression cleared and she took a step back herself. "You're married, aren't you?"

Even at the risk of her knowing it wasn't true, he thought about telling her he was, but there was enough deception between them already. "No," he said gently, "I'm not married. It's not that."

"Then what?"

"I'm not the person you think I am, Jennifer. I tried to tell you this before but I obviously didn't do a very good job. If you knew me better, you'd cross the street to get away from me."

"Why don't you tell me who you are and let me decide that for myself?"

Reaching out, he ran the back of his knuckles down the side of her face, his hand stopping at the hollow of her neck where he could feel her pulse.

"I'm sorry," he said softly. "But that's one thing I can't do."

He left her standing by herself and retreated below
deck where he started working on an engine that needed
nothing done to it. His mind returned to their situation
and at the end of the day, he knew they had to leave.

If he'd heard Jennifer's transmission, then it could
have been picked up by anyone in the vicinity. It'd been
nothing but sheer luck that he'd heard her radio plea and
even more luck that he'd been able to break into their
channel and disrupt the call. He wasn't willing to trust
that luck any further.

If he had maps, leaving would have been a nonissue,
but without them, taking off would be a crap shoot. The
marina at the fishing camp might have some charts, but
whoever showed up looking for him and Jennifer—and
someone would sooner or later—would know immediately which ones he'd bought and therefore which direction they were going. They'd get the information
one way or another.

He pondered the idea until the sun slipped beneath
the western horizon, a plan slowly coming together. It
had only one flaw. He'd have to take Jennifer with him
or risk another phone call. They were running short on
time and options, though.

He waited as long as he dared, then Stratton hoisted
the anchor and started the engine.

IT WAS AFTER MIDNIGHT, and Jennifer was digging
around in the refrigerator looking for something to eat
when the boat's engine rumbled to life. She wasn't hungry, but she couldn't sleep so she'd decided food might
fill the hole Stratton had left when he'd stepped away
from her. Every self-help diet book she'd ever read

warned against this kind of thing, but right now, she didn't give a damn. She'd wanted to take their closeness to another level and he hadn't. If that didn't justify double chocolate-chip fudge ice cream she didn't know what did. Unfortunately they'd been fresh out of that at the *groceria* so she was searching for a substitute. Grabbing a pickle and closing the door, she scrambled up the stairs toward the wheelhouse.

"Are we going back to Veracruz?"

Stratton shook his head.

She waited for him to elaborate, but as usual, he said nothing. "Where are we going then?"

He kept his eyes on the water. "You'll see when we get there. It won't take long."

Ten minutes later, he cut the boat's engine and running lights. They drifted in silence, the black night swallowing them. Jennifer could make out the outline of the island but the friendly lights of the camp were no longer in view. They'd been swallowed by a dark that felt ominous and foreboding. Just as Jennifer began to feel smothered, a streak of lightning split the sky. Blinded suddenly, she held her breath.

The next thing she knew, Stratton was behind her. She asked just to be sure. "Is that you?"

Instead of answering, he put his hands on her shoulders and even though she was expecting him, she jumped.

"Steady," he said, squeezing her shoulders. "I'm right here."

And that, she thought, *is the problem.* He stood so close, she could feel his chest move as he breathed, the steady rise and fall distinctly different from her own.

She wanted to blame the darkness for her nervousness but she couldn't. The sun could have been shining brightly overhead and she would have been just as jumpy.

"I can't see," she said defensively.

"Close one eye when the lightning strikes. That'll help maintain your night vision."

She nodded and he turned her around, his fingers resting in the hollows of her collarbones. An inch separated them.

"We're going ashore," he said quietly. "How good a swimmer are you?"

She swallowed. "Fair. How far is it?"

He looked over her head. "Quarter mile, probably less. Think you can make it?"

"I'll try," she said. "But why can't we take the Zodiac?"

"I don't want to make any noise." His words were as relaxed and easy as his breathing. Another streak of light lit the sky. "I'm going to break into the marina and steal something. You're going to stand watch."

She blinked as cannons of thunder rolled over the water. "I wouldn't depend on me for that. I—I don't see so well at night. Not even with both eyes open."

"You'll do fine." Bending down until their gazes met, he held her stare, his fingers now gripping her tight. "Just think about the Mexican jail we'd be thrown in if we're caught and you'll be surprised at how much your vision will improve."

"Can't you just buy whatever it is you want to steal?" The question sounded desperate but Jennifer didn't care.

"We need some charts and I don't want anyone to know I have them."

"But all they have to do is count their inventory. Then they'll know some are missing."

"Trust me. They have no idea how many are there, but they would remember what I bought. We're leaving the minute we get back to the boat but sooner or later someone's going to come looking for us and if they know what maps we have, they'll know where we've headed."

"Who would tell them?"

He nodded toward the camp. "That isn't a gentleman's club, Jennifer. It's a bunch of thieves and murderers and rapists who're hiding from the law. They'd sell their mothers for a cold beer." He let the silence grow then he spoke once more.

"It's every man for himself in my world, Jennifer. Try and remember that fact. It might come in handy later."

CHAPTER FIFTEEN

AFTER SHE'D HEALED from her wreck in high school, Jennifer had gone to the local pool daily to swim and strengthen her leg and the habit had stuck with her. Now she was glad she'd kept up her watery exercise. From the boat, the swim hadn't seemed like such a big deal but once she was in the water, she felt as if a giant hand was pushing the island farther and farther away with every stroke she took. Finally, they made it, Stratton stepping from the waves like a Greek water god, Jennifer gasping for breath like a beached whale in distress.

He gave her no time to recover. Holding out a hand, he helped her up then tugged her into the vegetation up the shoreline. Her legs still quivering, Jennifer followed as Stratton started down the beach, his path keeping them as close as possible to the cover the tall sea grasses offered. They walked for fifteen, maybe twenty minutes, then he held up his hand.

"The camp's right over this rise," he whispered, pointing to a large dune ahead of them. "The marina faces the opposite direction so we'll be approaching from the back. There's a loading dock off to the right with a rear entrance. I'll enter through that door and while I'm inside, you're going to stand outside and keep watch."

She nodded her understanding as he pulled something from one of the pockets of his cargo shorts and handed it to her. The walkie-talkie he'd put in her palm was tiny.

"If you sense anything—anything at all—that doesn't feel right, push the red button." He pointed to the unit's display. "I've got another one and mine will vibrate."

Jennifer started to speak when a chain rattled in the camp behind them. A chill of fear froze her in place.

"Take it easy! It's just the flagpole," Stratton said. "The breeze hit the cable against the pole."

As if to prove his point, a second gust of wind came along and the sound was repeated. Now that she knew what it was it reminded Jennifer of abandoned school yards.

"How long will this take?"

"Five minutes or less," he said confidently. "If it looks like it's going be any longer, I'll buzz you."

Behind them the cable clattered again but this time Jennifer was grateful—the noise covered up the knocking of her knees. In contrast, as always, the closer they got to danger, the smoother Stratton became. His expression was as calm and unworried as it could be, the sharp angles and harsh shadows of his face showing no concern whatsoever.

He looked down at her. "I'll be back before you even know I'm gone."

She considered that highly unlikely, but he made her forget her doubt with a kiss. A moment later, they were climbing over the dune and heading straight for the dock.

They scrambled up and then over the wooden platform and dashed toward the marina, Jennifer able to keep up with Stratton out of fear of being left behind more than any kind of ability. After they reached the cover of the building, Jennifer leaned against the nearest wall and waited with a roaring pulse while Stratton picked the lock. He had the job done in two seconds, and she exhaled.

His eyes connected with hers for one long moment, and then he was gone. Jennifer wondered once again what kind of man Stratton really was. He obviously did this kind of thing all the time, but why? Who had taught him? Who did he work for? Who was he? Her mind whirling, she tried to listen but she wasn't sure she would have heard anything over the pounding of her heart. Depending on her eyes instead, she swept her gaze across the area before her.

A lamp pole tilted off one side of the rotting dock, its light clearly dark for many years. The gaping holes in the wooden boards beneath it looked as if they led straight to Hell, but it was the aroma of old beer and stale cigarette smoke that really got to her. The smells so completely permeated the wall she stood against that they defeated even the fierce sea breeze that had sprung up. Jennifer hadn't been to the camp since they'd arrived and now she was glad. If it was this awful in the dark, she could only imagine how it would appear under the harsh sun.

In the distance an eye-popping flash of lightning rent the sky, reaching all the way down to the water. Jennifer snapped one eye shut, then thought what the hell and closed them both. The thunder came quickly—way too quickly—and she cursed without thinking. Sure enough, the minute the rumble faded, a dog began to bark and she tensed, her back going stiff against the wall. If someone came out to look...

She held her breath but everything stayed quiet.

A lifetime passed.

More lightning hit. More thunder sounded.

The dog barked again.

Jennifer's hand began to ache where she was gripping the walkie-talkie. Uncurling her fingers, she tried to relax, then she heard another sound.

She went perfectly still and strained to listen as the whispery shuffle was repeated a second later. It took her a moment to place the sound, but when she did, she pressed the button of the little unit so hard, she expected her finger to come through on the opposite side.

Stratton appeared almost instantly and her moment of fear was replaced with a wash of foolish relief.

The footsteps she'd heard were his.

JENNIFER MET STRATTON as he came out of the building.

"Back so soon?" she asked casually.

With his right hand, he held up the charts he'd found. "It was easy. They were just behind the counter." In his left, he raised the walkie-talkie. "Did you set this off? It's vibrating."

Her eyebrows went into twin peaks. "I must have accidentally hit the switch. I'm sorry."

She was lying, but why? He frowned and started to speak, but she beat him to it.

"Okay, okay," she confessed. "I heard you walking this way, all right? It scared me and I thought maybe—"

He held up his hand. "You heard me?"

She nodded guiltily.

"I can't believe that," he replied, his surprise genuine. "No one's heard me take a step in years. You *are* good."

A warm flush spread over her face but he was already moving on. "We need to get out of here." He started pulling her back down the dock. "Half the damn island is probably passed out but I don't want to rouse them. They're ugly drunks. The weather's getting nasty, too."

They ran down the beach, a trail of lightning and thunder marking every other step. When they reached the point where they'd first hit the shoreline, Stratton stopped and pulled a plastic bag from one of his pockets while Jennifer sat down on a nearby log and caught her breath. Stuffing the charts he'd stolen into the bag, he glanced up at the sky. Some serious clouds had begun to boil overhead—it was going to start to rain any minute. If the wind kicked up along with it, their swim wasn't going to be as pleasant going back as it had been coming in.

He glanced at Jennifer. "You okay?"

"I'm fine," she answered stoically, repeating his own reassurance from a moment before. "No problem."

"You're a trouper, Jennifer," he found himself saying unexpectedly. "I'm impressed with you. And not just because you heard me, either. You're…" He fumbled for the right word, then settled on the first one that came to mind. "You're tough."

"Wow, you really know how to flatter a girl." She grinned unexpectedly. "Actually, I was afraid you might leave me behind if I didn't keep up."

"I wouldn't do that." He crammed the plastic bag back into the pocket of his shorts, smoothing down the Velcro closure. Holding out his hand, he pulled her to her feet then brought her against his chest, her eyes going wide as she found herself in his arms. "You kiss too well."

She attempted to lighten the moment. "Wait till you see me rob a bank."

"We won't be doing that."

"You never know," she countered softly. "Some pretty unusual things have happened to me lately. They might begin happening to you, too."

Stratton didn't tell her so, but they already had. A kiss hadn't rattled him the way theirs had in a very long time.

"I appreciate the warning," he lied, "but it's been a while since anything's caught me by surprise. I doubt your problem will rub off on me."

Jennifer looked away first. Stratton felt a tug of regret when she did so, but he choose to ignore it. He took her hand and headed for the water.

They were standing in the waves waist high, just about to start swimming, when he first heard the sound.

Stratton gripped Jennifer's fingers and stopped her plunge at the very last second. She turned with a frown, and he held his fingers to his lips. Over the waves, the putter was barely audible, but then a lull came in the roar of the surf, and he heard it again—the faint buzz of a diesel engine, chugging slowly through the waters.

Had someone spotted them or was it just a late-night fisherman? Stratton studied the horizon but the line of darkness remained unbroken. Whoever was out there was running without lights. A bad sign, he decided.

The waves tossed her slightly, and Jennifer grabbed his arm, trying to maintain her position. "Is that a boat?"

"Sounds like an engine to me. Do you see anything?"

"No." Beside him, she stared intently, then he heard her pull in a sharp breath.

"What?"

"Look out there." She pointed toward the spot where they'd anchored their boat. "Right there! I thought I saw something shine, like a light." She looked up at him, her forehead furrowed. "You didn't leave anything on, did you?"

"No," he said grimly. "I made sure all the lights were off. Not a safe thing to do but I had to."

"There it is again!" She floated up with a big wave but held on to Stratton. "Did you see it?" She turned back to him. "Stratton, someone's on our boat! That *was* a flashlight!"

He stared at the outline of their own vessel till the light glinted again. She was right, dammit. Someone *was* onboard.

He would have liked to be surprised, but Stratton had expected this. That's why he'd fluffed up their pillows and stuffed extra blankets under their sheets. If anyone managed to get on board, he'd wanted them thinking they weren't there alone.

"Do you think it might be the Coast Guard?" Jennifer sounded worried.

"They don't patrol this late at night—they're tucked

into their own bunks and sleeping off their cervezas—
and why would they be there anyway?" He shook his
head. "The boat's too small to use as a smuggler and
we've been anchored out there for days. The *Guardia*
would have already looked at us if they'd been interested."

Squinting in to the darkness, Stratton thought through
the other possibilities. The lightning had let up so it wasn't
that. Curious fishermen? Not at this time of day. Pirates?
Unlikely. They could be found in these waters, for sure,
but they generally went for larger boats and bigger hauls.

He was left with only one real option and that was the
one he'd prepared for. Someone had tracked them here.
Someone who knew how to use a gun and throw a knife.

"What are we going to do?"

Stratton kept his eye on the barely visible shape of
their hull. "We're going to wait here until they leave,
then we're swimming back to that boat and getting the
hell out of here."

They stood in the water for ten minutes, maybe fifteen, then they heard an engine rev. The profile of a
small speedboat quickly came into view as it turned
north and headed straight for the mainland.

With their visitor's craft still in view, Stratton and
Jennifer plunged into the water and began to swim,
matching each other this time, stroke for stroke. Whatever had held Jennifer back earlier had now disappeared. She either sensed Stratton's unease or she
wanted to be on her way as badly as he did.

They were halfway there when it happened.

Stratton thought at first that lightning had struck but
a heartbeat later, he knew that wasn't the case.

The flash was blinding but the noise was even greater. The deafening explosion pressed them under the water, the waves caused by the blast too powerful to fight. Clutching Jennifer's fingers, Stratton fought to keep her with him as they were pushed beneath the waves. Tumbling deeper and deeper, he didn't think he could halt their helpless descent, but he finally managed to regain control and slow the spiral. Kicking backward, he pulled Jennifer with him and turned under the waves, striking out as hard as he could toward shore. As they swam, pieces of the boat rained down, some of it on fire. A large chunk of metal splashed through the water above, barely missing them as it plunged to the ocean's floor. Stratton watched it sink, thinking but not believing, that the blackened and fused piece of steel looked like part of the engine block.

Still underwater, stroking with all he had, he put as much space as he could between them and the boat but at length, Jennifer tugged on his hand and pointed above them. She had to have air.

He kicked upward and they broke the surface, Jennifer gasping and coughing, Stratton supporting her with one arm while treading water with the other. Jagged hunks of wood and fiberboard floated past but they'd come far enough to dodge most of them. He didn't want to look back, but when Jennifer finally got her breath, Stratton turned around.

The flickering red and orange flames allowed them to see clearly. Nothing but an oily patch of wreckage marked the spot where their boat had been.

IF STRATTON HADN'T BEEN holding her up, Jennifer would have gone under and never come back up. He tucked her under his arm, though, and brought them both back to shore.

They neared the beach and Jennifer's feet hit the sand, but Stratton continued to support her, finally sweeping her into his arms and carrying her the rest of the way. He didn't put her down until they were well hidden in the sea grass on the beach.

Her ears ringing, Jennifer looked at Stratton and started to speak but his hand came over her mouth. Only then did she realize she couldn't hear him—or herself. He pantomimed quietness and pointed over his shoulder toward the camp, using his fingers to make her understand. People were running down the beach already, the explosion bringing them out to see what had happened. She nodded then lifted her hand to touch her neck, a stab of pain searing a path behind her right ear. Her fingers came back smeared with something dark and she gasped without thinking.

His frown fierce, Stratton whipped his head around to silence her once again. When his eyes fell to her hand, whatever he'd been about to say was lost and his expression changed completely. Had she had better light, Jennifer might have even thought he paled.

He reached out and gently turned her head. Only after she heard his whispered "damn," did she realize her hearing had returned.

"What happened?" she said with alarm. "Am I bleeding? It hurts."

"Shh." She could feel his breath when he spoke. "You got hit with something. I can't see well enough to say what, but it's still there. Don't touch it."

At his words, Jennifer felt faint. "It's still there? What the hell does that mean?"

His eyes jumped to her neck then came back to her face. "Something's pierced your skin, right below your ear. I can't tell if it's a sliver of wood or something metal." His stare hardened. "Either way, it's got to come out, or you're going to be in trouble."

"Then do it fast," she instructed.

Supporting her firmly, he held her still then she felt an insistent tug. Red-hot pain followed. Her reaction was involuntary—she opened her mouth to scream, but somehow anticipating the problem, he covered her lips with his and swallowed the sound. Holding her tightly, Stratton kept his arms around her until she went limp, lifting his mouth from hers only enough to speak.

"God, I'm sorry, Jennifer." As if he could absorb the pain, he continued to kiss her, his apology and his caresses melting into one sensation, the sting of whatever he'd done fading into a dull burn.

"Jennifer? Jennifer?"

His arms felt too good to give up, but she could hear the distant sound of voices. They had to hide. "I'm okay. It wasn't that bad. Really."

"Can you stand?"

She nodded, then wished she hadn't, the world suddenly whirling as she struggled to her feet.

He caught her just before she hit the sand.

JENNIFER WOKE UP in a room that looked like a cross between a clinic and a kitchen. The nauseating smell of fried fish hung in the air, but so did the scent of rubbing alcohol. The strange combination made no sense but her eyes found Stratton's face, and she relaxed, the sound of his voice and another man's reassuring. She wasn't completely out but she'd obviously been given something to dull the pain. She let her eyes close once more.

"I don't give a damn what you *want* to do. You're going to take us to the mainland." Stratton's tone dropped ominously and Jennifer flinched, despite her drugged state. "If you don't," he continued, "I can guarantee you the medical authorities in Veracruz are going to start asking questions about why you're over here, practicing medicine without a license."

"They haven't so far." The voice was smug.

"That might be the case," Stratton conceded coolly. "But it won't be after I tell them about you."

"You don't want to do that, O'Neil. You'll be opening the door to your own closet and it isn't exactly free of skeletons, is it?"

"No," Stratton answered, "but I don't give a damn what they find out. I'll be long gone by then and you'll be the one who has to come up with the answers."

Her head woozy, Jennifer gave up trying to make sense of the conversation. She felt herself drifting off, their voices growing distant.

"I did what you wanted and cleaned her up, dammit! Why the hell can't you just crawl back in the hole you climbed out of? Go kill somebody else's fa—"

The table where Jennifer lay was suddenly jostled, the legs wobbling uncertainly. She held on to the edge, her eyes jerking open in time to see Stratton reach across her to grab something. She shifted her gaze and realized he held a handful of shirt. The man whose scrawny neck rose out of the wadded fabric wore a look of abject fear but it was Stratton's expression that held her captive. He looked like he'd been punched in the gut, a sick expression washing over his features, his eyes narrowing into slits of anger. They seemed to know each other, but she wondered all at once if the other man would make it out of the encounter alive.

"I can't compete with you in that department, Schwartz." As he spoke, Stratton's lips curled in repugnance. Jerking his head toward the room where they stood, he spit the accusation out as if it were about to choke him. "You've murdered more people with your scalpel than I've ever thought about killing."

The man paused momentarily, and Jennifer could sense Stratton's building reaction. She braced herself as the stranger started to reply.

"Don't go there," was all Stratton said.

For anyone else, it would have been enough, but the skinny man continued, clearly oblivious to where he was heading.

"Don't get hot! I only meant—"

"I don't give a shit what you meant." Stratton shook him like a dog would a rat. "Are you going to take us across the bay without any more crap or am I going to have to hurt you first?"

"All right, all right!" He threw up his hands. "I'll take you, calm down already."

Stratton opened his fingers and the man staggered back. He smoothed his wrinkled shirt with a prissy gesture then glared at Stratton. "We'll go tonight."

Stratton shook his head. "We'll go right now."

"It's almost dawn! Someone could see me! When I get back, it'll be daylight."

"That's your problem." Stratton stepped back from the table. "I only care about taking care of this woman and that means getting away from this shit hole as fast as I can."

Closing her heavy-lidded eyes, Jennifer listened to the man snort angrily then walk away. A moment after that, a door slammed shut. She had a thousand questions for Stratton, like who the man was and how they knew each other and most importantly what he had been about to say before Stratton had silenced him. But they faded into oblivion, along with her consciousness. The last thing she felt was Stratton leaning over the table, his breath warm on her cheek.

"Be okay," he whispered. "Please be okay."

THE SECOND TIME she came to, Jennifer was much more alert. She remembered nothing except for Stratton's plea. When he'd commanded her to be all right, his voice had held a tone she'd not heard before. She wasn't sure she'd *ever* be able to forget that.

She sat up slowly, her fingers going to her neck.

Stratton jumped from the chair where he'd been sitting and came to her side. "How's it feel?"

"I'll survive." Gingerly tracing the outline of the bandage, she looked up at him. "Where are we?"

"I brought you to the clinic on the island. It doubles as the doc's kitchen."

"What happened?"

"You caught a piece of debris from the boat explosion." He raised his hand and gently touched her neck. "I'm sorry, Jennifer. I shouldn't have let this happen."

Startled by his response, she shook her head. "It wasn't your fault."

"Maybe so," he answered, "but things are getting more complicated than I thought they would. I should have sent you somewhere safe." He nodded grimly. "We're both getting out of here. I've arranged for transportation."

Snippets of his conversation with the stranger came back to her. "That's good," she said. "You know this guy, right?"

"Our paths have crossed before," he said without elaboration. "He agreed to help after I explained our situation to him."

Footsteps broke the silence between them and the man she'd seen earlier entered the room. "We're ready," he said. Flicking his gaze in Jennifer's direction, he looked at her bandage. "You okay?"

The offhanded question wasn't posed as if it'd come from a doctor.

"I'm fine," she said.

"You won't have a scar," he assured her. "I worked on movie stars. I was a famous plastic surgeon in Hollywo—"

"She doesn't need your curriculum vitae." Stratton broke in with forbidding abruptness. "All we need from you is to get us the hell out of here and keep your mouth shut after we're gone."

CHAPTER SIXTEEN

FOR TWO GOOD REASONS, Stratton didn't tell Jennifer where they were headed until they were in the air. He needed more time to think about what was going on, for one thing, but primarily he said nothing because his concern was so great. First there had been the woman with the knife, now this. Jonathan Cruz, the fourth member of the OPS, had been their silent killer, but ironically one of the things he also knew a lot about was explosives. He could have easily wired the boat.

If his old friends were involved in this situation, Stratton had more trouble on his hands than he was sure he could handle.

The Cessna broke through the clouds to a perfect blue sky, the ride smoothing out immediately. Stratton glanced at the pilot in the front seat—the very rich pilot in the front seat. The good doctor Schwartz only accepted cash from his patients so he'd had plenty on hand. Stratton had relieved him of most of it, the majority of which was now in the pilot's pocket as payment for smuggling them in to the States. The man wore a set of heavy earphones and a mouth mike; he couldn't hear any conversation.

Stratton turned to Jennifer, wincing at the sight of the

bandage on her neck. He didn't want to let himself think about what would have happened if she'd been hit an inch lower but the thought came anyway. Meredith had told him once that a bleed-out death was so painless and quick the victim hardly had time to realize what had happened but that was little consolation if the victim was someone you cared about.

"We're going back to Houston," he announced. "You've got to get me Leonadov's files."

Her eyes rounded, and she asked the exact question he'd known she would.

"But what about Mr. Barragan? We can't leave him hanging in the dark—"

"I called his office before we left Veracruz." Stratton held her eyes with his. "He never made it out of Tel Aviv, Jennifer. He's dead."

After a moment of shock, her body seemed to deflate, her shoulders slumping against the leather seats, her face falling in despair. "Oh, my God. I can't believe this. Was he shot?"

Stratton shook his head. "Hit by a car."

"Was it an accident?" Hope glinted in her eyes, but it was false because she already knew the truth.

"He was murdered, Jennifer. Just like Singh, just like Leonadov, just like Wilhem. Once the bad guys realize there aren't any body parts in that boat wreckage, we'll be back on that list, too."

"But why?" The question was as rhetorical as the previous one but she asked it regardless.

"You knew the five of them and the killer thinks you know why they were meeting—"

"They were friends...."

He shook his head. "It's more than that, Jennifer. It has to be. And that's why we're going back. Whatever those men had going, there might be some kind of documentation about it. You said yourself Leonadov was writing checks on his own. That means he didn't want you to know about it, whatever *it* is. At the very least we have to find out who those checks went to and why."

Without saying a word, she nodded, her fingers going to her neck. An hour later, she turned back to Stratton and asked one more question.

"Why do you care?" She gripped his arm. "And tell me the truth this time, Stratton. I deserve to know."

He looked into her deep brown eyes and felt his resolution melt. She was right. She *did* deserve the truth and he had to give it to her.

"I'll tell you what I can," he promised. "As soon as we get to Houston."

THEY LANDED ONCE for gas and food but Jennifer had no idea on which side of the border their wheels touched down. She assumed they were still within Mexico but the lines between Texas and its southern neighbor were blurry at best; in the air, things got even more dicey. At one point, the pilot took them down so low, she thought she heard the tops of the mesquite trees scrape the bottom of the plane. Looking out, all she could see was a rush of red dust and pale rock then they regained altitude. She had no idea how long they'd been in the air when the man behind the controls pushed back his headphones and gestured to Stratton.

Popping off his seat belt, Stratton leaned between the

seats and they talked briefly. When the conversation ended, Stratton refastened his seat belt and spoke. "We're going to land in half an hour. You might want to tighten your seat belt. Things could get a little rough."

Her stomach lurched and she glanced out the window in distress. "Is the weather turning bad?"

"Not that I know of," he replied, "but we aren't landing on what you'd call a 'real' runway."

She blinked. "If it's not a 'real' runway, then what the hell is it?"

"If I were pressed, I guess I'd probably call it—" he paused "—a road."

"We're landing on a road?"

The pilot turned around and grinned. Even with his ears covered, he'd heard her question. Stratton shrugged.

"What about the traffic on this road?" she asked in panic.

"There isn't any to speak of," Stratton answered. "It's not paved."

She felt faint even though she was sitting down. Less than three weeks ago, she'd been afraid to step inside a 767 with a professional pilot and four hundred other passengers. Now she was flying in a tin box with wings that was about to land on a dirt path. She closed her eyes.

Then Stratton's hand covered hers.

"It'll be okay," he promised.

The rumble of his voice so close to her ear made her shiver. She opened her eyes, and everything disappeared but Stratton.

"How do you know that?" she whispered.

He pushed a curl away from her face, his fingers lingering on her cheek before he spoke. "Have I ever lied to you, Jennifer?"

"Yes," she said. "You *have* lied to me. Several times as a matter of fact."

"I only did it for your own good."

"That still doesn't make it okay." Her words sounded prissy but she didn't care. "Lying is never right."

"A lot of things aren't 'right,'" he answered, "but they have to be done. That's the way of the world. Haven't you figured that out by now?"

Without waiting for her answer, he moved closer and put his lips over hers. The desire she'd felt building the past few weeks took another leap forward and suddenly the wall she'd built between them came tumbling down. She could *see* them in bed making love, she could *smell* the scent of his body, she could *taste* his skin beneath her tongue. She gripped his shoulders tightly, their kiss deepening. All at once she didn't care where they were or what they were doing or even who was watching. All she cared about was the feel of Stratton's mouth on hers and the possibilities of what might develop between the two of them. He kissed her back as if he could sense the change in her emotions and wanted to take advantage of the opportunity before him.

Several moments passed before Jennifer noticed the stillness. She pulled back with a start then looked out the window. Instead of blue sky, she saw red desert.

They'd landed and she hadn't even realized it.

THEY WALKED A MILE OR SO into the nearest town then took a bus from there. Every few hours, Jennifer swallowed the pills Stratton gave her, washing them down with a bottle of water they'd bought at the bus station. She knew they were back in the States because the highway signs were in English but other than that, she saw no indications of civilization. The road stretched ahead of them with deadly monotony, never changing direction, and she finally fell asleep, her head on Stratton's shoulder.

She woke up with him shaking her shoulder.

"We're here," he said.

She blinked in the bright lights. The bus had stopped under a metal-roofed terminal. There were parking places for a dozen more vehicles, but theirs was the only one. The station was deserted, except for two exhausted-looking couples with screaming kids, four empty-eyed teenagers and one old lady who seemed completely lost.

"Where's 'here'?" she asked.

"Red River." Stratton stood then pulled her to her feet. "It's a lovely little town, but don't get attached to it. We won't be staying long."

She wanted to ask him exactly how they were going to do that minus money or resources, but she knew she'd get no answer. He led her out of the bus and they crossed the sizzling tarmac to enter a frigidly air-conditioned terminal. There were more folks inside than out but it still wasn't packed. Jennifer sensed an emptiness to the place that had been there for so long it'd taken up residence.

She headed straight for the restrooms. There wasn't much she could do with the elastic-waisted pants and T-shirt the doctor had grudgingly given her to put on over her top and boxers but she could at least wash her face and slick back her hair.

She entered the bathroom then suppressed a groan of disbelief when she looked in the mirror. A weathered hag glared back, her hair sticking out in sixteen directions, a smudge of dirt beneath her chin, two bandages on her neck. Jennifer couldn't believe no one had called the police when they'd walked into town and boarded the bus, then she remembered the clerk who'd sold them their tickets. He couldn't have cared less.

She cleaned up the best that she could, used the toilet, then walked back out, heading for the bench where she'd left Stratton. But he was nowhere in sight. A moment's panic hit her before she realized he'd probably gone to clean up, too. Glancing around, she sat down on the plastic seat to wait and that's when she spotted him.

He was standing on the other side of the station, talking to a woman. She was young and beautiful but you had to look carefully to realize it, past her worn housedress and frizzy hair, past the flip-flops and two toddlers she was trying to corral. She carried a beat-up leather purse but had a navy backpack at her feet. She nodded as Stratton spoke then seemed to get angry all at once. Their voices rose slightly—they were speaking Spanish—but Jennifer couldn't distinguish the words. The woman crossed her arms and shook her head furiously.

The fight continued for several minutes, then it seemed to lose strength. Stratton said something with a smile and tugged at her arm then she seemed to relent and smiled back. Glancing in Jennifer's direction, the woman nodded once and Stratton then leaned over and kissed her cheek. Jennifer certainly had no claim on Stratton nor he on her but the intimate exchange left her so confused she could hardly think. Good God, was she jealous?

No, she decided quickly. Stratton wasn't the kind of man a woman would have to worry about in that department. That was good, she thought, but why did she even care?

The answer to that question came much more slowly than the one previous, but when it did, it rocked her. She was developing feelings for Stratton that she shouldn't have. Sure, they'd shared a few kisses, and she'd imagined them together, but her lustful fantasies had been just that—fantasies. Until this very moment she hadn't had the time to realize there was something more, something of substance, behind those daydreams.

And Stratton himself was that something.

He was a man who knew the difference between right and wrong and he'd proven that time and time again. By saving her life, by protecting her. Even when she hadn't understood and she'd protested, he'd been firm in his convictions and because of him, they were both alive.

He acted as if just the opposite was the case, though. Puzzling over her realizations, Jennifer could only surmise that somewhere along the road, he'd taken a wrong turn that had made him lose faith in himself, but she, seeing him from a different perspective, could see the truth clearly.

STRATTON CROSSED the terminal and came to Jennifer's side. Over the past few days, they'd hit quite a few rough spots, but she'd hung in there. He didn't know too many men who would have survived what they'd experienced, much less come out of it looking as great as she did right now. Her hair pulled back, her face scrubbed, she was the all-American girl. The one who still believed in the truth.

He sat down on the bench and she turned, her dark eyes locking on his. "I saw you." She nodded in the direction he'd been. "Who was the woman?"

"I don't know her," he said, opening the backpack at his feet. "A friend sent her."

"You don't know her?" Jennifer's voice was incredulous. "You had a fight. You made up. You kissed her. How could you not know her?"

"It was a setup. If you'd been closer, you would have heard the 'argument.' *Mi hermana* is not happy with me but she agreed, one more time, to give us some help." He reached over and patted Jennifer's stomach. "For the *chico*," he added.

A look of embarrassment suffused Jennifer's face. "I thought you knew her," she said faintly. "I just assumed..."

He shook his head slowly, her reaction intriguing him. He'd file it away and think about it later. "How many times have I told you not to do that?"

"Several," she admitted.

"Then maybe you need to start listening. You can't figure me out. Give up trying."

"But how..."

He looked at her until she fell silent then he began to check the contents of the bag. Halfway through his task, she spoke again.

"Well, why did she..."

Once again, he raised his eyes to hers and once again, she stopped talking. When he was sure the silence would continue, he returned his attention to the backpack.

Everything he needed was there, he saw with satisfaction. Money, weapons, a passport. When he'd been with the Operatives, it'd been SOP to keep boxes like this stashed at mail pickups. All it took was a single phone call and he had a new life. He would have used the one in Rio to get them out of Brazil but he'd had to have a passport for Jennifer, as well. Here by the border he'd gone even further and had a "sister" in place to deliver the box if necessary. He hadn't been sure this stash would still be there, but thank God, it had been. The woman had even included some clothes for Jennifer as he'd instructed.

He got to his feet and looked down at Jennifer. "I'm going to rent a car. Don't go anywhere."

TWENTY MINUTES LATER they were driving away from the bus station. They didn't get too far, though. In the next good-size town, Stratton pulled into the parking lot of a motel and shut off the engine. Jennifer turned away from the window to see him rubbing his eyes.

"We're getting a room," he announced. "I need some sleep before I do something stupid."

"I can drive," she offered.

"You don't have a driver's license," he said. "All we need is to get stopped one time by a bored cop."

"But we haven't done anything wrong."

He looked at her with a bloodshot gaze. "You're wanted in three countries, Jennifer. By the time that got sorted out, we'd probably be dead. Whoever's out there killing diamond dealers has clout and they're getting closer."

His explanation made no sense. At first. Then she understood and her whole body went cold. "You think they could get to us, even in jail?"

Staring through the windshield, he had to force himself to loosen his grip on the steering wheel. "When someone wants you killed, nowhere is safe."

Jennifer shivered at his words. "Voice of experience?"

"It's the truth," he said quietly. "That's all."

She shivered again, but Stratton didn't notice. He had already opened his door and was walking to the office of the motel. He emerged five minutes later with a key in his hand. Moving the car to the rear of the building, away from the highway, he backed into a parking spot at the end of the row then pointed upward. "We're on the third floor."

The room was small and dark. A table and two chairs sat beside a curtained window and a bed, an enormous bed, took up the rest of the space. Jennifer didn't bother to question the arrangement. At this point, it hardly seemed to matter and Stratton wouldn't have answered her anyway.

He locked the door then wedged one of the chairs beneath the knob. "Ladies, first," he said, tilting his head toward the bath. "Go ahead."

She didn't argue this, either. Inside the tiny bathroom, peeling the doctor's grungy clothes off with disgust, Jennifer stepped under the stream of water before it could even run warm. She didn't care; she simply wanted to be clean. Ten minutes later, she was. Her hair still dripping, she combed it with her fingers, wrapped a towel around her body and opened the door. Stratton was stretched out on the bed. "Your turn," she announced.

He didn't move.

She crossed the room on tiptoe to stand beside the bed. His eyes were closed and his breathing was even. He was fast asleep. She'd never seen him in such a relaxed state and would have expected him to look younger but just the opposite was the case. He seemed to be on guard even more, his forehead furrowed, his body tense. The only time Stratton relaxed was in the middle of danger. Freed from the burden of his scrutiny, she leaned closer to study his features.

In a flash, his hand snaked out and circled her throat. Before she could draw a breath, she was flat on the bed and he was on top of her, straddling her with his legs, one hand still on her neck, the other stretching her arms over her head.

She would have screamed but she was too scared.

He blinked then rocked back on his heels, both his hands going slack as he realized what he'd done. "Dammit to hell, Jennifer! Don't ever sneak up on me like that again. I could have…" His voice trailed off, his meaning obvious.

"I didn't sneak up on you! I was trying to see if you were asleep or not."

"Well, I was," he said. "But I'm not anymore."

At that moment Jennifer became aware of their position, the realization clearly hitting Stratton, as well. The feel of his legs on either side of hers, the way he loosely held her wrists, the heat in his stare. Jennifer knew what would come next and she didn't try to stop the need that rose between them. It had been denied for way too long.

Without a word, Stratton moved his hand to the towel still knotted at her breasts. His fingers were cold when they brushed her skin, but Jennifer didn't notice. The desire inside of her held all the warmth she needed. Her thoughts from the bus terminal came back to her, and she found herself admitting what she hadn't been able to acknowledge then. She wasn't just "falling" for Stratton.

She was falling *in love* with Stratton.

He undid the knot and coherent thought fled. Her hands going to his shirt, she fumbled at the buttons but managed to unfasten them before moving on to his belt. Their clothes ended up in a pile on the floor, hanging off the bed, flung to one side. When they were both naked, Stratton wrapped his arms around her. Jennifer figured she knew what would come next, but when he brought her to him, nothing was familiar. He took her hands and made them his, took her mouth and refused to give it back. The whole experience of making love suddenly became foreign to her, the excitement of his touch overcoming what few inhibitions she had left. She felt her desire crest, his intensity the greatest aphrodisiac she'd ever experienced. A moment later, he reached into the backpack he'd brought inside and pulled out a condom.

A murmured groan, a few strokes, a second's worth of touching and then he was inside her.

His mouth covered hers as he thrust deep inside her.

Jennifer held nothing back and welcomed every push, her legs around his hips. Squeezing her eyes shut let pure sensation overtake her and in that instant, just as it'd been in the plane, nothing mattered but Stratton.

Would anything but him ever matter again?

She had the thought, then gave herself up to the moment. But as she cried out his name, a realization came to her. She'd been wrong, desperately wrong.

They were much more alike than they were different, and nothing could have scared her more.

CHAPTER SEVENTEEN

THEY SHOWERED TOGETHER then made love a second time, Stratton falling into a light sleep that lasted almost an hour. On his own, he would have never stayed that long in bed, but he didn't want to disturb Jennifer. The tenderness that swelled inside his heart when he looked down at her curled in his arms scared the hell out of him so he made up excuses for what they'd done.

The tension of the moment had brought them together, and that was it, nothing more. A man and a woman couldn't experience the stress they had without releasing it somehow. He'd been in these situations before and he knew the drill.

He swept a finger over Jennifer's cheek and she smiled in her sleep, murmuring something unintelligible. They'd just had the kind of sex you had after a funeral, he rationalized, the kind you had in order to reassure yourself you weren't the one who'd been put in the ground. The encounter meant nothing more.

And that, he told himself a moment later, was the biggest crock of shit he'd heard in quite a long time.

They'd given each other much more than mindless pleasure and he knew it. They'd shared something that went beyond the physical. He was afraid to admit that he cared so much yet he had to acknowledge his feelings, no matter how deeply they sliced or how badly they stung. Life didn't cut you any slack in that department. You could face the truth now or later but one way or another, you faced it.

And the truth was—he was falling in love with Jennifer.

So what in the hell was he going to do?

He watched the steady rise and fall of her breasts as she breathed and accepted that for the first time in his life, he didn't have a solution to a problem. He wasn't prepared, he didn't have a Plan B, he had no idea of how to proceed.

Her eyes opened and their warmth pulled him straight back to the place he'd just left. He tried to resist but he couldn't and emotions he'd never planned on feeling again hit him.

She stared at him without saying anything and after a moment, he realized she was trying to figure out where they stood. He didn't know their status himself but he suddenly found the answer to his question. He didn't have a plan because he didn't need one.

When he told her his past, there would be no decisions left to make.

He sat up and swung his legs to the edge of the bed.

"We've been here too long." He spoke over his shoulder as he headed for the shower. "We need to head for Houston."

Silence filled the moment that followed and Stratton could almost hear Jennifer's thoughts. She wasn't the kind of woman who made love with a man then rolled out of bed and forgot about it.

He knew he needed to keep walking, but he was dying inside so he turned around. She'd gotten out of bed and was standing, her beautiful back a slim, straight shadow in the dimness of the room. "Jennifer?" was all he could say.

"I'd better get dressed, then," she said in the darkness. "Give me ten minutes and I'll meet you at the car."

JENNIFER DIDN'T SAY anything when she slid into the front seat. What was there to say? She felt more for Stratton than he did for her. Otherwise, he would have said something besides "We've got to hit the road."

For half a second, she'd considered confronting him but she had her answer so there was no point in prolonging her humiliation.

Stratton drove east, the Texas night so clear Jennifer felt as if she could reach up and grab a star. She figured they'd go the whole way in silence, but after an hour of traveling, she was startled to hear Stratton speak. *What* he proceeded to say shocked her even more.

"I haven't been fair to you, Jennifer. I promised to tell you more and I haven't. I think it's time you know the truth."

He spoke with such determination, a forbidding undercurrent to his words, that her mouth went dry.

She'd wanted to know his secrets but now that the time had come, she was no longer sure it was such a good idea. She didn't have a choice, though. He continued as if he had a real and sudden purpose in mind. He *wanted* her to know now, but why?

"After I left the Marines, I went to work for an organization called the Operatives. There were only four of us. The woman I've already mentioned, Meredith, and two other men I'll call Cruz and Armando. Meredith started the group and asked each one of us to come work for her. We'd been independents until then, but our business is a small one and we all knew each other since we did the same thing."

Jennifer tried to act casual. "Is this the business you mentioned before? The trash-collection agency?"

He turned his head toward her, but she could only see the motion in the darkness. His expression stayed hidden. "We didn't collect trash, Jennifer. We killed people."

Jennifer couldn't help herself; she almost laughed.

She'd suspected many things about Stratton, but not this. Assassins were people you heard about in the movies or read about in spy books. They weren't real.

But in the echoing stillness that settled between them, she realized Stratton was not lying. She'd shared his bed—and unintentionally, his soul—and she knew he was telling her the plain, unvarnished truth.

"Tell me more," she said.

He exhaled slowly then spoke. "Meredith arranged everything. Her father was in Naval Intelligence and she was actually a spook for a while."

"A spook?"

"She worked for the CIA," he explained. "She got out because she felt the agency screwed up more times than it was successful, and she was tired of seeing the bad guys get away. She contacted each of us and laid out the deal. We all signed on."

"And the law be damned?"

"There isn't a *law* against political assassinations."

He spoke calmly, as if they were discussing the weather. "Gerald Ford signed an executive order prohibiting them after a series of congressional hearings in the mid-seventies. Carter and Reagan expanded the order to include anyone working for the U.S. government. Problem was, no one ever defined 'assassination.' President Bush signed a new order when the U.S. started looking for Osama Bin Laden, but it still limits the use of covert activities." He glanced across the seat at her. "In any event, the orders only apply to the United States government. That leaves plenty of other countries—and individuals—willing to take care of their problems through unorthodox methods." He stopped for a moment, then continued. "If they had the money, we had the solution."

The night sped past their windows, as she absorbed what he'd told her.

"Are you shocked?"

"No." She paused then spoke again. "Yes." She stopped once more and shook her head. "I'm both, I guess."

And she was. If he'd told her this at the very beginning, she would have taken off as fast as she could in the opposite direction, even if he could save her life. She would have immediately assumed—as he always told her not to do—that he himself would have been behind Ami's murder.

At the same time, though, she knew that she was right about Stratton. He *was* the man she thought he was, regardless of what he'd just said. He *was* someone who could recognize the difference between evil and good. He *was* a person who cared what happened and why.

She formed her answer carefully. "I'm shocked that people like you actually exist but I'm not shocked at what you do and why you do it."

He threw her an incredulous look. "You're the woman who says lying is wrong but you're okay with sanctioned killing?"

"The world is better off with some people gone." She looked into the empty blackness that surrounded their car. The stars didn't seem quite so close now. "That's why SWAT teams have snipers. That's why the military has sharpshooters. Those men are brave and good and courageous because they're doing something that few people actually can. We need to be grateful they're there."

She turned in her seat and faced him. "I may not be familiar with your world, Stratton, but I'm a realist and I know there are good guys and there are bad guys. When things go right, the good guys win by stopping the bad guys. When things go wrong, just the opposite occurs." She sighed heavily. "If anyone believes otherwise, all they need to do is ask an Auschwitz survivor. Ami would have been happy to set them straight."

STRATTON GRIPPED the steering wheel with both his hands, his hold on the molded plastic so tight he thought it might bend. At one time, he'd used the same terms she was using to describe himself and the others. Courageous. Brave. Heroic. They were going to save the world and that's why he had joined Meredith. He'd thought he was doing the right thing.

Until he'd screwed up.

"I knew there was more to the situation than you'd

let on." Jennifer's voice brought him back to the present. "What I can't understand is how you got from the Operatives to helping old guys who didn't trust the police."

He started to make up something, then stopped himself. If he'd gone this far, he might as well tell her the rest. Things had gotten too damn complicated for anything else.

"Ami didn't hire me to find out who killed Singh," Stratton said. "I'm working for the IDDA, Jennifer. They hired me so they could calm down the rest of the dealers and reassure them that they were doing something about Singh's death. They wanted to be able to tell them everything was under control."

Jennifer was silent for so long, he thought she hadn't heard him, then she spoke. "Why didn't you just tell me that?"

"I couldn't. You were a suspect. You don't tell suspects you suspect them."

He wasn't sure what he'd expected but her silence was not it. "You don't seem surprised."

"That's because I'm not," she answered. "I knew Ami hadn't hired you. He would have told me if he had." She shook her head. "What I couldn't figure out was why you were sticking around. Don't you remember me asking you why you cared?"

He nodded.

"That's why I asked. I knew something was wrong. But one way or the other, who your employer is doesn't change anything. We're both targets now. You should have quit while you were ahead."

"That's not how I work," he said in a hard voice.

They went a few more miles on the endless black-top before she spoke again.

"So what do they think?" she asked. "The IDDA always struck me as being on top of things."

"I don't know what they think. I haven't spoken with my contact there since Ami died."

"Why not?"

"I don't trust them."

"You aren't alone in that," Jennifer responded. "The organization has a bad reputation but there's nothing the dealers can do about it. It's the old golden rule, you know." She waited a beat. "He who has the gold makes the rules. There's never been another option for the dealers."

Her cliché sent Stratton's thoughts in a totally different direction. He considered this new idea for a few minutes, then he turned to her, chastising himself for not seeing the possibility earlier.

"Maybe that's it," he said slowly.

"That's what?"

"Maybe Ami was trying to change the rules."

She frowned. "Like how?"

"Who knows? Maybe he and the others were starting some kind of cartel themselves. Maybe they wanted to challenge how the IDDA did business. That would shake up the status quo."

"The IDDA wouldn't have hired you if they didn't like whatever Ami was doing. They take care of their own problems. They'd want to keep any kind of investigation quiet while they took care of it themselves." She shook her head again. "That doesn't make sense."

"From our point of view, you're right, it doesn't. But

everything can be seen from a hundred different angles and nothing's going to look the same from each."

Stratton's eyes met Jennifer's in the glow of the dashboard light. He'd seen her guilt over her sister's accident and had thought it unreasonable, had seen her fear of flying and had thought it was silly. He'd expected her to be horrified by his history but she'd taken it in stride. Now he understood the truth of those things because he was looking at her from a different angle, the angle of a lover. Now he knew how deeply she cared and how brave she really was.

What you saw always depended on where you stood.

THEY HIT THE OUTSKIRTS of Houston sometime before dawn. Even on Saturday Houston's traffic was bad, especially on the freeway coming into town from the west. Constantly under construction, every lane was congested with bumper to bumper vehicles and their progress slowed to a crawl. Stratton maneuvered the rental with caution. He obviously didn't want to attract any attention although most Houstonians drove just the opposite way, changing lanes, running red lights and turning abruptly, all without the benefit of a signal. Jennifer was impressed by his restraint.

Her thoughts went right back to where they'd been for the past six hours. Sure, she'd been shocked at his revelation, but men and women who put themselves on the line to fight evil were heroes in her book.

Stratton was a man of conviction—and that made her feel good—but as the miles had passed, she'd become less shocked and more curious. He'd told her the truth, but he hadn't told her everything. Stratton was holding back something. What could it possibly be? What could be worse than what he'd already told her?

She didn't know but the question made the distance between their two worlds seem even greater. The paralysis she'd sensed inside him had been put there by a violence she couldn't begin to imagine. He'd left the Operatives for some reason but not for a normal life. That wasn't an option for him. A man like that didn't suddenly decide to settle down, have a family and start playing golf. He'd be miserable. Or he'd go nuts.

His voice pulled her back into the present, and she was surprised to see the progress they'd made.

"Where do I go from here? We're on Westheimer."

She directed him to a small hotel on a nearby side street, just off Richmond. They couldn't go back to her apartment, he'd explained, or anywhere else Jennifer was familiar with because those places would undoubtedly be under surveillance. Especially once it was verified no body parts were floating around in Veracruz Bay.

They'd hide out until late that night, he'd said, then go to Ami's house where Stratton would retrieve Ami's spare key to the office. If no one had modified the alarm's code, they could slip into the office undetected.

That was a risk, she'd told Stratton, after revealing the key's whereabouts, but she doubted Thomas even knew how to change the number. Jennifer had been in charge of things like that.

Once again, Stratton checked them in, received a key and drove them to the back parking lot. An eerie carbon copy of the one they'd left hours before, the room was just as small and just as dark. And the bed,

Jennifer noted as she walked up to it, was just as wide. She turned, her eyes meeting Stratton's.

A moment later, they were in it, forgetting what was behind them and ignoring what lay ahead.

A FEW HOURS LATER they were still wrapped in each other's arms. This was getting way too messy, Stratton told himself. When it came time to leave, there would be hell to pay.

He felt her gaze and turned his head to meet it.

"What are you thinking?" Jennifer asked. "You look as if you're a thousand miles away."

He couldn't duck the issue anymore. "I am," he said, "or I will be shortly." Kissing her gently, he pulled back. "When this is all over, I'll be out of here, Jennifer. I can't lie to you about that. You need to know—"

She covered his lips with one finger and silenced him. "I know everything I *need* to know," she said. "For now, let's leave it at that."

Her request confused him but he respected it. "What will you do?" He balanced on one elbow to look down at her. "You don't have a job, your life's been turned upside down. Do you have a plan?"

"I was already at a crossroads with Julie gone." She shrugged. "I guess it'll be a fresh start—if I stay alive and don't end up in a South American prison."

"You will be alive. I'll make sure of that." The thought of anything else was something he couldn't consider. He shook his head and smiled, forcing a lighter moment. "Can't guarantee anything about that prison problem, though."

"Will you visit me, at least?"

"I don't know. I'm not too crazy about that part of the world. I'll probably give it a wide berth for a while." Pausing for a moment, he spoke quietly, his mood changing quickly. "It wasn't my favorite place to begin with."

She threaded her fingers through the hair on his chest. "Why is that?"

"You don't want to know."

She sat up, pulling the blanket with her. "I do want to know. I wouldn't have asked if I didn't." She paused. "There's more to it than what you told me last night, isn't there?"

Her question didn't surprise him. Jennifer was a smart woman. He looked down at the wrinkled sheets then back up at her. He'd never actually told the story to anyone before and he'd never planned on doing so, either.

But when she reached out and touched his jaw, Stratton knew the time had come.

"I was on a job in Cartagena," he began slowly. "It's a beautiful city with beautiful women but like a lot of things down there, Colombian politics can be violent. They play rough and if you can't keep up, you're out of the game."

As he spoke, his voice changed, becoming lower. Jennifer held back a shiver of unease.

"The drug cartels are changing everything. They're gaining control of the country, piece by piece. They buy power and influence where they can and when their money won't work, they kill whoever stands in their way. Before too long, they're going to be in control of the whole country, and they'll be there legitimately. No one will be able to stop them."

"What do you mean?"

"They're putting their people into the government itself. When a city mayor or the governor of a state comes up for reelection they approach him and try to convince him not to run again. He either takes the money and escapes, or he stays and wakes up dead. They set their man in his place and he's always elected."

"Rigged elections?"

Stratton shrugged. "I doubt they bother to count the votes. If he's on the ballot he wins. No one can get him out after that. They don't have recalls."

Her mouth became dry as the importance of his words sank in. "But they *do* have assassinations."

"You catch on fast."

"I'm learning." She brought her knees to her chest and hugged them tightly, a coldness gradually coming over her that felt unlike anything she'd experienced before.

"But something went wrong," she said. "What was it?"

"A man named Juan Castillo went wrong," he said. "The drug people got rid of the local guy and put Castillo on the ticket. I had an informant inside his operation because he was a pretty big player. My man got hold of Castillo's itinerary, which was kept a secret for obvious reasons. It listed all the dates and stops he was making for his 'campaign' trip. Right before he would arrive, the locals would be informed he was coming, then they were all supposed to show up and cheer for him. My guy didn't know Castillo's organization had gotten suspicious of him, though. They set him up with some bad information. He paid for it with his life and I almost did the same."

"How did it happen?"

Stratton's expression shifted. "The list he found contained one extra stop. He passed on the time and place to me. I got there, he got there, but Castillo was nowhere in sight. Next thing either of us knew, the square where I'd set up my equipment was closed and we were trapped. I almost didn't get out."

The chill seeped into Jennifer's bones. "But you did. And then you went back."

"I hadn't finished the job."

She waited in silence as he reached for the bottle of water she'd left on the night stand. After taking a long drink, he resumed his story.

"Meredith got me more equipment and I set up again, making sure the information was correct. It was actually easier the second time because they'd decided no one in their right mind would stick around after failing." He glanced at Jennifer. "After they caught my informant, they cut out his tongue."

Her stomach rolled. "Just like Gomez's maid?" she whispered in a horrified voice.

"Not exactly," he said. "They let her live. This man was hung in the square. *After* they mutilated him. Castillo himself did the honors. I watched."

Jennifer's heart felt like it was caught in a vise, and she realized she didn't need any more explanation. She knew what he'd been holding back. Like any sane man, Stratton had reached his limit and he'd walked away. But Stratton was Stratton and quitting had maimed him. He saw it as a failure.

"I understand," she said softly. "Good grief, Stratton, no one could continue after witnessing something so awful. You had to stop."

He laughed without humor. "Oh, Jennifer, if only it had been that simple."

She went still, the sarcasm—and the agony—in his voice paralyzing her.

"Seeing that scumbag get his tongue ripped out didn't bother me in the least. He was a longtime loser but he'd just been 'promoted.' They were going to send him to the States for a little upper management training. If the cartel hadn't gotten suspicious of him, he'd be in Houston right now, running product from here to the East Coast." Stratton curled his lip in disgust. "Believe me, he's one of those people whose departure left the world a better place."

She leaned closer, her attention solely on Stratton. "Then what happened?"

"I followed Castillo to the next town and set up there. Everything was ready and in place. His entourage showed up, he went into this school to give his little speech, and then he came out. I didn't know he'd been joined inside by his family." Stratton's voice turned mechanical. "Castillo's bodyguard came out first, as he usually did. I set up the shot, took a breath, then squeezed the trigger when Castillo came into view. But the second before I fired, he turned to say something to his wife. She was standing right behind him, holding their five-year-old daughter."

He looked down at his hands and Jennifer's eyes followed his movement. He'd wrapped the sheet so tightly around his fingers that his knuckles were now bloodless.

"I killed her and the child with one shot. He was elected a month later."

CHAPTER EIGHTEEN

RELIVING THE MOMENT, sick to his stomach, Stratton pushed the sheets away and got up without saying another word. He didn't look back as he stalked into the bathroom. He didn't want to see the disgust he knew would be on Jennifer's face. He saw enough of it in his own reflection every damned morning.

A moment passed and then another. Finally he heard her bare feet padding up behind him and he raised his eyes. The blanket she'd wrapped around her body trailed after her like a train. Her hair was disheveled and her lips were swollen. The skin above her breasts was red from the irritation caused by his stubble.

He forced his gaze to her face then blanched. Her expression was not one of disgust; it was worse. Her brown eyes were filled with sympathy, her forehead furrowed with concern.

She spoke softly, her voice husky from the impact his words had had on her. "Why didn't you tell me this sooner, Stratton?"

"And give you even more reason to run?"

"How do you know I would have done that?"

"It's what I would have done if I were you."

"Well, you aren't me," she said flatly. "But it hardly

matters because this isn't something you can escape. This will haunt you forever."

"No shit," he said.

She stood beside him and shook her head, her eyes closed. He could only imagine her thoughts but he knew for certain they weren't good.

"You must have felt…" She stopped then opened her eyes. "God, Stratton, I can't even think of how horrible that must have been. You must have been devastated."

"Maybe so, but who cares? I'm still alive. They aren't."

"But you weren't trying to kill them—"

"God help me, no!" His eyes locked on hers. "Never. Never. I'd never deliberately take out a mother and her child, Jennifer. Think what you want to, but know that's the truth."

"Then you made a mistake," she said. "A tragic, terrible mistake, but a mistake all the same."

"It shouldn't have been made period."

"You're right again, but unfortunately you aren't perfect. No one is."

He faced her, his words scathing in their condemnation. "I killed an innocent woman and a five-year-old girl, Jennifer. I took a man's family. He was a son of a bitch, yes, but they didn't deserve what happened to them."

"Of course, they didn't." She put her hand on his arm but he shrugged it off and her fingers fell limply to her side. "You weren't aiming for them, though. You said you didn't even know they would be there."

"I didn't know," he confirmed, "but I should have.

Instead I was in a big damn hurry and wired to the max because of the way things had gone the last time. I didn't do the prep I should have. In fact..."

The sentence drifted off, and he stared into the distance over Jennifer's head, remembering things he didn't want to remember.

"In fact what?"

He let the silence build until he couldn't stand it a moment longer then he turned around so he didn't have to see her. He started to speak like that—his head hanging down, his gaze unfocused—then he realized what he was doing and he forced himself to look her in the eye.

"In fact, I'd been drinking." His confession was like a knife against silk, rending the space between them into two distinct parts. His. And hers.

"I was mad and uptight and the night before I'd tied one on. I knew better but I ignored the rules and that morning I was paying the price. I felt like shit and my aim was for shit."

This time her expression was one of pure shock. He'd finally managed to make her see what kind of man he really was.

"Go ahead," he said in a slow and deliberate voice. "Say what you're thinking. Tell me what a horrible, rotten bastard I really am. Tell me what a failure I've turned into. Tell me how I don't deserve to be alive."

Silence, thick and heavy, grew between them. Finally, Jennifer broke it.

"I don't have to tell you that. I have the feeling you say it to yourself often enough for the both of us."

His self-censure was immediate and unforgiving. "I

was paid to do a job and I didn't do it. Instead I murdered two defenseless people. I need to remind myself, Jennifer. Someone should. It's the least I can do for them."

"Will punishing yourself for the rest of your life bring them back?"

"Do you have a better idea?"

She put her hands on her hips, her gaze measuring his. "So you just walk away and let the bad guys win? That's it?"

"Yes, dammit to hell, that's it." His jaw became tight and so did his chest, the air in the bathroom suddenly too heated to breathe. "I walked away and I won't be going back. They can win. They can take the prize. They're the victors." He pulled in a ragged breath. "If you don't like that, then take a number and stand in line because I've disappointed plenty of people before you. I'll just add your name to the list."

JENNIFER STEPPED out of the bathroom, closing the door behind her. Retrieving the clothes she'd left scattered about, she got dressed under a cloud of confusion and chaos. She'd tried not to let Stratton see the hole that had opened up inside her heart at his revelation, but she wasn't sure she'd been successful. Or even if she should have tried. She'd told him she believed in what he did but this... This was different. This was horrible.

This was unforgivable.

Or was it?

Stratton had obviously made a terrible mistake but did that make him a terrible man? Did actions determine fate or did intention matter more? Her mind went blank and she opened the door to the hotel room, walking into the parking lot in a daze.

She didn't have an answer. She didn't even have a clue. Hell, she wasn't even sure what the question was.

On the freeway, the traffic droned with relentless determination. She crossed the asphalt and headed toward their rental car, her brain refusing to function. For several paralyzing minutes, she stood beside the automobile, then slowly, so slowly it barely registered at first, a realization began to form.

If Stratton didn't care so much about what he'd done, the tragedy would have left him with little more than regret. As it was, he treated the deaths of the woman and her daughter like wounds that would never leave him, touching them constantly, keeping the injuries fresh and raw. He was a penitent, but the guilt that had lodged deep inside would never fade because he wouldn't let it.

Guilt was such a pointless emotion, she thought unexpectedly, whether it was deserved or not. Regret and reproach did nothing useful. Nothing at all. Those people were gone and as Stratton had said, nothing was bringing them back.

Sadness welled inside Jennifer, sadness for Stratton, sadness for the mother and her child, even sadness for herself because hadn't she done the very same thing? There was no reason for Jennifer to feel guilty about Julie's accident, but Cissy had been right—she did all the same.

Stratton had made a horrible mistake and the results had been tragic, but he was brave and fearless and willing to risk his own life to make the world a safer place.

He achieved his goals in a way she hadn't expected but deep down, his motives were pure.

And she loved him.

The knowledge made her close her eyes and moan. She might feel that way for all the right reasons but so what? How did you live with a man who did what he did? She could only imagine the conversation.

"I'm sorry we can't come to your party next week. My husband had to go out of town on business. He's in Uzbekistan knocking off an evil dictator, but he'll be back on Friday."

With a heavy heart, she started back to the room. She was in serious trouble. Stratton wasn't a person who would ever settle down. Kids, dogs and mortgages weren't part of his world. He knew it, too. That's why he'd finally told her what he had. The determination she'd sensed in his voice had reflected his purpose, as well. Telling her the truth had created an easy out for him. He didn't want any entanglements and he'd known his past would make Jennifer's decision a quick and simple one.

Lost in her troubled thoughts, Jennifer turned the corner then gasped in fright as Stratton unexpectedly materialized before her. He was shirtless and shoeless, his jeans unbuttoned. He'd obviously just realized she'd left and rushed from their hotel room

He grabbed both her arms. "Where do you think you're going?" he asked roughly. "You shouldn't be out here—"

"I needed some air." She looked him square in the eye. "I had some thinking to do."

His eyes narrowed into two slits of anger, but the reaction was a cover-up. Underneath the anger, she saw the uncertainty.

Unfortunately, it made her love him all the more.

NOTHING ELSE WAS SAID as they waited for dark. Stratton kept to his side of the room and Jennifer did the same. From time to time, he would leave her and patrol the perimeter of the small motel but everything stayed quiet. The passing time stretched out as the silence grew, the tension between the two of them expanding along with it. A storm of emotions continued to attack him, from raging anger to bitter disappointment and everything in between. He wanted to be furious at Jennifer for what she'd pointed out, but how could he? Everything she'd said was the truth but for the past two years, all he'd been able to think about was the damage—the immutable damage—he'd caused.

At 1:00 a.m., Stratton stood. "It's time. Let's go."

Obviously as relieved as he was to finally do something, Jennifer jumped up from the chair where she'd been sitting. Ten minutes later they were in the car and heading for Ami's house.

SITTING IN THEIR VEHICLE and scanning the neighborhood, Jennifer watched as Stratton picked the lock then slipped inside Ami's garage. Thomas's BMW sat in the driveway but the house was dark. Had he moved in? She wouldn't be surprised if he had. Located in the Bellaire section of Houston, Ami's home had been a showcase in the fifties when he'd bought it. He'd kept it in pristine condition. The place was so retro perfect, she couldn't imagine what it might sell for now.

Stratton reappeared, key in hand. He climbed inside, shut the door without a sound and tossed something into her lap.

"I found a stack of those in the garage, right beside the safe where you said the key would be," he said. "Thought you might find them interesting."

Jennifer unfolded the newspaper he'd given her. The issue was over a week old, but she immediately understood why Thomas had kept it. A large black-and-white photo of him was featured prominently on the right side, above the fold. He wore a suit and a solemn expression. She read the caption underneath out loud.

"Local Man Grieves for Murdered Father. Assistant and Cache of Diamonds Still Missing."

"Your buddy Thomas has been busy. There were papers from other days in there, as well."

She scanned the article then tightened her lips. "I can't believe this! He's telling everyone I killed his father." She read a bit more then tossed the newspaper to the backseat. "And I went out with that son of a bitch! What was I thinking?"

"You dated him?" Stratton shot her a look. "You never told me that."

"You didn't ask," she said tartly. "But in any case, I'd hardly call it 'dating.' We only went out once, and I did that because Cissy practically blackmailed me into it. It happened right before I went to Rio with Ami. I don't even know why he asked me to go anyway—all he did was pump me for information about the business."

Stratton frowned. "Cissy blackmailed you? What do you mean?"

"Not literally!" She corrected him quickly. "She just

said I needed to date more, and I was crazy not to let him take me out."

"Why would she say that?"

"Who knows?" Jennifer shrugged. "Cissy can be weird sometimes. She just wanted me to have fun, I guess. I'd been sad because of Julie and I just gave in."

Stratton's questions about Cissy and Thomas didn't stop until they reached Westheimer. If he'd been anyone other than who he was, she might have thought he was jealous about Thomas but Jennifer knew Stratton was too self-confident for that. No, he was suspicious of Thomas and Cissy.

From the street, the office loomed darkly above them, except for several floors right in the middle. They were brightly lit for the cleaning crews. As he parked, Stratton sighed with what sounded like relief.

"What is it?" Jennifer asked.

He stated the obvious. "The janitors are here."

"So?"

Instead of answering, he asked another question. "Do you know the night guards?"

"Not the ones on the late shift," she said. "They're paid security men. We have cops during the day."

"Good," he said shortly. "Wait here. I'll be right back."

He ran directly to a white van parked under the overhang in the back of the building. From where she sat, Jennifer had difficulty reading the sign on the side but she finally made out the words. Williams Cleaning.

He was back a minute later.

He handed what turned out to be a pair of coveralls to her. "Put that on," he ordered. "I don't plan on anyone seeing us, but if they do, we might pass with these." They slipped into matching sets then quietly left the car.

The side door was propped open with a trash can but the security guard was sitting only a few feet away. He could have stopped anyone from coming in, if he'd cared to, but he looked up, saw the uniforms, then looked back down, his attention fixed on the small television in front of him.

Jennifer was trembling as they headed to the stairwell and climbed to the fourth floor. Stratton had timed the cameras when he'd been there before, he told her in a whisper, and they only had two minutes between sweeps of the lens to make it from the stairwell to the inside of Ami's suite.

Her hands sweating, Jennifer clutched the key and nodded. Stratton cautiously opened the door an inch, no more. He waited a bit, then counted down, marking the seconds. Jennifer wondered if he could hear her heart beating. The sound was deafening to her, but it got even louder when Stratton grabbed her hand and yanked her into the corridor. With him counting the whole time, they raced toward the outer door of the office where Jennifer stabbed the key at the lock, repeatedly hitting the door. After three tries, she finally managed to get the damn thing into the keyhole. The heavy cylinders clicked, and she pushed the door open, Stratton right behind her as they entered the security vestibule. They were out of range of the cameras in the corridor, but if anyone were inside the office, they were now in big trouble. Jennifer glanced up at the wall-mounted camera and said a quick prayer. Thomas's car had been at the house, but who knew? Explaining to Ami's son why they were there at two in the morning might be difficult.

Unlocking the interior door, Jennifer ran to the security box where the alarm was located. Her fingers shook as she punched in the code. A lifetime had passed since the last time she'd been there and suddenly, despite the danger, she was flooded with memories of Ami. She could have sworn his aftershave still lingered in the air. The alarm buzzed as the computer accepted the numbers, then all went quiet.

Jennifer let out her breath, her shoulders slumping against the wall. Standing right beside her, Stratton looked down and she thought she saw a glint of sympathy in his eyes.

She straightened her shoulders in response. "Ami's office is back here."

Entering his private suite brought Ami's memory back even more sharply, but Jennifer forced herself to ignore it. She went straight to his closet and opened the door. Pushing aside an overcoat and a broken umbrella, she leaned down and tapped on a corner of the molding.

The entire panel swung open and a light came on automatically. A small space was revealed.

Stratton whistled lightly. "I searched this office from top to bottom. I didn't have a clue this was here."

She wasn't as surprised by his revelation as she might have been at one time. "A lot of the suites have safe rooms." Jennifer pointed to a small shelf positioned on the back wall. It held a half-dozen water bottles, a telephone and a .38 Special. "He had everything he needed in case someone managed to get in and try and rob him. He could hide and call the police."

Stratton nodded toward the gun. "Or handle it himself."

"He told me he didn't even keep bullets in here," she said. "I doubt he knew how to use it."

Stratton checked the pistol's safety, then gave the cylinder a quick twist. Every chamber held a round. "I think your boss had lots of secrets." Replacing the weapon, he tilted his head to the filing cabinet that sat just inside the door. "Shall we see what else he might have been hiding?"

The filing cabinet was locked but Stratton had it open quickly. Pulling the top drawer out, he stepped back so Jennifer could see, too. She read labels on the files, murmuring as she touched each one. "Medical Tests, Salaries, Social Security..."

She'd flipped through a dozen or so when Stratton reached around her and pointed to one she'd already passed. "Wait! What's that? It doesn't seem to fit in."

She read the label out loud. "'Ioao Industries.' I have no idea."

"Hand it to me."

She did so, then continued to look through the others as Stratton scanned the file's contents. When he cursed sharply, Jennifer turned.

"I think I found something." Stratton held the file open for Jennifer. "You sure you never heard of this firm?"

"I'm positive."

"Read this." He pointed to an official-looking report. "And check out who wrote it."

She glanced at the signature on the last page. "Joaquim Ioao," she gasped. "That was the man Ami was meeting in Rio. The one who was killed."

Stratton nodded.

She looked again at the papers he'd given her but after a minute she shook her head. "I don't get it," she said. "You're the chemical engineer. You tell me what it means."

He pointed to a paragraph and read slowly.

"The linking of a number of carbon atoms into a three-dimensional diamond lattice results in a puckered hexagonal ring of atoms. This octahedral direction in the crystal is imperative, but the atomic forces between the layers are weak with a resulting bond of 3.35 angstrom units, shearing easily. Due to the longer creation period and high heat of said process, intense pressure allows significant nitrogen atoms to be trapped in the lattice structure and therefore able to migrate into groups, producing a viable range of types of diamond, beyond the Type Ib or Type II, which are normally available only in nature."

Jennifer stared at him with what she knew was a blank expression. "You lost me somewhere in the first sentence."

"If he was doing what I think he was doing, then Ami definitely wasn't following the rules. I can see how the IDDA was unhappy. And it's got nothing to do with how stones are sold."

"Then what *was* he doing?"

Stratton's expression was a mixture of surprise and admiration. "Ami was making diamonds." He waved the piece of paper. "This is the proof."

"That isn't a big deal, Stratton." She spoke slowly as if to a child. "Fake diamonds have been around forever. I know you don't have much time for TV, but haven't you seen the Home Shopping Network? Diamondique and all that? Zirconia, rutile, Spinel?"

"I'm not talking about fake diamonds," he said equally patiently. "I'm talking about *synthetic*. There's a huge difference."

"I know there's a difference, but—"

Stratton moved a step closer, putting his hand on her shoulder. "Ami was producing real diamonds, Jennifer. He obviously had this company making stones that were indistinguishable from genuine ones. Indistinguishable under any and all circumstances. *Real* diamonds," he repeated.

She shook her head again. "I hate to disappoint you, but that's been done before, too. Diamonds can be made. It just takes a lot of time and money."

Stratton went through the report until he came to a certain page. Lifting it out of the folder, he handed it to her. "You didn't understand the chemical analysis," he said, "but you'll understand that. You managed the accounts."

Jennifer skimmed the spreadsheet. When she reached the bottom number, she inhaled sharply then looked up at Stratton.

"They were turning out diamonds in batches. Ioao had obviously found a way to make the process profitable and Ami, along with some kind of help, probably financial, from Wilhem and Barragan, was going to sell them. Singh must have had a piece of it, too." Stratton tapped the folder he held. "Ami wasn't going to challenge the IDDA, Jennifer. He was going to put them out of business."

NOT REALLY SURPRISED by what they'd found, Stratton stuffed the file into the pocket of his jacket and headed for the vestibule while Jennifer closed the closet behind them. Deleting the record of their entry noted by the alarm, she rearmed the system while Stratton waited anxiously. He'd suspected from the very beginning that Lucy Wisner had lied to him when she'd hired him and now he knew why.

The whole thing had been a ploy. The IDDA hadn't wanted him to uncover the truth about Singh's death because they were actually behind it. They'd wanted just the opposite and that's why they'd hired him. They'd needed someone they thought was totally incompetent. The appearance of doing something constructive had been their goal. That was all.

So the tables had been turned and he and Jennifer had become the hunted, instead of the hunters. The IDDA had assumed Jennifer knew what Ami was doing so they'd had to get rid of her, but after Stratton had figured out enough to show up in Rio, they'd had two problems. Even though he'd proved them wrong, Stratton's ego stung at their assumption.

He pushed aside his thoughts for later as Jennifer stepped into the vestibule. Timing their move just as they had before, they had almost reached the door of the stairwell when the bell announced the elevator's arrival. Trapped between Ami's office and the doorway to the stairs, Jennifer turned to Stratton with a terrified expression. He grabbed her arm and pulled her toward the end of the hall but escape was impossible.

"Jennifer! I'm so glad to see you! I was getting worried about you."

Jennifer stopped and turned. "Thomas! I wasn't expecting to see you here."

"I bet you weren't." Ami's son had brown eyes but unlike Jennifer's warm ones, his were hard as marbles.

"We just got off the plane," Jennifer said lamely. "I needed my spare house key that I keep here at the office." She lifted a hand in Stratton's direction. "This is my friend——"

Thomas waved away her lie. "Don't bother." He continued down the hall until he stood right before them. "I don't need to hear some kind of ridiculous excuse. We both know what you've done. And forget the introduction. I know Mr. O'Neil, too, although he doesn't know me."

Easing his hand to the back of his pants, Stratton tensed and cursed their timing. A few more minutes and they would have been gone.

As if hearing Stratton's thoughts, Ami's son turned his focus on him. "Thank you for reaching for your weapon, Mr. O'Neil. Please place it on the floor beside you."

"What makes you think I'd do that?" Stratton asked.

"Because if you don't—" A woman spoke suddenly behind Stratton and Jennifer. "Then I'll shoot you myself. And with pleasure, I might add. You've caused me a lot of trouble."

Stratton looked over his shoulder to see Lucy Wisner standing in the doorway of the office next to Ami's. She held a small Smith & Wesson, one manicured finger curved behind the trigger pull. "Give up your gun," she ordered.

Stratton lifted his weapon out with one hand and placed it on the floor.

"Step back," Thomas instructed.

Jennifer and Stratton did as he said. Lucy came closer and kicked the gun, sending it spinning fifteen feet down the hall.

Stratton spoke quietly, Jennifer practically vibrating at his side with fear. "What are you doing here in Houston, Lucy? Your New York boyfriend get tired of you?" He looked at Jennifer. "This is Lucy Wisner. She works for IDDA, in case you've never met."

Lucy ignored his introduction. "I got tired of him.

After things got a little sticky, I gave it some thought and decided my fortunes lay in a different direction. I threatened to share a few things with his wife, and he agreed it might be best for me to handle this situation alone."

"Was that before or after you hired me?"

"After. But I did hire you on the recommendation of Mr. Leonadov," she said, nodding toward Thomas. "He has friends in low places."

"You'd already taken care of Singh and the other dealers were screaming." Stratton's expression hardened. "But you never expected me to figure any of it out."

"You're absolutely right." She smiled. "Unfortunately for us, though, it seems you caught your second wind."

"Do you have Singh's stolen stones?"

She looked pleased. "Actually we do. That was a nice little bonus for us to add back into the inventory, considering we'd already been paid off by the insurance company."

"Who was the woman in Buenos Aires?" Stratton asked.

"What do you care?"

"Who was she?"

"Her name is Farah. That's all I know. Ian found her."

Sometime in his past, Stratton had heard of her, a second-rate killer who worked for anyone. In his heart, he'd known the woman hadn't been Meredith, but at Lucy's confirmation he felt even more relief. "And the boat?"

"A nobody, a local, just like in Rio," she said with a careless shrug. "We wanted you both out of the way but when we discovered you didn't die in the explosion, I figured you would show up here sooner or later. Thomas had the alarm set to report at his house."

"Okay, okay," Thomas spoke abruptly. "That's enough chitchat. We're wasting time."

To her obvious consternation, he yanked the gun from Lucy's hand and waved it at them all. "Go to the elevator. We're taking a trip."

Stratton squeezed Jennifer's hand with what he hoped was reassurance, and walking slowly, they started down the hall, his brain in high gear. All he had to do was separate Thomas from the S&W. He could eliminate Lucy with a kick, then grab the weapon from Thomas in the confusion that followed.

Thomas hit the button when they reached the bank of lifts but instead of the down button, he surprised Stratton by tapping the one that would take them up. Smiling nastily at Jennifer, he spoke. "I know how fond of heights you are, Jenny. I thought you might enjoy the view from the roof."

Jennifer's fingers flinched inside Stratton's grip. "Why are you doing this, Thomas? You would have had the business when your dad died, regardless."

"Why wait for him to die? I would have been an old man myself before that happened." He nodded carelessly toward Lucy. "If you'd been nicer to me, you might be standing beside me right now instead of this loser."

"You're the loser," Jennifer said quietly. "And you always have been."

His face flushed but the elevator doors opened, and he swallowed his rebuttal. Inserting a key into the control panel, Thomas angrily stabbed the top button. The elevator doors closed and they headed for the roof.

CHAPTER NINETEEN

JENNIFER STARED COLDLY at Thomas. Because of him and the woman with him, Ami was gone, along with four of his friends. The old man had deserved so much better. A hell of a lot more. He might have been misguided in the direction he'd taken his business, but Thomas had never been the kind of son Ami should have had. What kind of man betrayed his own father?

Jennifer's gaze slid to the woman who stood next to Thomas. She was clearly furious about his remark to Jennifer, her hands fisted at her sides, her body tense to the point of trembling. Her attention had fled Stratton and Jennifer and she was glaring at Thomas. Jennifer wondered how he could fail to notice her rage, but he was clearly oblivious.

They exited the elevator, and Jennifer's heart contracted, her breath freezing as she looked around in terror. Nothing protected them from the edge of the high-rise. There was no barrier, no railing, no curb. Nothing. No one else seemed to be affected, but she couldn't get her feet to move. She felt anchored to the spot where she stood, but paradoxically she knew the sensation was a false one. She wasn't tied to anything. A few steps and she could be over the edge.

Stratton took her hand, put his arm around her waist and guided her forward. "Close your eyes," he whispered. "And hang on to me."

She gripped his hand with bruising strength but she couldn't close her eyes. He looked down at her and she shook her head. He held her gaze and nodded, his lips forming the words. "You can do this. Come on."

Lucy spoke unexpectedly, drawing Jennifer's attention, as well as everyone else's. "You're an idiot." She spat the words in Thomas's direction, her voice filled with contempt and disgust, her face a mask of fury. "I should have kicked you out of my office the day you showed up."

Thomas sent Lucy an offhanded look. "And miss out on everything I had to offer? I don't think so. You like expensive things just like I do. Problem is, neither one of us wants to work for them."

Jennifer's eyes jumped to Stratton's then back to the arguing couple.

"I've worked all my life," she snarled. "I just went about it the wrong way. I thought I needed a man to provide the cash but I should have depended on myself. In the end you can only trust yourself."

Thomas actually seemed puzzled by her words, a flash of hurt crossing his expression. "You can trust me."

She looked at him in disbelief. "You're an idiot, a complete idiot! I knew the minute you tried to hook up with that woman you didn't have what it took."

Through the fear that had rolled over her, Jennifer clutched Stratton's arm. Now she understood the "date" Thomas had insisted upon.

"Jennifer could have helped us."

"Help like hers I can do without."

"You didn't give me a chance," he whined.

Thomas topped Lucy by a good three inches but he seemed threatened by her. "You're just like every man I've ever known. You take and take and take, then you take some more. All you wanted was to get in her pants. She couldn't have given us squat because she didn't know anything. Can't you see that now?"

She pushed at the center of his chest with a finger. There couldn't have been too much force behind her action, but Thomas stumbled backward, moving closer to the edge of the roof. Jennifer staggered in response, a sickening dizziness sweeping over her.

When it passed, she realized Stratton had led her away from the place where she'd been stuck. The elevator was at least fifteen feet behind them and they were much nearer the precipice of the building than she'd thought.

"You didn't care about anything else, did you?" Lucy stabbed her finger into Thomas's chest again and raised her voice, drawing Jennifer's eyes once more. "Did you?"

Thomas was more prepared this time and he tried to stand his ground, but Lucy was past furious. Even in her fright, Jennifer could see the emotion behind the woman's anger was fueled by something—or someone—other than Thomas. It had been building for a very long time.

"You're a man," Lucy cried. "And you're all alike!"

Rushing toward Thomas, she lifted her hands and put both of them on his chest, giving him a push that almost sent him to his knees. Thomas dropped the gun and in the scuffle the tiny S&W went over the edge. Thomas sent a startled glance toward the space where it'd disappeared then seemed to buckle in fear.

"Lucy, please! You're not thinking straight—"

"My thinking is perfectly clear. In fact, I can see things better now than I ever have."

There was no pause, no warning, no hint.

Lucy screamed then propelled herself at Thomas again, all of her pent-up anger focused on him.

Gasping in shock, Jennifer wanted to close her eyes and turn but she couldn't.

Paralyzed, all she could do was watch as Thomas dodged to one side...and Lucy went over.

STRATTON DARTED FORWARD but he wasn't fast enough.

He grabbed only air where Lucy Wisner had been standing a second before. Her scream was high and terrified and it sent a skittering ripple down his back. Thomas scrambled to his feet behind him and Stratton pivoted, Lucy forgotten.

Leonadov held a blade. The wickedly curved blade gleamed in his hand and Stratton recognized it as the kind of tool that carpet layers used. Thomas had probably found it on the roof, maybe grabbed it when he'd fallen.

"Put it down," Stratton said calmly. "Lay the cutter at your feet, Thomas, and step back."

"I'm finished with people ordering me around." He tilted his head toward the spot where Lucy had been. "Do you want to join her?"

Stratton took a step closer and Thomas backed up, but not much. "Just drop it," Stratton said. "We've had enough killing already."

"You'd know, wouldn't you?" Before Stratton could answer, Thomas slashed at him. For a second Stratton felt nothing, then the sting hit him. Thomas had somehow managed to slice both Stratton's palms. Blood instantly welled.

"Don't make me hurt you," Stratton said through gritted teeth.

Thomas laughed wildly and jumped at Stratton again, but this time, Stratton caught the man's arm and twisted him backward, both of them falling to their knees. Stratton's now bloody hands were slick, though, and Thomas slithered out of Stratton's grasp.

"Your time's up, O'Neil," Thomas said, his chest heaving. "I'm going to finish you off."

Jennifer spoke softly but everyone heard her. "I don't think so, Thomas."

Both men scrambled to their feet but Thomas's eyes fell to Jennifer's hands and when he saw what she held, he knew it was over. He lunged for Stratton one last time.

A heartbeat later, he was down, a tiny hole in the center of his chest. Stratton lifted his gaze in shock.

Over the barrel of Ami's gun, Jennifer's eyes met his.

IN FRONT OF THE BUILDING, the local television station had already set up their cameras. They were prepping the janitor, who'd seen Lucy Wisner's body fly past the window, for an interview. "Details to come during our morning breakfast hour," the reporter explained cheerfully to the camera. They'd already filmed the attendants rolling Thomas Leonadov's corpse to a waiting hearse. His wounds had proven fatal, the reporter announced in an equally upbeat voice.

The medics tended to Stratton's cuts then the police moved in. Sequestered in one of the first-floor offices, Jennifer and Stratton were questioned separately until they were exhausted. Jennifer heard their queries and gave them her answers but she didn't feel as if she were actually present. She was stuck in the moment when she'd aimed the pistol and fired. Shooting someone in real life wasn't like watching it happen in the movies.

Regret lodged itself in the middle of her gut, the acid of its existence etching a hole deep inside her. Thomas had died and Jennifer was responsible.

The police wanted to hold them downtown but Jennifer called Rusty Tippin and when the high-powered attorney showed up, the lieutenant threw up his hands in disgust and waved them off. The diamond engagement rings Tippin had given each of his four wives had been selected by Jennifer and hand delivered to his office. An old friend of Ami's, he hugged her and said the process would take longer than any of his marriages had lasted but he would fix her problems eventually. He knew people, he said confidently. People in South America.

"And the missing diamonds?" Jennifer had asked.

"I'll find them, sweetie." He'd glanced at Stratton. "I'm sure Mr. O'Neil can help us there. Don't worry."

The rest of their conversation was cut short with the arrival of Cissy. Throwing her arms around Jennifer, she hugged her tightly and began to cry, her speech garbled, but her love obvious. "I was watching TV," she said, "and I saw you and I couldn't believe it and I nearly died. These cops were staying with me, but I started crying, and they gave up and brought me here."

Jennifer let her friend continue until she ran out of steam. Then she introduced Cissy to Stratton.

As he hugged her gently, Cissy looked over his shoulder at Jennifer and rolled her eyes, mouthing the words, "Oh, my God!"

Despite the past few hours, Jennifer grinned at her friend.

Stratton released her and stepped back, his usual un-smooth style in place. "Did you drive over here?"

Cissy nodded. Jennifer had never seen her speechless but Stratton had clearly affected her.

"Then you can divert the press out front while Jennifer and I slip out the back. Tell them you're her spokesperson or something. When it cools down, drive around to the street behind the building and pick us up."

She nodded compliance then Jennifer gave her another quick hug. With their arms wrapped around each other, Cissy whispered in Jennifer's ear. "He's incredible! I told you travel was good for you!"

Jennifer just shook her head, then she and Stratton headed for the rear of the building while Cissy started for the front. In her element, she called to the press and they flocked to her as Jennifer and Stratton escaped.

The summer heat was intense as they walked toward the park behind the office. Crossing the street, Jennifer thought blankly about what a different person she'd been just a few weeks before. She'd watched the nannies stroll with their charges here and been totally unaware, blissfully unaware, of the intrigue, death and passion that had been ahead of her. She wondered what she would have done had she known.

The cicadas sounded louder than usual but what did

that mean? A heavy winter or a hot summer? She couldn't remember.

"Jennifer?" Stratton's finger against her cheek startled her. Sending him a puzzled look, she copied his movement and touched her face. Her cheeks were wet. She was crying and hadn't even realized it.

Pulling his crumpled handkerchief from the pocket of the filthy coveralls he still wore, he offered it to her. Jennifer stared, the effort of accepting it too much for her to handle on her own.

He wiped her face then stuffed the square away.

"You carry a handkerchief," she said in a daze. Ever since he'd whipped it out in Wilhem's office, she'd wondered about it. "Who carries a handkerchief nowadays?"

"You should always carry a handkerchief," he advised stoically. "My father taught me that. 'Be prepared for everything and you can handle anything.' Words to live by."

"They do sound good," she agreed. "But I'm not sure if that advice covers people getting pushed off buildings and unexpected shootings."

Taking her frozen fingers in his, Stratton captured her gaze. "Who cares?" he said. "I'm just glad as hell you took that target shooting class with Cissy. But what made you grab Ami's gun in the first place?"

"I don't know," she said. "For some reason, it seemed like a good idea."

"Maybe Ami was watching over you."

"That wouldn't surprise me one bit."

From the swing set in the park behind them, a little girl cried out. "Faster, faster!"

Stratton spoke quietly. "You saved my life back there, Jennifer."

"And I took Thomas's in the process."

"Would you rather it have been the other way around?"

His logic didn't register. "I killed a man, Stratton."

"I know," he said, "and if you hadn't, he would have killed me."

"That's true, but—"

He placed a finger against her lips. "There are no *buts* in these situations. You did what you had to do. If you hadn't, I would have been the one under the sheet. And then he would have killed you."

She dropped her gaze and stared at their intertwined fingers. She knew what Stratton said was the truth. In the split second she'd had to decide on her actions, she'd weighed the options. She knew she'd done the right thing, but it didn't feel that way.

It felt bad.

It felt like the guilt she'd suffered over Julia's accident only a hundred times worse.

"You didn't have a choice, Jennifer." Stratton paused, a combination of regret and relief coming over his hard features. "You didn't have a choice—just like I didn't have a choice two years ago. You're in the moment, you make the decision and then you have to live with it. Don't make my mistake and second-guess yourself. We both did all we could with what we had and one way or the other, there's no turning back. You're the one who finally made me see that when we argued at the hotel and it's the truth."

His words sank in slowly and as they did, something

eased inside her. The movement was so slight she would have missed it if she hadn't been hoping so desperately for something just like that to happen.

"Will I ever forget?" she asked.

"I hope not," he said, surprising her, looking off into the distance. "Taking a life is a serious thing, an irreversible thing." He faced her again. "I've never done it without thinking about the consequences. I've never done it lightly and certainly not without proof."

He pulled her to him and wrapped his arm around her shoulder. "If you hadn't shot Thomas, he would have killed me and then he would have killed you. We did what we had to, Jennifer. Just like I did in Colombia. I had to take the shot because I thought at the time it was the right thing to do. Castillo made the decision to use his family's presence for his so-called campaign and he's the one who put them in the line of fire—just like Thomas was the one who came here tonight with murder on his mind. Lucy and Thomas made that choice, not you. There were plenty of other ways they could have handled Ami's discovery other than death."

His voice dropped then softened. "You're a special woman, Jennifer. You're brave and honorable and from the very beginning of this ordeal, you've done nothing but impress me." He smiled in a way that made her heartbeat faster. "I've come to see a side of you I bet you didn't even know existed." He paused. "And I love you for it."

She closed her eyes and for just a second, savored the sweetness of his words. "I love you, too," she said quietly, staring at him once more. "But where do we go from here? I don't see how a relationship between us can ever work, Stratton. We're alike in some ways, but our lives are so different, our ways of thinking are different—"

"I disagree."

"But don't you see—"

"Shh." He followed his quiet admonition with a heart-pounding kiss that made her forget all her objections. How did he do that? How could he take away reality and replace it so thoroughly she couldn't even tell the difference?

He pulled back and stared at her. "Listen to me, Jennifer. Between what you said at the hotel and what we did tonight at the office, I realized something. I do have skills I should be using. But not with the Operatives. It's time for me to move on and I want to make a fresh start. I think you should, too. Even before the problem in Colombia I'd been thinking about opening a security firm to help people just like Ami." He hesitated then forged ahead. "What would you say if I suggested we do that together?"

She started to tremble again, but this time not from fear.

He rushed on. "You're an incredible woman, Jennifer, and I know I'd be gaining more than you would, but I have to at least ask or I'd never be able to live with myself. Between your abilities and my talents, we have a perfect fit." He tightened his embrace and smiled. "Not as perfect as the one we've got right here, I'm sure, but a good one, nonetheless. We could be partners. Would you consider it?"

She felt overwhelmed. And confused. And frightened. And hopeful. "Are you asking if I'd consider *you* or if I'd consider a business venture?"

"Both," he answered, "but to be honest, mainly me. You understand me better than anyone. You know all my secrets and all my weaknesses. And you still love me, just like I love you. I want us to have a life together and I think we can overcome the differences. Somehow. Somewhere. What do you say?"

Jennifer gripped his arms and let herself fall into his eyes, an unbelievable excitement sweeping over her at the possibilities ahead. Stratton could lead her into a whole new life, she thought, then she realized he already had. The truth of that hit her, and there was only one way she could answer him.

"I say 'yes' and 'yes.' I love you, too, and I've got proof that will be all I'll ever need. It might be rocky, but what the heck?"

He grinned and she kissed him this time, her ardor taking away his breath and her own. When she finished and pulled back, she paused, a frown knitting her forehead.

"What is it?" he asked in alarm.

"If it's all the same to you," she asked, "could I have a ruby instead of a diamond for an engagement ring? I'd just as soon never see another one of those for as long as I live. Real, fake, or anything in between."

He laughed. "You can have anything you want, sweetheart. Anything you want, as long as you take me, too."

EPILOGUE

Six months later
Houston Chronicle

A LIEUTENANT in Houston's global crime task force announced the recovery today of over ten million dollars in stolen diamonds.

"We owe a lot of our success to the police force in Rio de Janeiro, and especially to Detective Roberto Angelo," Jack Chico said at a press conference held early this morning at police headquarters. "Without his help, this case would have never been solved."

The diamonds were stolen after their owner, Ami Leonadov, was murdered in Rio in June, one of a series of deaths that took place last year within the diamond community. An international hunt was initiated at that time for Leonadov's assistant, Jennifer Rodas, but she was later cleared. Leonadov's son, Thomas Leonadov, and an associate of the International Diamond Dealers Association from New York, Lucy Wisner, are presumed to have been responsible for the murders but authorities cannot confirm this. Leonadov and Wisner were both killed during an attempt on Ms. Rodas's life.

Ms. Rodas, who has since married, said she was glad

the diamonds were recovered and can now be included in Ami Leonadov's extensive estate, which he left entirely to a local charity.

An associate chemist from a well-known firm, Ioao Engineering, in Rio claims the recovered stones are man-made but IDDA's president, Ian Forney, scoffed at this notion. "Man-made diamonds are not economically feasible at this time," Forney said, "and even if they were, our clients would not be interested in them. Diamonds are meant to reflect the purity and steadfastness of a loving relationship. What would a woman think if she found out her husband had given her a fake diamond? She'd believe his love was equally suspect. Man-made diamonds will never be a viable alternative to the real thing."

Everything you love about romance...
and more!

*Please turn the page for Signature Select™
Bonus Features.*

Bonus Features:

BONUS FEATURES

Not
WITHOUT PROOF

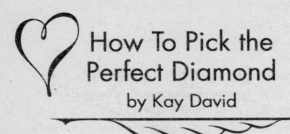

How To Pick the Perfect Diamond
by Kay David

Perfection, to some extent, has a different meaning for everyone. We all have our own preferences for almost everything, and those choices determine our standards and desires.

This theory applies to diamonds, as well. The perfect diamond for you might be totally unsuitable for the woman two feet away at the very same jewelry counter. That's why a good jeweler is part salesman and part psychologist. The stone he helps you select should fulfill not only your needs, but your desires, as well.

To find your perfect stone, you should first understand the standards by which diamonds are judged, otherwise known as the four C's—carat weight, cut, clarity and color. I've added a final C for you to consider as well, and that is cost.

Carat weight is determined by weighing the stone on a jeweler's very precise scale. One carat equals one-fifth of a gram, or 200 milligrams.

4

This weight can also be expressed by describing the "points" of the stone. This term has nothing to do with the facets of the diamond, only the weight. A "ten-pointer" is a stone that weighs one-tenth of one carat. Think in terms of dollars and pennies. One dollar equals one hundred pennies—same thing for carats and points. One carat is equal to one hundred points; therefore, a half-carat diamond could also be referred to as a fifty-point stone.

One last thing about carat weight. Carat with a C always refers to the measure of weight. Karat with a K refers to the purity of a metal, such as gold or platinum.

The **cut** of a diamond refers to the shape of the stone, but it also refers to the proportions and finish. *(See Figure 1, which shows the various cuts that are currently popular.)* Through the years cuts have changed, and this can provide an interesting clue to the age of the stone when you're buying estate jewelry.

The round, or brilliant, cut is the most traditional and the most popular. This is also one of the safest shapes in terms of wearability. It's far more difficult to damage a round stone than it is to damage a marquise, for example. The "perfect" stone for a banker would be a different cut than the "perfect" stone for a landscape artist simply because of the work they do.

6

Oval

Marquise

Emerald

Round

Pear

Princess

Heart

Popular Diamond Shapes
©2001 HowStuffWorks

Figure 1

Another factor to think about is that different cuts appeal to different personalities. A more conservative woman who dresses accordingly will be more likely to select a round or emerald-cut stone than say someone of a less traditional bent. A potter might appreciate the way a pear-shaped stone balances against her fingers, whereas a movie star might want the flash and dazzle of a huge marquise.

The desired proportions of each shape differ greatly but one fact is universal—a poorly cut stone will not be as brilliant and will exhibit much less "fire" than one that has been properly shaped.

The presence or absence of naturally occurring flaws within a diamond determines its **clarity**, the third C, which can best be explained by *Figure 2*. Using the Gemological Institute of America's scale, diamonds are rated for their clarity, and these standards are set by the GIA.

This factor also impacts the brilliance of the stone. Flaws can be defined as mineral inclusions, either light or dark, and cleavage cracks, among other things. They impede the light as it travels through the stone and therefore affect how the stone shines.

The fewer inclusions, the better. If they're small, whitish and located away from the center of the diamond they have less impact than flaws that are large, black and obvious to the naked eye.

Perfectionists usually want stones that fall into the F or VVS category. They don't care if the flaw can be seen only under a jeweler's ten-power loupe—*they* know it's there and that's what counts! Less demanding diamond buyers may be willing to sacrifice clarity in order to afford a bigger stone or a whiter stone. If the flaw is invisible without a loupe, then they're pleased.

One factor in determining your perfect stone vis-à-vis clarity is to take into account where the stone will be worn. Only Aunt Ethel might lean close and examine your earrings, but almost everyone will take your hand and gaze at your engagement ring.

CLARITY	SCALE
Flawless or Internally Flawless	F/IF
Very, Very Slightly Imperfect	VVS1/VVS2
Very Slightly Imperfect	VS1/VS2
Slightly Imperfect	SI1/SI2/SI3
Imperfect	I1/I2/I3

Figure 2 Clarity Table

The **color** of a diamond is very difficult to judge, but this is one of the most important qualities of a stone. *(See Figure 3 for GIA scale.)* In theory, the assessment is simple. The whiter the diamond, the better. No hint of any color should be visible. With the exception of what are called "fancies," (J.Lo's famous pink diamond, for example), the perfect diamond, colorwise, has none. Think of ice.

A loose stone (not set) shows its color more easily than a mounted one, and this is why you should always buy your diamond first and then select your mounting. Turn the diamond upside down on a piece of perfectly white paper and compare it with a stone that is priced differently. The stone that shows any shade of brown or yellow should cost less, all other factors being the same.

Once the diamond is set within a piece of jewelry, color is difficult to ascertain. Two stones that will show their difference on the paper will look identical once mounted, unless the difference is three to four grades.

Consumers are generally presented with stones in the I-J-K range because they're plentiful and affordable. If you can perceive the color, then ask for a diamond in the G-H range. If you still aren't happy, go up to the D-E-F category, but be prepared to pay.

Another factor that impacts color is the setting of your jewelry. Up to a certain point, a yellow stone will appear whiter if mounted in white gold or platinum. If you really want a yellow gold ring but want the diamond to look whiter, tell your jeweler to use a two-toned mounting. The prongs that hold the stone will be white gold, but the shank (the part of the ring that goes around your finger) will be yellow gold.

COLOR	SCALE
Colorless	D/E/F
Near Colorless	G/H/I/J
Faint Yellow	K/L/M
Very Light Yellow	N/O/P/Q/R
Light Yellow	S/T/U/V/W/X/Y/Z
Fancies	Color

Figure 3 Color Table

The final C to consider is **cost.** Few people have unlimited budgets. For those lucky enough to be in that circumstance, you can skip this. The rest of us must find a stone that fits inside the boundaries of our circumstances.

Like everything else in life, this is accomplished by compromise. Decide which of these five C's mean the most to you and focus on that factor.

Want to impress your friends, but don't care if your stone has flaws? Concentrate on size, buying a stone that may have some flaws but none that are really obvious to the naked eye. Get an I-J-K in color and set it two-toned or purchase one of the flashier cuts. A one-carat marquise looks much more impressive than a one-carat round. Look for shallow-cut stones, too. The more surface area, the larger the diamond will appear, but be careful. Stones cut too flat will not have any sparkle.

If clarity is more important to you, use a different set of rules. Stick with either a round or emerald cut. Rounds are plentiful, so it's simple to find a very clean stone. Emerald cuts are frequently very clear stones, too, because flaws are easier to spot in the large, flat facets that define this shape.

Reputable jewelers want customers who are educated, because it's the best way you can end up with a stone that's perfect...for you. So educate yourself, have fun, then go shopping!

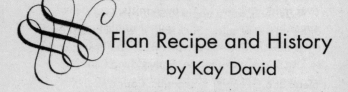

Flan Recipe and History
by Kay David

*Flan (pronounced "flahn") is a puddinglike dessert,
the name coming from an old French word, flaon, the
roots of which are Roman. Regardless of where the
word originated, however, the delicious treat is a*
12 *favorite in many cultures. The version I've given below
is typical of one you might taste in Mexico or any
Latin American country in that it's baked in a water
bath and turned out upside down for presentation.
Usually there is no other flavoring besides vanilla, but
I like this almond version. ¡Buen provecho!*

FLAN

1/2 cup sugar
1 2/3 cups sweetened condensed milk
1 cup milk
3 eggs
3 egg yolks
1 1/2 tsp vanilla extract
1 cup slivered almonds, coarsely chopped

Sprinkle sugar evenly in a 9" cake pan; place over medium heat. Using oven mitts, caramelize sugar by shaking pan over burner until sugar is melted and turns a light golden brown; cool.

Combine remaining ingredients in blender; blend at high speed 15 seconds. Pour over caramelized sugar.

Cover pan with aluminum foil and place in a larger shallow pan that is filled with 1" of hot water.

Bake for 55 minutes at 350°F or until knife inserted near center comes out clean.

Remove pan from water and uncover; let cool on wire rack at least 30 minutes. Loosen edges with a spatula. Place service piece upside down on top of cake pan and quickly invert. Chill before serving.

Kay David's

Travel Tale...

My Time in South America

When my husband came home several years ago and announced we were moving again, I wasn't surprised. He worked in the oil business at the time and moving is a way of life in that field. When he told me where we were going, though, I had to get out the atlas. It took a while, but I finally found the little dot on the map that indicated the location of Comodoro Rivadavia, Argentina. The town is in the Patagonia region of South America. Think of pampas and gauchos and wind. Lots and lots of wind.

The trip between our home in Texas and Comodoro took twenty-four hours, doorstep to doorstep. Various modes of transportation were employed, including cars, planes, buses and taxis. In short, just about everything except donkeys. Since there is no time change between the two countries we never had jet lag, but we certainly had "travel lag." The journey was a grueling one. And familiarity never changed that.

It's never easy to travel a great distance, but throw in a seasonal change and you're really confused by the time you arrive. I would leave Houston either completely bundled up in layers I could shed or wearing shorts and carrying layers I could add. Winter to summer in the space of twenty-four hours is strange, to say the least.

Because the town of Comodoro is on the Atlantic seacoast, very near the Falkland Islands, the wind blows continually. This is not the "jungle" part of South America. The landscape is very dry, very barren and, oh yes, did I mention windy? Very, very windy. If you've ever been to Odessa, Texas, you have an inkling of what I mean. I couldn't wear lipstick outside because my lips would be covered in dirt within seconds. When we first arrived, I told my husband one day that the house was swaying, but he said I was crazy. When I dragged him into the bathroom and pointed at the water moving in the toilet, he believed me.

Spanish is, of course, the official language of Argentina and as a guest in that country, I tried my best to learn it. My skills simply do not lie in that area, however. Fortunately for us, my husband's first language is Spanish, so we didn't starve or get lost.

There were two other American couples living in Comodoro when we arrived. Shortly after, they both left and my husband and I were the sole Americans.

We stayed for two years, our time broken up with trips back home to see family and friends. The hardest times for me were the holidays, especially since the seasons were reversed. Christmas just didn't feel like Christmas when it was in the nineties outside. Of course, the same thing can happen in Texas, but it's different somehow when you're a world away.

Working at home, writing my books, I felt isolated in a way I've never experienced before or since. I was very lucky to have my career or I would have ended up talking even *more* to the cat than I already did. In fact, he probably would have started to answer, at least in my mind!

The day we left for good, we flagged down a taxi and headed for the airport. Passing the same neighborhoods we had when we arrived, we said goodbye to the city and its inhabitants. On the last corner going out of town, a man waited for the bus and I'll never forget seeing him as we drove by. He had a chicken under his arm, and I still find myself wondering just where in the heck he and his feathered friend were going.

Here's a sneak peek...
at the next book in
The Operatives series, coming
in October 2005.

Not Without Her Son
by
Kay David

CHAPTER 1

San Isidro, Colombia

JULIA VANDAMME-RAMIREZ studied the crowd milling about her living room. Sipping drinks and eating hors d'oeuvres, all dressed expensively, if not tastefully, her guests mingled and laughed, clearly enjoying themselves. She smiled tightly and waved to one of the women, the motion catching her husband's eye. Miguel Ramirez followed Julia's gesture, then he turned in her direction and gave her a slight nod.

Julia acknowledged him and took a deep breath, relief washing over her at his approval. The woman at her side, Meredith Santana, looked at Julia and raised an eyebrow. She was Julia's best friend. Julia's only friend.

"Who's the old broad?" Meredith asked.

"That's the governor's wife." Her mask of gaiety intact, Julia spoke out the side of her mouth. "Miguel told me to be nice to her. I guess he wants something from them." She acknowledged another official, then added under her breath, "But if I don't get out of here in the next two minutes, my head is going to explode."

Meredith mimicked Julia's nod to Miguel and smiled graciously, her slow drawl reflecting the Southern past they shared. "Can we go outside to the patio? If you're gonna do something messy, we might be better off out there."

Julia grinned, her expression real this time. "Good point." She tilted her head to the French doors at their back. "Let me grab another glass of wine, then we can meet on the patio. We have a lot of catching up to do. It's been way too long."

Meredith murmured her consent, then slid away soundlessly. Handing her empty flute to a passing maid, Julia waded into the crowd and continued to greet as many people as she could, her spirits lifting as she anticipated visiting with her friend. The last time they'd seen each other had been at Julia's wedding, almost four years before. She still couldn't believe her good luck—if she hadn't walked out of that department store in Bogota at just the right time, their paths would never have crossed and she would have missed Meredith. As it was, Julia had cried out her friend's name then grabbed her in a tight hug, insisting she come to their party a few nights later.

Reaching the bar, Julia accepted a new glass of merlot, then headed for the rear of the room. She was almost to the doors when Miguel put his hand around her arm and pulled her to a stop.

20

"You aren't going outside, are you, darling? We have other guests in addition to your friend, you know."

His voice was low and measured, as full of charm as ever. Julia's heart skipped a beat.

"I don't think those other guests would appreciate it if I threw up on them." She met his black gaze and wondered how she'd ever thought it sexy. "I'm getting a migraine. I need some fresh air."

"I'm sorry," he said politely. He always spoke this way to her. Anyone who listened would be impressed by his smooth civility. She had been when they'd met. "I hope it doesn't intrude on your time tomorrow with Tomasito."

The threat rippled over her with sickening awareness, just as he knew it would. Miguel controlled everything in her life, including the amount of time she spent with their three-year-old son, Tomas. When Julia didn't behave as Miguel thought she should, he punished her by cutting her visits short or eliminating them altogether.

Her mouth went dry. "Tomas expects me, Miguel. I already told him we were going to the beach."

"Then you'd better not break that promise." To make his point even clearer, he tightened his grip on her arm. Refusing to flinch, Julia gritted her teeth and endured his painful touch.

"Please visit with my guests," he said. "And I mean *all* of them."

SNEAK PEEK BONUS FEATURE

He left her standing alone and shaken. With no other options, she sent a quick look out the windows at her back. Meredith had seen the encounter and clearly understood. She nodded to Julia and mouthed the words "Go on," then pointed to a side door and held both hands up, her fingers splayed.

Meredith was older than Julia by almost four years, but they'd been roommates at the University of Southern Mississippi. They'd made this their code for skipping out of class. It meant "ten minutes." Julia nodded, then held her own hand up, adding five more. Miguel would expect her to do exactly as he'd instructed and he'd check to make sure she complied, but if she put on a show for at least fifteen minutes, she'd be all right. He would be involved in something else by then.

Sure enough, by the time she'd made a second circuit of the room, Miguel had disappeared. She glanced up the staircase to his office. The lights were on and the doors were closed. He was obviously holding one of his endless meetings. If she had still thought he was the Colombian diplomat he'd claimed to be, she wouldn't have given his absence another thought, but she noticed it now, because she knew the truth.

Picking up the hem of her beaded dress, Julia hurried through the kitchen and walked outside. She had crossed the patio and was headed for the side door when a shadow materialized from the darkness by the house.

Julia stumbled back in fright, putting a hand to her chest as she finally recognized her friend. "Good grief, you scared me half to death, Meredith. When did you learn to be so quiet?"

Meredith shrugged and waved off Julia's comment. "Miguel didn't look too happy. I didn't want him to see me." She tilted her head to the window above. "He's in his office, isn't he?"

"You've become observant, too." Julia looked up, then nodded. "He's having some kind of meeting. He does that a lot when we entertain. I hardly see him anymore, even when he's here, which isn't often."

"That's too bad." Meredith's voice was neutral in the darkness. "You must get lonely."

Julia knit her fingers together, then looked down at her hands. There was no one she was closer to than Meredith, but Julia's relationship with her husband had never been a topic of discussion between them. For one thing, Meredith didn't like Miguel and Julia knew it. For another, she'd been raised not to air her dirty laundry. Vandammes didn't talk outside the family, especially about trouble.

Even as she had these thoughts, however, Julia acknowledged, at least to herself, the real reason she'd stayed silent—she was embarrassed. How could she have made such a horrific mistake? How could she have missed the monster beneath the facade?

"It's a quiet life," Julia finally replied. "But I have Tomas."

"What about friends?" Meredith asked. "We haven't talked for a long time. Have you gotten close to any of the women inside?"

"They're very busy," Julia said. "Everyone has so much to do with the children and everything."

"The children?" Meredith didn't bother to hide her skepticism, her voice turning sharp. "They've all got nannies, Julia. Nannies and cooks and maids and God knows what else, just like you do. How busy can they be?"

On edge already, Julia felt her throat go tight. She turned away from her friend. She couldn't explain. Not now.

"Oh, shit. Julia, honey, I'm sorry. I didn't mean anything by that...."

She reached out to turn Julia around, her fingers pulling at Julia's right elbow. Julia winced without thinking as a streak of pain raced up her arm.

Meredith froze. "My, God, what's wrong? Did I hurt you?"

"It—it's nothing," Julia lied. "I—I fell against the door the other day and my arm's still bruised, that's all."

Meredith's eyes locked on Julia's and without saying a word she pulled back Julia's sleeve. Even in the faint light that fell from Miguel's office, the fingerprints were obvious. Meredith let the fabric drop, then she raised her suddenly hard gaze to Julia's. "What in the hell's going on here? A door doesn't leave a bruise like that."

"It's nothing," she insisted.

"Nothing, my ass." Meredith shook her head in disgust, then jerked her thumb toward the window above them. "He did that to you, didn't he?"

Julia debated how to answer, a heavy silence building between the two women. After a moment she spoke. "You can't do anything about this, Meredith. It would be best if you forgot what you just saw."

"Best for who?" she snorted. "Not you, I'm sure."

During their college years everyone had called Meredith Superwoman because she'd righted every wrong she came across, regardless of the consequences. The last thing Julia needed was Meredith getting involved in her problems. The very last thing.

"I'm not important here, Meredith. Okay? And nothing is going to change that. Not even you."

"If you're not important, who is? The wife beater up there?"

"My son is," Julia said, her tone vehement. "And I have to remember that above everything else."

"Take him and leave."

"It's a little more complicated."

"Nothing's *that* complicated," Meredith retorted. "Unless he keeps you a prisoner or something."

With three glasses of wine and nerves stretched wire thin, Julia felt her defenses slip. Meredith's opening was too perfect to resist. "Not 'or something,'" she said grimly. "A prisoner is exactly what I am. He has my passport, all the cash, everything. I can't leave."

Meredith's eyes showed so little reaction it made Julia wonder, but there was no stopping her now, her reckless words rushing out in a torrent. "It's been that way from the very beginning. I hate Miguel Ramirez with every bone in my body. If I could, I'd kill him with my bare hands and never look back."

Meredith stared at Julia with a gaze so steady it was unnerving. Between the sudden tenseness and the dim light, she almost seemed a stranger. "Tell me more," she commanded.

26   "There's nothing more to tell," Julia answered, her anger changing into bitterness. "Miguel is a very controlling, very angry man and I do what he says because I have no choice."

"C'mon, Julia Anne. Everyone has a choice—"

Julia held up her hand, Meredith's use of her middle name bringing back their dormitory days and all the whispered confidences they'd shared in the middle of the night. Back then, their biggest problem had been how to arrange the loss of Meredith's virginity. As she thought of the hell her life had become, a bubble of hysteria formed in Julia's throat, but she pushed it down.

"Tomas is all I care about, and I would never leave him."

"Take him with you."

"I can't. I have no funds, no assets, nothing. Even if I did manage—"

"Do your parents know what's going on? I can't believe they wouldn't help you."

Julia's jaw tightened. Her father had argued against her dating Miguel, but she'd ignored what she thought of as Phillip Vandamme's overprotectiveness and married Miguel within weeks of meeting him. She'd come to wonder if the impulsive act—so out of character for her—had been an unconscious effort to escape her parents and their restrictive nature. If it had been, the trick had backfired. She'd hurt no one but herself.

She shook her head. "I haven't heard from them in months and frankly, even if I did, it wouldn't make any difference. All the money in the world wouldn't keep us safe. Miguel would find us, and when he did…"

"When he did…what? There are laws that protect people like you and Tomas."

"Laws mean nothing to Miguel, Meredith. You don't understand—"

"He's a diplomat, for God's sake, not a hit man. He may have some privilege, but that doesn't mean he can do what he likes."

Julia stepped closer to her friend and dropped her voice. "He's not what you think, Meredith. He has the ability and the power to do anything he wants, and he has what amounts to a virtual army at his beck and call. He's a dangerous man and—"

She broke off abruptly and fell silent, her pulse going wild as a sudden breeze rippled over the garden. Meredith started to speak, but Julia held a finger to her lips and the other woman went still, the leaves whispering around them. Julia let out her breath a moment later, the wind brushing past them with a quiet exhalation that matched her own.

Meredith raised an eyebrow.

"I th-thought I smelled Miguel's aftershave," Julia explained. She shook her head then rubbed her temples, the sudden onslaught of adrenaline waking her up to the danger of her indiscretion. What did she think she was doing, telling Meredith these things? If Miguel were to overhear, Julia didn't have to imagine what he'd do. She knew.

Meredith stepped closer and put her hand on Julia's arm. Her breath was warm, her expression concerned. "What can I do to help, Julia? You can't go on like this. There's got to be a way—"

"There's nothing anyone can do. Miguel will never let me go without Tomas, and I'm not leaving my son."

AFTER THAT Julia went silent. There was too much at stake for her to be talking like this and she was a fool for sharing what she already had. She shook off the rest of Meredith's questions and the two women went back inside to find the party beginning to break up, a few people already drifting outside to their cars. Standing in the entryway, Miguel was telling everyone good-night, his second in command, Jorge Guillermo, beside him as usual. Half bodyguard, half counselor, he watched Miguel's back as well as his bank account. On occasion, Julia thought she saw sympathy in his eyes when he glanced at her, but deep down she knew that was only wishful thinking. Guillermo was Miguel's shadow and loyal to a fault.

Both men looked up as Meredith and Julia walked into the living room and Julia's stomach turned over as Miguel caught her eye. No one else would have seen his displeasure, but she had learned to read the subtleties behind his every expression. He was angry because she'd been in the garden and not at his side.

She walked swiftly to where he waited and began to bid her guests good-night. Meredith was the last in line. Miguel extended his hand to Julia's friend, but when she took it, he pulled her closer and brushed both her cheeks with a kiss.

"I'm so glad you could come this evening. I know you and Julia had a lot to talk about. I hope she said kind things about me."

Julia held her breath and watched as Meredith smiled warmly at Miguel. "Kind things? She bragged relentlessly and made me envious of her good fortune. Great husband, wonderful home, beautiful child. She has it all. You're both very lucky."

SNEAK PEEK BONUS FEATURE

Miguel put his arm around Julia's waist and drew her close. "We make our own luck in San Isidro." He looked at Julia and smiled slowly. "Julia would be the first to tell you that, yes?"

"Of course," she murmured.

Meredith leaned over and kissed Julia's cheek. "I'll be in touch," she whispered.

As the front door closed behind Meredith, a sweep of exhaustion came over Julia. She hid it until the last of the stragglers were gone, then she turned and headed for the stairs. When she was halfway up, Miguel's voice stopped her progress and then her heart.

"I'd like to see you in my office, Julia. Please change your clothes and meet me there."

She turned slowly, her mouth dry. Had he heard her talking to Meredith? "I'm really tired, Miguel. Can it wait until tomorrow?"

He seemed to consider her request, but both of them knew it was an act. "I'd prefer to discuss this tonight," he said thoughtfully. "The only time I have open tomorrow is when you're supposed to see Tomasito. Would you rather we talk then?"

She fumed, but silently. "If those are my choices, then I pick tonight."

He nodded and smiled. "Good."

Fifteen minutes later she was in his paneled study, but Miguel was nowhere to be found. He often made her wait so she wasn't surprised, but his lack of con-

30

sideration bothered her more than usual. She wasn't sure if that was because she'd shared her situation with Meredith or because the headache she'd faked was now becoming real. She crossed his office to stand beside the window and stare at the mountains.

In the valley below, the lights of San Isidro twinkled romantically. When Miguel had brought her to the tiny Colombian village, she'd been enchanted. Quaint streets, red-tiled roofs, charming children. That first day, they'd strolled the twisting sidewalks and Julia had been so happy. She'd thought she'd finally found true love and was looking forward to starting a family. Everything had seemed so perfect.

A normal woman would have closed her mind to the memories that rose inside her, but Julia no longer considered herself normal. She'd become something else, something that had no name. Miguel had taken away the person she'd been and replaced her with this new being who wanted to remember what had happened because the details fueled her fire.

Closing her eyes, she let the pain roll over her and relished it, the haunting images as fresh now as they'd been four years ago. They'd had a wonderful meal, then she and Miguel had gone upstairs to his luxurious bedroom. She'd been looking forward to making love with her husband, and she'd moved eagerly into his arms with anticipation. He'd ripped her clothes off and what had followed was something she *did* blank out.

In shock, Julia hadn't known what to do except run. The first time she'd gotten to the gates of the compound. The second time she'd made it to the village. The third time, well, she couldn't remember how far she made it the third time. Miguel had caught her and locked her in a room somewhere inside the villa. She still didn't know where it was. He'd kept her there and "visited" until she'd gotten pregnant.

Tomas had been born that summer.

Julia had begged for her freedom.

Miguel's answer had dumbfounded her. "Go ahead," he'd said. "Leave whenever you like."

For a second she'd let herself think about it, then he'd stood from behind his desk and come to where she waited. "If you do go, however, you will go alone. Don't even consider taking Tomasito with you. Should you try, I will hunt you down and bring my son back. I want to raise him here, in San Isidro, to follow in my footsteps."

"But he's my son, too," she'd argued foolishly. "What if I don't want him brought up that way?"

The look in his eyes had been merciless. "What you want or do not want is irrelevant to this discussion. My son will grow up as I desire. You have no say in this matter."

"You can't do that to me," she'd said.

His reply had been simple and irrefutable. "I already have."

Despite the warning, she'd taken Tomas and tried

one more time. The punishment for her foolishness had been so painful and humiliating she knew the scars—figuratively and literally—would never disappear. Miguel was a master at abasement and her psyche would never be the same. In the end, though, he'd be the one to pay. She'd forged her humiliation into a rage so deep, it had had nowhere to go except inward. Once there, it had become a determination, the likes of which she'd never felt before.

She *would* escape and she *would* take Tomas with her. Miguel would burn in hell before she'd allow her son to become his father's victim, too.

But explaining all this to Meredith would have been impossible. To begin with, it would have taken more time than they'd had, but secondly, Meredith would never have understood how Julia had gotten into this position, because she would never have allowed it to happen to her. Meredith was incredibly strong and assertive and smart. She'd barely been twenty-five when she'd started her own international business, a firm that did something financial, she'd explained vaguely. Meredith would have somehow dealt with Miguel and ended the nightmare immediately. Julia couldn't risk taking her offer of help, though. She'd be damned if she put anyone else in jeopardy because of her own foolishness.

In the end, it didn't really matter anyway. Julia would rather her friend think she was some kind of helpless idiot than jeopardize the plans she'd begun to make.

From behind her, Miguel's voice broke the silence. Her heart pounding painfully, she trembled as she turned.

"Why the shivering? Are you cold? Would you like me to close the window?"

She recovered quickly. "What I would like is to go to bed."

His expression stayed the same, but in his eyes something shifted.

Julia kept her face a mask. He hadn't touched her since before Tomas's birth, but she worried relentlessly about him coming into her bedroom.

34

"Just tell me what you want, Miguel." Her voice stayed steady. "I'm exhausted and my headache is getting worse."

He waited a moment and she held her breath, then he spoke. "I'm leaving town tomorrow. I'll be gone for several weeks and I'm taking Tomasito."

The taste of fear mixed with a flood of nausea. There were worse things Miguel could do to her than what he'd already done, and taking Tomas was one of them.

"Where are you going?" It was hard to get the words past the lump in her throat.

"Where isn't important. All you need to know is that I expect you to remember whose wife you are.

You may go into town to visit Pilar, if you wish, but not alone."

Pilar Lauer was an older woman in San Isidro whose son worked for Miguel. She and Julia had developed a friendship despite their age difference. Miguel's generosity went unnoted. All Julia could think of was her son. "I assume you're taking Mari?"

"No, Mari will not be going. You coddle the boy too much. He can do without his nanny for two weeks."

"Miguel! He's only three—"

"I will handle him."

The words cost her dearly, but Julia said them without reserve. "Then take me with you. I'll watch Tomas for you and you can do whatever it is you need to do."

He seemed to weigh her words, then he dismissed them without even answering, heading for the door instead. At the last minute he turned. His profile looked like stone in the lamplight. "We're leaving early. If you want to say goodbye, I suggest you keep that in mind."

...NOT THE END...

Look for NOT WITHOUT HER SON *in October 2005 from Harlequin Superromance.*

SAGA

Coming in August…

A dramatic new story in
The Bachelors of Blair Memorial saga…

USA TODAY bestselling author

Marie Ferrarella

SEARCHING
FOR CATE

A widower for three years, Dr. Christian Graywolf
knows his life is his work at Blair Memorial Hospital.
But when he meets FBI special agent Cate Kowalski—
a woman searching for her birth mother—the attraction
is intense and immediate. And the truth is something
neither Christian nor Cate expects—that all his life
Christian has been searching for Cate.

**Bonus Features,
including:
Sneak Peek,
The Writing Life
and Family Tree**

Where love comes alive™

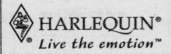

COMING NEXT MONTH

Signature Select Collection
VELVET, LEATHER & LACE by Suzanne Forster,
Donna Kauffman and Jill Shalvis
Hot new catalog company Velvet, Leather & Lace is launching a
revolution in lingerie—and partners Jamie, Samantha and Mia
are coming apart as fast as their wispy new underwear! At this
rate, they might get caught with their panties down. And the
whole world will be watching!

Signature Select Saga
NOT WITHOUT PROOF by Kay David
When hired assassin Stratton O'Neil is framed by a dangerous
drug cartel, he is forced to protect Jennifer Rodas, who is also
a target—which means drawing her into his dark world of high-
stakes murder and intrigue.

Signature Select Miniseries
THE BEST MEDICINE by Marie Ferrarella
Two heartwarming novels from her miniseries, *The Bachelors
of Blair Memorial*. For two E.R. doctors at California's Blair
Memorial, saving lives is about to get personal...and dangerous!

Signature Select Spotlight
MAKING WAVES by Julie Elizabeth Leto
Celebrated erotica author Tessa Dalton has a reputation for her
insatiable appetite for men—*any* man. But in truth, her erotic
stories are inspired by personal fantasies...fantasies that are
suddenly fulfilled when she meets journalist Colt Granger.

Code Red #12
JUSTICE FOR ALL by Joanna Wayne
Police chief Max Zirinsky's hunt for a serial killer leads him to
Courage Bay's social elite. He needs a way to infiltrate their ranks,
and turns to hospital chief of staff Callie Baker. Her solution:
pretend they're dating. But the attraction is all too real, and
neither of them can "pretend" for long. But the killer sees
through their relationship. And for that, Callie will have to die....